The alien press agents clamored for answers

"Is it true," a spindly blue crustacoid from Haik Thirteen demanded, "that your Terry females outweigh their mates three to one, and devour the males immediately after mating?"

"An exaggeration," replied the Terran Director of Public Relations soothingly.

"But what about this rumor that Terran females are capable of driving you helpless males right around the bend, merely with a single glance?"

"Yeah, how about it?" reiterated a small, cootie-like wire rep from the Goober Cluster. Others joined in the clamor until the PR man raised both hands in a placating gesture.

"One or two at a time, *please!*" he chided. "I mustn't be quoted directly, now, but I think I can give you a specific 'perhaps' on that one. That's all for today, chaps."

KEITH LAUMER
RETIEF
AND THE
PANGALACTIC PAGEANT OF A PULCHRITUDE

BAEN
SCIENCE FICTION
BOOKS

RETIEF AND THE PAN-GALACTIC PAGEANT OF
PULCHRITUDE

This is a work of fiction. All the characters and events
portrayed in this book are fictional, and any resemblance to real people or incidents is purely coincidental.

A Baen Books Original

Baen Enterprises
260 Fifth Avenue
New York, N.Y. 10001

First printing, March 1986

Part of this book has appeared previously as "Retief's
Ransom," © 1971 by Keith Laumer.

ISBN: 0-671-65556-6

Cover art by Wayne Barlowe

Printed in the United States of America

Distributed by
SIMON & SCHUSTER
TRADE PUBLISHING GROUP
1230 Avenue of the Americas
New York, N.Y. 10020

Book

ONE

RETIEF AND THE PAN-GALACTIC PAGEANT OF PULCHRITUDE

I

"Retief!" Magnan wailed from his perch on a ledge in the cave wall. "I'm s-s-scared!"

"Certainly, Mr. Magnan," Retief replied from his seat on a boulder. "You'd be a damn fool if you weren't."

"DO something, quick!" Magnan urged. "Nothing rash, of course. Why, if you were killed, I'd be here all alone with *that*."

"With that thought in mind, how can I fail?" Retief said.

"Gracious," Magnan lamented. "How did an inoffensive diplomat like myself come to find himself, er, myself, that is, in such a situation?"

"Don't you remember, Mr. Magnan? You volunteered."

"Why, how in the world did you kn—, ah, ever get a silly idea like that?"

"Since I was stuck with the detail as Project Officer," Retief pointed out, "I made it my business to know what was happening."

"If you had carried on in strict accordance with regulations, your paperwork would have kept you too fully occupied to bother with details like personal ... ah ... intervention," Magnan rebuked mildly. "But then, of course that was too much to expect." Magnan broke off to eye the monstrous

3

quadruped which paced the floor below, pausing occasionally to yawn mightily, exposing impressive yellow fangs.

"Somehow, Retief," Magnan said sadly, "I can't help feeling you know more about that ferocious creature than is appropriate for a sound diplomat to know."

"A little," Retief agreed.

"Then tell me: what in the cosmos *is* it? The Post report didn't say anything about a great big diplomat-chasing animal here on Glorb XIV, with big sharp hooks on all its feet and all those awful pointy things in its mouth. It looks almost like a picture I saw once of an extinct Terran beast called a tiggle, or something like that. Somehow those dreadful black and yellow stripes make it look even more sinister."

"Good thinking, Mr. Magnan," Retief said. Magnan yelped as the big cat reared suddenly, placing its forepaws against the wall only inches below the terrified bureaucrat's feet, stretching its neck to sniff the scuffed toes of his bright-polished boots (issue, top three grades, for the use of on informal occasions).

"Retief!" Magnan shrilled. "It's about to eat me!" He tried in vain to climb higher up the vertical wall. "Well, tell mother I died game," he requested quietly, while the feline dropped back to all fours and used a hind leg to scratch behind its small, round ear.

"Imagine!" Magnan said in a stricken tone. "A loyal bureaucrat devoured by an extinct prehistoric monster!"

"Except that it's not *quite* extinct," Retief pointed

out. "*Panthera Tigris*, commonly known as the Royal Bengal Tiger. One specimen was preserved at the Berlin Zoo, you may recall."

"Yes, I once saw a special on vanishing life-forms," Magnan almost babbled, gazing down in horrified fascination at the huge feline as it approached once again. "Pity, in a way, I suppose," he went on gamely. "A healthy female, and no male extant to father a brood. Though why anyone would want to perpetuate *that* horrid, bitey carnivore, I can't imagine." Magnan paused to chew his lip. "It's the same group that carried out the 'Save Our Anopheles' campaign last year, I imagine," he concluded.

"Why so hostile, Mr. Magnan?" Retief inquired cooly. "After all, she hasn't even nibbled you yet."

"Thanks entirely to my agility," Magnan snapped. "I was *so* enjoying our stroll in this alien landscape, until *it* came along. It seemed so reasonable to take refuge here—but now it's clear this is strictly a two-man or one-tiggle cave. And I thought we were so cleverly concealed. How did it find us so quickly? ESP?"

"She trails by scent," Retief explained. "She can smell us, Mr. Magnan, even smell the spots on bare stone where we stepped."

"Retief! Are you deliberately trying to be offensive?" Magnan scolded. "Why, I assure you I took my sono as usual this morning."

"She has a very sensitive smeller," Retief said. "And of course she's extra-keen, since after she stepped out of her cage she's been on her own all day here on Boondock—"

"Retief!" Magnan cut in severly. "The official

designation of this world is, as you well know, Glorb. That offensive nickname is hardly proper terminology for a diplomat accredited to the planetary government."

"Glorb or Boondock," Retief pointed out, "there's nothing here for Gertie to eat. She missed her usual morning feeding, and we represent the only edible food for her within several dozen lights— unless you want to count the boys back at the ship, or the staff at the Embassy over at Furtheron; and even Gertrude can't smell that far."

"Gertrude? But that's the name . . . Retief! You *didn't!*"

2

"Sure I did. Why not?" Retief replied affably. "I had my instructions: to go over the list of finalists and select the most beautiful female native to Terra. And I picked Gertrude."

"But that wasn't. . . . I mean, yours was to be a purely rubber-stamp function. You were supposed— after all, Ambassador Grossblunder thought. . . ."

"I can't argue with that," Retief admitted.

"You . . . you deliberately tricked me. I mean you let me think—"

"Mr. Magnan, be calm," Retief urged. "When you offered to serve as chaperone for our candidate, I hinted to you that Miss Gertrude was something of a spitfire."

"Indeed you did. Those casual remarks of yours about her uninhibited behavior during those long tropic nights, and how she loved to be petted to help her get to sleep, and always enjoyed having her back scratched in the bathtub—why, that was all calculated to lead me on to folly!"

"You assured me you were motivated solely by your dedication to bureaucratic method," Retief reminded his senior.

"Bureaucratic method, indeed!" Magnan snorted. "When word reaches Ambassador Grossblunder that his protege, that little Peaches Ripetree, I think her name is, is to be left out, while we transported this ravenous beast all the way here to Boondock, as Terra's entry in the P.P.P., why, I dread to contemplate his wrath."

"In that case, Mr. Magnan," Retief soothed. "I suggest you think about something else." As Gertrude reached the far end of her pacing pattern, Retief stepped quietly down to the cave floor. The big cat, near the entrance to the twelve-foot cave, turned quickly to face him.

"Retief," Magnan said coldly, drawing in his feet even further as the carnivore strolled back across the cave floor and wrinkled its nose at Retief, who scratched her behind the ears, eliciting a distinct, though *basso* purr. "Retief, how is it the tiggle isn't eating you? Surely you're as edible as I?"

"I took the precaution of making friends with her during the trip out," Retief said. "If you'll come down, maybe you can do the same."

"I rather think not," Magnan said. As he shifted position, Gertrude glanced up at him and growled, a sound like a gallon of ball bearings spilling on a hardwood floor. Magnan edged aside hurriedly, hugging the rock and watching the cat's lazy movements as it stretched, its claws scraping the stone floor with a sound like chalk squeaking on a blackboard.

"Making friends with *that* monster," Magnan said harshly. "So that's what you were doing all those times I noticed you slipping away from the group at odd hours. I thought—and so did Ambassador Grossblunder, I fear—that you were carrying on an illicit liaison with Miss Ripetree."

"Did you give His Excellency that idea?" Retief inquired. "Or was it a case of independent inspiration?"

"Oh, I may have commented casually on your zeal," Magnan acknowledged. "I felt your devotion to, ah, duty shouldn't go unnoticed."

"I wondered why he ordered me under close arrest."

"And here you are, Retief, not merely trapped by a hungry tiggle, but braving the wrath of an aroused Ambassador!"

"Now, Mr. Magnan," Retief said, stroking the tiger's sleek head. "As I've shown you, Gertrude isn't always as ferocious as she looks."

"That's all very well for *you*." Magnan sniffed. "But the moment *I* set foot down there, that monster will rend me limb from limb. I presume she's one of those—I believe 'man-eaters' is the colorful term they used in the old days."

"She'd rather have a truckload of horse guts than a slender diplomat," Retief pointed out. "But no doubt she'd settle for you in the absence of a dump truck."

"So—I repeat:" Magnan yelped. "*Do* something! Gracious, Retief, this time we're really in a pickle!"

I thought we were goners that time on Roolit I when those two beaked horrors sprang out at us—and again, the time at Verdigris when we found that ancient tomb full of homicidal machines. And what about that awful moment when we saw Renfrew—that ghastly mummy, strapped into his pilot's seat in the jungle at Yudore? But of course all eventuated quite nicely," he went on more calmly, "else we'd not have survived to be mauled by *that* horrid great monster!" Mangan stared with fascinated disapproval at the big cat who looked up at him and yawned.

"So much for reminiscence," Magnan concluded. "But this time I fear there's little hope of rescue. His Excellency and the entire staff are totally involved with the preparations for the pageant, and contending with the press, so that our absence won't be noticed for hours—if not days. It does seem a cruel fate for harmless diplomats merely out for a stroll after the ordeal of a long crossing. And however do you suppose Gertrude happened to be roving loose at the same moment?"

"As to the latter point," Retief offered, "I was feeding Gertie when your urgent summons was delivered. I requested a half-hour's grace, I'm sure you recall, but you were quite adamant."

"I had no intention of venturing out on the surface of a virtually unknown world alone," Magnan stated firmly. "And of course, I assumed you were as eager as I to breathe a bit of fresh air, even with its slight chlorine content. Naturally, I had no idea that you had just stepped out of the monster's cage when your escort arrived, leaving the door ajar."

"It wasn't precisely ajar, Mr. Magnan," Retief corrected. "Just on half-latch, since I intended to return immediately: that was before the armed guard arrived to escort me. Gertie was lonely, so she broke the latch and followed."

"It was essential to seize the opportunity for our constitutional while weather conditions were favorable," Magnan explained impatiently.

"You mean while His Ex wasn't looking," Retief suggested.

"Well, of course, one dislikes to trouble an Ambassador Extraordinary and Minister Plenipotentiary with trifling requests for permission to disembark," Magnan pointed out. "But enough of these recriminations: what are we to do now?"

Before Retief could answer, the stillness was broken by a yowl from beyond the cave mouth, a long-drawn-out cry which started as a shrill scream and descended the scale to a low rumble.

"Oh, dear," Magnan blurted. "It appears there is local wildlife as well as our imported form. I don't suppose there's a back way out of this cave?"

At the screech, the tiger had spun to face the entry and crouched, her striped tail lashing, her jaws agape. At a second cry, she advanced, stood for a moment silhouetted in the opening against the greenish sky. Then, beyond her, a great maned beast came into view, its bared fangs even longer than the tiger's.

"Great Heavens, Retief!" Magnan blurted. "Do you suppose that creature is going to come in here? Why, it's even bigger than Gertrude! And at least as ferocious looking. Actually, it looks rather like her, except for being green with pink spots, of course."

Gertie growled, gathering her feet under her for a rush.

"Retief! Stop her!" Magnan yelped. "She'll be killed! Though of course," he went on after a moment's reflection, "then we'd be safe—unless, of course, that awful creature should attack us next. Somehow, I prefer Gertrude." Magnan broke off to call soothingly to the tiger. "Down, Kitty, just relax; no need to venture out there just now."

The tiger acknowledged Magnan's attentions by looking back over her shoulder at the slightly-built diplomat perched above her; then she returned her attention to the intruder now coming warily into the shadowy entrance to the cave. Gertie advanced a step to meet it, sniffed, then turned and retreated to the cave's deepest recess. The newcomer came forward a step, then lowered its haunches, wrinkled its nose and uttered a purr even louder than Gertrude's.

"Worse and worse," Magnan mourned. "It appears to be settling down for an extended visit—and even the tiggle is intimidated by it. Retief! You'd best come up here with me—at once, before it notices you."

From the dense blackness of the niche where she had taken refuge, Gertie uttered a low, moaning growl, then emerged suddenly and bounded past the pink and green beast, accidently bowling him over with a glancing blow of her hindquarters. The alien carnivore scrambled up with a yowl, but Gertie was already gone, out into the glare of sunlight. Cautiously, the intruder followed, sniffing audibly; as it passed beyond the entry, Gertrude sprang from concealment, struck an almost playful blow with one mighty paw, knocking the pink and green horror aside; it leaped after her as she bounded away, out of sight. A moment later there was an outburst of snarls mingled with screams, and the sounds of heavy bodies impacting.

"Good lord, she'll be killed!" Magnan wailed. "The last of her kind, dying on a minor planet, done in by a casual passer-by. Too tragic."

"Maybe not," Retief replied as he reached the cavemouth and looked out. "She seems to be holding her own, at least."

Magnan came up to peer over his junior's shoulder. The two great meat-eaters were facing each other at a distance of six feet, breathing hard, tails lashing.

"A remarkable example of convergent evolution," Magnan commented. "But then I suppose the optimum mechanism for catching and eating animal life is bound to be much the same anywhere Terrestrial-like conditions obtain."

"It looks like a draw," Retief said. "Neither one seems inclined to attack."

"And we can seize the opportunity to slip away," Magnan pointed out. "Quietly, now, Retief, while they're not looking."

As Magnan stepped past Retief and started across the flat, rocky ledge before the cave, a harsh voice called after him in bad Terran:

"Hey, you in the fancy pants! Hold it right there! I got a couple questions to ast you boys." Magnan whirled, an astonished query on his lips, to see the alien combatant approaching him, a purposeful look on its cat-like face. For the first time Magnan noticed a broad leather strap across the creature's chest, adorned with a large, shiny badge. Gertrude sat where she had been, calmly licking her fur.

"Merciful heavens," Magnan wailed. "It would seem that the tiggle has assaulted a member of the local constabulary! Ah, sir," he went on, more briskly, "it's all a trivial misunderstanding. You see, my colleague and I were simply admiring some unusual geological formations in the cave just here, and—"

"You got maybe a license you should go prospecting on Glorbian turf?" the cop demanded belligerently.

"You mistake my meaning, sir," Magnan pointed out, using a modified 397-B (Righteous Outrage Under Strict Control by Superior Strength of Character).

"Don't overdo that three-ninety-seven, Mr. Magnan," Retief suggested. "He might mistake it for a six-oh-two."

"Knowledge of Moral Rectitude Pushed Beyond Endurance?" Magnan queried, shocked.

"No, more like Resisting Arrest Without Enough Muscle to Make it Stick," Retief corrected.

"That's enough backchat, you two," the visibly annoyed constable cut in. "What kind life-form are you, anyways?" The big alien feline wrinkled its pink and green face at them.

"Goodness," Magnan blurted, backing away. "I hope it doesn't bite—"

"Not unless the prospective bitee has got more meat on it than you, skinny-britches! By the way, what's the idea calling me 'it', instead of 'he'? You think I'm some kind animal or something?"

"Not at all, Chief," Magnan put in soothingly.

"But I *was* deeply impressed by the fashion in which you interacted with Gertrude."

"You mean that yeller-an-black female that give me a dislocated mooby-bone?" the cop demanded, turning to eye the tiger which was now hovering moodily in the middle distance.

"She's a looker, I'll give her that, in spite of the funny color-scheme—not that I'm one of them racists," he finished almost defensively. "What's she doing, hanging out with you boys?"

"Just friends, sir," Magnan explained.

"Somebody oughta tip the kid to watch out for bad companions," the cop grunted.

"It's been charming, chatting with you, sir," Magnan gushed, edging away. "But my colleague and I must be off now. We've preparations to make for the pageant, you know."

"I shoulda figgered you outlanders was here for the big cheesecake show," the officer conceded. "Me, I'm in that project, too. In fact, I'm my union's rep on the Preliminary Panel. We weed out the real dogs, you know. By the way, Yong's the handle," he told Magnan. "I'm a member of the noble tribe of Vang," he went on. "Now you aliens have to understand the situation here on Boondock IV—or Glorb, the skinny five-eyes decided to call it, just because the spot they happened to land and build their town on was in the territory of the Glorbs—now, they're stubby little devils, used to live by dacoit attacks on peaceful villages and trade caravans. Us other six or eight tribes had no use for 'em. But the Groaci set up this like planetary government, they call it, and put the Glorbs in charge. Worked out a deal with the little skunks to help 'em loot Boondock in return for being the top tribe. They been harrassing the rest of us native Boondockers ever since—but I guess you boys aren't interested in our problems—"

"On the contrary, my dear Constable," Magnan rebutted. "As diplomats it is precisely such chicanery on the part of the Groaci, the ferreting out of and rectifying of, to which we are dedicated!"

"Huh?" Yong commented. "I guess maybe you're talking too fast, pal. I didn't quite catch that. Well, ta."

The now affable cop turned and moved with feline grace across to where Gertrude turned to meet him, fangs-first. The cop stopped short of combat and uttered a plaintive-sounding cry, to which Gertrude replied with a lift of her nose and a curt twitch of her tail, before turning to stroll away, disappearing among the gullies of the craggy landscape.

"Heavens!" Magnan commented behind his hand, "imagine that uncouth flatfoot included among those sitting in judgment on the Galaxy's premier beauties! Shocking!"

3

Ten minutes later, back at the bustle of activity among the colorful pavilions erected by the landing crew around the base of the Corps Transport, in position in line with the other visiting vessels, Magnan, pausing only to recommend to Retief that he see to the recaging of Gertrude at once, hurried away in search of the Director of Public Relations.

"Ah, there you are, Roy," he cried on espying the short portly ad man, who was surrounded by a varied assortment of alien reportorial personnel, all clamoring at once for a reply to some vital question. These were couched in some three dozen totally unrelated languages, a circumstance which had caused the translator to fuse its main unscrambler circuitry to the accompaniment of an emission of pungent fumes, occasioning an outburst of coughing, likewise in thirty-six alien modes, ranging from the shrill whistles of a diminutive Phip to the basso roars of a hulking, shaggy green Hondu sports editor.

"Is it true," a spindly blue crustacoid from Haik Thirteen demanded in a momentary lull, "that your Terry females outweigh their mates three to one, and devour the males immediately after mating?"

"An exaggeration," Roy soothed the excited stringer blandly.

"But what about this rumor that Terran females are capable of driving you helpless males right round the bend, merely with a single glance?" Other voices were stilled, as all present awaited the reply to the Haikan wire service rep's query.

"Yeah, how about it?" reiterated a small, cootie-like chap from the Goober Cluster. Others joined in the clamor until Roy raised both hands in a placating gesture.

"Fellows, fellows," he chided. "One or two at a time, *please*! As to Bumchik's interesting question, ah, as to that, one might almost say, now, I mustn't be quoted directly, you understand—not that the point has any strategic significance, of course: some feel—or so it is sometimes said—well, anyway I can give you a specific 'perhaps' on that one. Now, that's all today, chaps; kindly disperse if you will, so as to allow His Excellency to disembark."

"Nice going, Roy," the Mission Press Officer offered, slapping the PR man's narrow shoulder as he passed, pushing through the departing throng, his voice rising above the chorus of disappointed muttering. "That ought to hold 'em till press time," he added, shying as a passing Reeb spurned the press hand-out he proffered.

One aggrieved reporter turned to confront the Terran flack. "Hows come we don't get a look at the Terry entry?" he demanded. "All the other competing powers give us a good look at theirs." He waved a horny manipulative member, indicating the row of alien craft parked in the designated Registered Personnel Only area, each surrounded by its complement of groundcrew besieged by eager journalists, all bathed in the glare of multi-banked polyarcs punctuated by the flash of actinic photoflares. At the foot of the nearest ramp could be seen the iridescent form of the Bloovian finalist, a white-feathered peacock-like being spreading a silvery fan of tail-plumes, each adorned with a jewel-like blob of color.

"Wow, Grossblunder's little number is going to have to go some to beat out that Bloovian princess," Roy muttered, his remark overheard and repeated by a number of the jostling departures.

"Oh, boy, 'Terry manager predicts his girl will bow to Bloovian'," the Bloovian video chief composed his headline enthusiastically.

"Here, I never said that!" Roy yelled in vain as

the report of Terran defeatism spread at a velocity in excess of that of the propagation of electromagnetic radiation in a vacuum.

"What about that dish from Krako Eight?" somebody yelled. All sense-organ clusters turned as one to watch as, at the debarking port of the second vessel in line, a sinuous, jet-black Ophidian with brilliantly polished scales slithered into view, raising a wedge-shaped head adorned with a golden, plume-like frill to look imperiously over the lesser mortals below.

"She's got that Bloovian babe beat by a country zop," someone commented reverently. Roy mumbled, not even bothering to practice his 753-D (Politely Amused Contempt).

"Never mind, Roy," Magnan managed to hiss in the harassed press man's ear. "Remember they haven't seen Terra's entry yet."

"Where ever *is* Miss Ripetree?" Roy moaned. "I was assured His Excellency would introduce her to the press this morning—that's why I came out here to confront these riff-raff."

" 'Terry Official Calls Press Corps 'riff-raff'," an agile Groaci scribe muttered in a stage whisper, into his recorder.

"I did *not*, Thif!" Roy objected. "I only—"

"To have heard you with my own auditory membranes," Thif countered saucily. "Oh, boy: 'Terry Official Denies Public Statement'."

"What can be keeping Miss Ripetree?" an assistant code clerk wondered aloud. "She'll put these showy strumpets to shame."

"Could be maybe she ain't so hot after all," a wrinkled gray Yill suggested cynically.

" 'Showy Strumpets'," Thif recorded dutifully, keeping pace with the little group of Terrans, while manuvering to remain up-wind to avoid the peculiar meaty odor of the alien beings.

Magnan clutched suddenly at Retief's arm. "Retief! Whatever are we to do? They're demanding to see Peaches! Miss Ripetree, that is. Wherever could His Excellency be keeping her?"

At that point, Jerry, the supply room clerk, popped up at Magnan's elbow.

"A slight hitch, Ben," he whispered loudly. "It seems like nobody told His Ex Peaches'd hafta show up in the nood. 'No concealing wrappings', is the way His Groacian Excellency, that little creep Shilth put it."

"I heard that!" Thif hissed. "Groacian Ambassador Extraordinary and Minister Plenipotentiary characterized as 'creep' by Terry spokesman!"

"I did *not*!" Magnan snapped. "You can't go picking up every little casual wisecrack by mere CDT reserve personel as official Terry policy, Thif! Gimme a break!"

"Terry official dismisses mortal insult as 'wisecrack'," Thif recorded. "Attempts to disavow barbarity as casual. Demands break!"

"Worse and worse," Magnan moaned. "Retief, what can I say to remedy matters?"

"You might try keeping your lip zipped," Retief suggested, "with respect, Mr. Magnan."

"Terry underling tells senior to shut up," Thif put in happily. Retief plucked the compact recorder-transmitter from the Groaci's fingers, squashed it flat in his fist, and tossed it into a convenient rubbish receptacle.

"Flimsy equipment, Thif," he commented as the Groaci dithered, speechless. " 'Inferior transmitter fails'," he added.

"Oh, boy," Jerry gloated, craning for a better view of the debarcation ramp from the Terran transport.

"For once old Shilth has a good idea. A fellow don't often get a chance to see a classy broad like Peaches strolling around in the sunshine, starkers!"

"Nor will you today, Jerry, you leering Thomas!" the resonant tones of Ambassador Grossblunder boomed out from the exit lock. "Miss Ripetree is indisposed, alas, and in any case will certainly not display herself in any immodest fasion. You may as well all move on," he shifted targets to the crowd of attentive newshawks straggling along toward the next vessel in line where the iridescently feathered Bloovian princess was being bundled into a waiting limousine while glare-bulbs flashed.

"It's all right, Percy!" a tearful feminine voice was audible in a lull in the disappointed mutterings. "I'm prepared to sustain Terran honor at whatever cost." All oculars went at once to the top of the ramp where a shapely Peaches Ripetree, wrapped in a gossamer negligee, was striking a demurely provocative pose.

"Wow!" Jerry sobbed. "I can't hardly stand the suspense!"

" 'Terry menial finds prospect of spectacle of undraped contestant unendurable'," Thif duly reported.

"You misunderstand, Thif!" Magnan protested, not diverting his gaze from the nearly nude girl. "Jerry only meant—well, the fact is, a dish like that *does* get the old juices flowing!"

There was a brief scuffle at the top of the ramp as the dumpy Ambassador Grossblunder bundled his fragile protege back inside.

"Spoilsport!" Jerry called boldly after the departed Chief of Mission.

"I heard that, Jerry," the familiar Grossblunder tones came hollowly from inside.

" 'Menial publicly insults Terry Ambassador'," Thif reported. " 'AE and MP meekly acknowledges insult'."

Further deterioration of the Interplanetary situation was abruptly curtailed by the arrival of the boxy forty-foot-long, gold-plated and jewel-encrusted limousine of the Glorbian Minister of Culture, representing the host planet of the P.P.P. The short, lumpy, grayish-yellow driver darted around to open the door for the descent of the Minister himself, a stubby being scarcely distinguishable from his driver but for his brocaded toga and ceremonial quirt of office.

"Why, hi there, Mr. Minister," Magnan gushed, advancing to greet the local dignitary who shied violently and lashed out with his quirt, catching the eager Terran a smart clip across the jaw.

"Make way, impudent alien!" the Culture Chief commanded in a voice reminiscent of boots being withdrawn from deep mud. A second Glorbian, in a somewhat less ornately embroidered garment, pushed up beside his boss.

"Here, you—whatever you are!" he burbled in his glutinous voice—like that of a fat man who has just won a pie-eating contest. "Make way for his Excellency Minister Foob! Just who and what are you, fellow?" he demanded of Magnan who had shrunk back under the vigor of the verbal challenge, and was delicately fingering the welt across his jaw.

"Why, nobody, er, nothing, that is," Magnan cried in an unsuccessful attempt at a 373j (Insousiance Under Irregular Treatment Hardly Appropriate to Civilized Beings).

"Don't waste that 373 on me, fellow-me-lad!" the Glorbian burbled. "I'm not impressed. You look like one of those, a, 'Terrors', I believe they're called in their own barbaric tongue."

"Terran," Magnan corrected. "I have the honor, sir, to be Permanent Secretary to the Committee for the Pageant. And may I enquire as to your own august identity? And I don't think it's so barbaric."

"Mmm," the squat alien replied. "I'm Glud, Third Assistant to the Assistant to the Minister here. Why?"

"I simply need to know precisely whose career I am about to terminate when I report your savage conduct to my Chief," Magnan explained crisply.

"Your chief got nothing to do with the operation of Murphy's Law out here on Glorb!" the Assistant Assistant rejoined spiritedly, while Thif whispered at length into a new recorder.

"In fact," Glud went on, spurred by Magnan's 27-x (Speechless Indignation at Uncouth Treatment by Other Ranks) and his own chief's bland indifference to the exchange, "I gotta good mind to call a cop. Getting tough with a Glorbian official in performance of his duty and all." The squat A.A. stepped back up on the running board of the limo to scan the crowd.

"Yey! Over here, Yong!" he yelled before emitting a blast like a steam whistle. There was a stir in the crowd some yards distant; then the fearsome pink and green visage of the planetary police officer thrust between two dilatory bystanders. His yellow eyes fell on Magnan.

"Oh, it's you again!" he growled. Then, to Glud, "what's the beef, Mr. Assistant Assistant?"

"The impudent creature actually threatened to use influence to blight my career development if I failed to do as he bade," the little Glorb whimpered.

"Oh, yeah, Glud?" Yong commiserated. "And what did he bade?"

"Bid," Glud corrected. "He demanded an interview with His Excellency here, just come busting up and unbuttons his lip—and without making no appointment through channels, meaning *me*!" Glud paused to breath heavily and dash a drop of exudant from one tiny pig-like eye. "And he connerdicted me, too," he added. "Said Terry talk was *not* barbaric and all!"

"Geeze," Yong muttered, frowning down at Magnan. "Looks like you got yourself in pretty deep, pal. What you got to do, you got to learn how to talk to these here bureaucrats like Glud. You don't just say what you mean, like they was people or something."

"I myself am a bureaucrat of many years' standing, Constable!" Magnan replied, heatedly. "And I assure you I am a people! All I said was, ah, well, I don't exactly remember what I said, but it was certainly nothing prejudicial to the dignity of noble bureaucrats!"

"Say, Mr. Assistant Assistant," Yong addressed the driver in a confidential stage whisper. "Why don't we just kinda cool this one, you know, to show these here foreigners that Glorb bureaucrats has got some class? OK?" He turned to wink at Magnan, an expression so sinister that the First Secretary's knees momentarily failed him. Retief caught him and held him upright.

"Good thinking, Yong," Retief said. "Mr. Magnan will make a note of it in his daily Report of Local Atrocities and Other Incidents, I'll bet. That next promo's coming up soon, eh? No harm in making a few extra points."

"You and me could get along, Terry," Yong said heartily, "especially if you'd put in a word for a fella with that snazzy Gertie, which by the way, where is she? Ain't seen her since she give me the sprain in my moobybone yonder."

"You're not thinking of arresting her?" Magnan quavered. "She's only a naive young thing, and under diplomatic immunity at that."

"Naw, nothing like that," Yong disclaimed. "I got nothing on the kid—just high-spirited is all, you know."

"Most high-minded of you, Constable," Magnan congratulated the cop. "As to her whereabouts, she seems to have, um, strolled off to contemplate nature or like that. Perhaps you'd be so kind as to seek her out and escort her back here."

"Well, I dunno, it's not what you'd call line-of-duty," Yong objected feebly. "But I guess I could have a look around. I know these here badlands pretty good after twenty years on the beat."

"Now, Retief," Magnan addressed his colleague, drawing him aside from the most boisterous of the still-clamoring newshawks. "How are we to manage the substitution of Gertrude for Peaches? His Ex has a beady eye on the girl, we may be sure. It will be no simple matter to whisk her out of sight."

"Suppose we just let it ride for the present and see what develops," Retief suggested.

"You're right; it *is* close to tea-time," Magnan agreed. "After our little adventure, I'm famished."

4

Seated at the long table in the Senior Officers' Mess, Magnan cupped an ear attentively as Ambassador Grossblunder, at the head of the board, drew down the corners of his traplike mouth, glared along the line of faces miming Eager Interest Above and Beyond the Call of Duty (71-z).

"Don't strain a gusset, Ben," he advised Magnan, "I haven't said anything yet. And your seventy-one (about a weak *C*, I'd say) is lacking in zeal. Either that or your crumpet has disagreed with you."

"Not at all, Mr. Ambassador," Magnan reassured his chief. "The crumpets are superb. It was just that I didn't want to miss anything."

"Are you implying that I mumble?" Grossblunder demanded testily.

"Heavens, no, Your Excellency, not *you*!" Magnan improvised.

"Oh, you're suggesting I'm accustomed to yell," the Chief of Mission replied in the tones of one who has just solved a mystery.

"Who, me, sir?" Magnan whimpered.

"No, *me*, you idiot!" Grossblunder barked. "Better leave it at that, Ben; you're getting in deeper with every word. Now—" he dismissed the subject. "We're faced here, gentlemen—and lady," he added, with a smirk at Miss Flump, the junior assistant in the Cultural Attache's office. "Local regulations, it seems, are in direct conflict with Terran mores—to say nothing of common decency!"

"But, sir," Lacklustre of the Program Committee put in, "it's a basic of Corps policy, going all the way back to pre-space times, that native customs are to be regarded as sacrosanct to the point of the ridiculous, while one's own most treasured principles are to be abandoned at once in the face of a hint of alien disapproval."

"Certainly, Marvin," the great man acknowledged. "That's fine when it comes to eating aged Furthuronian Garg and like that, but these Glorbian barbarians are demanding that a shy, retiring, modest little *shicksa* parade around in front of a bunch of talking crabs and all, without a stitch to her back! Now, there's some things that ought to be reserved for a lady's husband or fatherly sponsor only. I'm putting my foot down: Peaches don't compete in the raw!"

"Still," Hy Felix of the Information Service put in, "it wouldn't look too good in the old record if Terra no-shows (no pun, boys) at this pernt."

"Say, sir," Magnan piped up. "I have a notion." He glanced around almost coyly at Retief before proceeding. "Why don't we substitute another candidate, one perhaps less inhibited than Miss Ripetree?"

"You saying Peaches got no team spirit, Ben? Nonsense, she's a good sport, just sheltered, is all. Anyway, where do you propose to scare up a replacement on about eight hours' notice? The big semifinal is at five pee em today, you know."

"Right, sir!" Magnan responded brightly. "And I imagine the farsighted and resourceful diplomat who produced a solution to the dilemma would rate an 'outstanding' in his effectiveness column next ER, eh, sir?"

"Ben," the Ambassador said sadly, "to dream of outstanding ER's at this point is visionary in the extreme, I should say." He jotted a note on his traditional yellow legal pad with one of the needle-sharp 2H pencils provided according to immemorial custom, snapping the point off short.

"Damn!" he snapped, tossing the offending instrument to the floor whence it was rescued and reverently replaced by young Marvin Lacklustre.

"Don't know why the Corps can't provide a decent electro-stylus instead of these damned charred sticks," he muttered, glaring along the table for signs of disapproval.

"Oh, I agree, sir," Magnan warbled as the icy glance seemed to hesitate for a moment on him.

" 'Critical of Corps policy,' " Grossblunder scribbled, snapping off a second needle-point. "But enough of these trifles," he decreed heavily. "Boys, we got to field a winner, pronto, and without giving Peaches chilblains, nor providing Thif with ammo for another smear."

"Why, Mr. Ambassador," Marvin offered eagerly, "why don't we just admit it's impossible, get off a dispatch to Sector so they won't find out from the morning pictonews, and get the heck out of this crummy place?"

"That will be enough out of you, Lacklustre,"

his Chief commanded almost quietly. "You're junior, remember, Marv, *very* junior, and your best strategy is to keep quiet and listen while your betters wrestle with the profound problems that beset the Galaxy."

"I don't see how Peaches showing her rump is so Galaxy-shaking," Marvin muttered under his breath, only partially drowned out by the simultaneous throat-clearing of three adjacent senior bureaucrats instinctively closing ranks to protect the young. Grossblunder looked startled, then shook his head dismissingly.

"Couldn't have done," he mumbled, then turned his 429-2 (Benign Paternalism, Sorely Tried) on Marvin.

"Any indiscretion uttered at this time under the stress of the moment will be overlooked, gentlemen," he intoned, adding, "you're lucky, Marvin, this time. See that you don't misinterpret charity as weakness."

"I've got an idea," Nat Sitzfleisch of the Econ Section spoke up briskly. "Suppose we wrap Peachy in bandages and claim she's got a skin condition that's highly contagious. That'll give 'em something to think about."

"Right, for about a zillioneth of a second," his Excellency replied sardonically, "then Thif will come up with his leader: 'Terries Impose Typhoid Mary on Galactic Beauties'."

"Heck, half of 'em don't even have skin," Nat muttered to himself. "With that oversized molluscoid babe from Yirg 19 and all them chitinous critters from you-name-it, and all the other ones with feathers and scales and all."

"It is precisely the *other* half which will raise the cry of contagion, Nat," Grossblunder pointed out, almost kindly.

"Don't be concerned, Mr. Ambassador," Magnan counselled dramatically. "I can assure Your Excellency that the matter will be resolved to the complete satisfaction of all."

Retief leaned closer to his supervisor to comment. "Too bad we don't know where Gertie is, eh, Mr. Magnan? Maybe I'd better go look for her."

"Not now," Magnan hissed. "Later, after Staff Meeting!"

"Ben," the Ambassador cut in, eyeing Magnan with a look as reassuring as an impending ice avalanche. "When you've concluded your chat, perhaps you'd return your attention to the problem you so lightly dismissed a moment ago."

"I didn't exactly dismiss it, sir," Magnan cried. "I only said I'm sure you'll resolve the matter satisfactorily, as usual."

"No, Ben," the Recording Secretary contradicted. "You said *you'd* clear everything up."

"Hardly, Fester," Magnan rebuked the clerk. "I but predicted a happy resolution of the affair, reposing full confidence in our chief, His Excellency the Terran AE and MP."

"Sure, that's OK for you, Ben," Grossblunder said grumpily, "but I'm the one's got to contend with Peaches, which I promised her she'd be the toast of the Eastern Arm. She's a demanding broad," he added, "and right now she's demanding my hide."

"Say, there's a Terry Mission over at Furthuron, only about six lights in-Arm," Colonel Underknuckle offered. "They prolly got a couple snazzy secretaries over there could stand in for this Ripetree dame if she's too shy to show. No pun intended, fellas."

"I think, Colonel, it might be difficult to explain that the Terran entrant had suddenly become twins," Grossblunder objected. "Even if, as I must assume, you have overnight developed a method of instanteous transfer of personnel."

"Now, nothing like that," the Attache objected, "I just thought—"

" 'Didn't think' might perhaps better describe your cerebral activity, Harvey," His Ex countered. "Now, back to your duties, gentlemen: we still have a few hours of daylight in which to come up with a solution which will doubtless go down in Corps history." He rose and left the room, attended by a cluster of his more image-conscious underlings, all talking at once. Retief slipped out by a side door and hurried away.

5

After dropping by the mess hall for a sandwich made from a slice of succulent haunch of frozen blurb-beast, Retief descended again to the rocky plateau, now nearly deserted, only a few discarded gribble-grub bags blowing in the hot wind to suggest that a crowd had dispersed only moments before. The featureless expanse of pinkish rock stretched away in all directions to a dark line of distant verdure. After ten minutes' brisk walk, Retief looked back: the visiting ships, some squat, some slender needles, had shrunk to insignificance. Ahead lay only more of the sun-baked terrain. He went on, scanning bare rock for a glimpse of Gertrude's sinuous form. Then, far ahead, Yong strolled into view from the shelter of a clump of tumbled rocks. Retief angled off to intercept the local cop, who changed course to meet him.

"You got any idear where she would of went?" Yong called. Retief shook his head. "Unless there's a patch of jungle not too far away," he suggested. "Gertie's used to dense vegetation."

Yong waved a front paw. "Sure," he said. "Right past the ridge yonder. This here's the only patch of desert this side o' the ocean. Government big shots didn't want to waste any useful real estate on a bunch of foreigners. Them Glorb are a bunch of small-timers, got no feel for public relations."

"You're critical of your government?" Retief commented idly.

"Not *my* gubment," Yong objected. "I ain't no Glorb. What I am, I'm a Vang," he declared with vehemence. "See, there's a number of mentational species evolved on Boondock. We used to eat 'em, yunnerstan', then the Groaci come along and set up the Glorbs in business as top dogs. Coulda wiped us out with them borrowed power guns, I guess, but these here Groaci—they're foreigners, like you. Well, not exactly like you, maybe worse. But they come along and stuck their snoots in. We hadda go along. They had all kinds o' zap-guns, yunnerstan'. But old King Zup the Sagacious, he sold 'em on a deal where we'd handle the rough stuff—army and all—and do cop duty. So now we coexist." Yong settled on his haunches and used a formidably taloned hind leg to dislodge a small parasite from behind an ear.

"Damn yutz-bugs," he commented. "Desert's full of 'em. You're lucky they can't use alien juices. That's one of our like grievances," he went on. "Damn Glorbs—or their Groaci pals—could exterminate the yutz-bugs any time—but they don't bother. Maybe old Zup didn't make such a neat deal after all. Well, let's go see if we can pick up her trail. I lost it on the rock-flats—but we oughta be able to find it on the sand if we quarter it pretty good."

Retief looked out across the sun-hazed expanse of wind-rippled dunes. "Let's try the jungle first," he suggested.

"No offense, pal," Yong offered almost diffidently, "but you don't look to me like you're designed for the desert work. Wanta ride? I wouldn't let no Glorb set on me, but hell, we're in this together. We'd make better time," he added.

Retief accepted, and a moment later the constable was proceeding by twenty-foot bounds toward the distant streak of green which marked the jungle's edge, the Terran astride and gripping the shaggy mane.

After a five-minute gallop, they were in the grateful shade of the towering fung trees, vine-draped patriarchs adorned with showy red-and-yellow blossoms the size of dinnerplates. Retief dismounted and thanked his steed for the lift. Yong nodded, his breathing hardly accelerated by the brisk run. "What we gotta do, Retief," he offered, "we got to look out for slangs—some of 'em run twenty foot and bigger around than me. Got jaws can snap up a boar mump in one bite, and got poison to boot. Nasty customers. Like to hang in the big fungs and drop on a fellow. Could squash a little guy like you accidental before he got a whiff and realized he couldn't digest you. Here, better let me go first." As the Vang thrust past his Terran ally, Retief glanced up at a scraping sound from the dark foliage above. He caught a glimpse of a sinuous neck supporting a head with a mouth like a dragline bucket, set with yellow fangs which dripped black venom. Then the head swooped, trailing an apparently inexhaustible length of yard-thick neck, uncoiling from the darkness. The heavy loops fell across Yong's back, staggering the powerful carnivore, then whipped around him in a crushing embrace while the head hovered, alert for the opportunity to dart in and inflict the fatal bite. As Yong screeched in pain and shock, Retief made a sudden movement with his right hand, and was holding a switch-blade poniard. He held it out to intercept a tarry glob of venom as it fell from the slang's jaws. Then he took a step forward, arm outstretched to intercept the attack. The knife sank to the hilt in the pale underside of the slang's throat. At once, the stricken monster recoiled, threshing with a fury that snapped off foot-thick boughs and tossed both Yong and Retief into the underbrush. Yong was first to speak:

"I seen that, Retief, neatly done, for a foreigner. How'd you know the only way to stop a slang is to knife him with his own venom?"

"We have a similar, though smaller creature back on Terra with a similar sensitivity," the Terran explained. "And in any case, I didn't have time to work out anything more sophisticated." He emerged from the tangle of vines into which he had been tossed by the slang's death-struggle to see Yong limp from cover, looking battered but intact.

"Like I said," the Vang commented calmly. "It don't pay to mess with a slang. That was a big one," he added. "Lucky, in a way; a smaller one'd struck first and broke up the bones after." He paused to rub awkwardly at his chest with a forepaw.

"Let me take a look," Retief suggested. He went over and gently palpated the big cat's side, eliciting a low moan of pain.

"We'd better get you back to the ship and see if our surgeon can tape you up," he suggested. "You've got at least three broken ribs there."

Yong turned to tug a length of the dead slang out into view. "It ain't et lately," he commented. "If it would've, there'd be a bulge. So maybe Gertie's OK. Unless it killed her by mistake, or just for meanness. We'd better find her as soon as we can."

"Let's start here," Retief suggested as he started off along a dimly marked trail.

"One spot is as good as another," Yong said. "These are animal trails. Like you said, we might as well start here." He went past Retief to lead the way into the black-green gloom; Retief followed, skirting the boles of giant buttressed trees, thrusting aside leafy fronds, ripping through clinging tangles of vine, to emerge on a tunnel-like path which twisted off into the deep jungle. Yong's camouflage was effective here, Retief noticed; his pink-and-green hide was invisible at a few feet's distance among the dark green shadows and glancing streaks of sunlight which penetrated here. The Terran was hard put to keep pace with his lithely slinking guide. After five minutes' headlong progress, Yong recoiled suddenly, turning quickly to face Retief.

"Bad luck, Terry; it's a tud. Great big frothy sort of creature; it can engulf you in a trice or two and dissolve you in nothing flat. By the way, I got that 'nothing flat' and 'trice' out of a phrase-book we had to learn at the academy. What do they mean?"

"Nothing much," Retief dismissed the matter absently as he went past Yong to look at what appeared to be a thick, yellowish blanket with a wet-glistening surface which bubbled and seethed here and there. Behind it stretched a trail of bare stems, denuded of foliage. A leaf fell on the heaving surface, and was instantly engulfed. The mass rippled and edged closer, extending a lumpy pseudo-pod toward Yong, skirting Retief widely. A dead branch fell on the tud, splashing fluid matter before it sank from view, smoking. As Yong recoiled with a yowl, slapping at a fleck which had spattered on his forelimb, Retief observed other droplets burning their way through foliage or deep into the boles of trees. A small gob had come to rest on his sleeve, he noted, but after an initial spasm it appeared quiesent. He flicked it away. There was no visible damage to the synthetic fibers of the jacket, he noted, nor did the tiny smear of fluid left on his fingertip appear to be active.

Yong had retreated a few yards along the trail. "We'll have to go around," he called. "Nothing can go over a hungry tud."

"Maybe I can," Retief countered. "I don't think the tud likes Terries for lunch any more than the slang did."

"Hold it!" Yong snapped. "This is different: chemical action, you know, not metabolic digestion. Step on that and you'll be shorter by a foot.''

Before Retief could respond, a shrill scream sounded from the deep jungle ahead With a crashing of underbrush, Gertrude appeared, upside down, enmeshed in the coils of a squid-like creature, deep red in color. The tigress was fighting desperately, raking deep-purple furrows in the smooth leathery hide of the thing that had seized her. Her yellow eyes fell on Retief and she redoubled her efforts, wresting both hind legs free of the muscular, sinuous tentacles; but now a great bone-yellow parrot beak was snapping bare inches from her flank.

"Too bad," Yong called. "That's a zuzz's got her. They can eat anything. She's a goner."

"Hang on, Gertrude," Retief called encouragingly to the embattled feline. He put a foot on the pulsating surface of the tud, which spasmed—then seemed to melt away underfoot as the creature withdrew its substance from contact with the alien matter. In four strides Retief was across and crashing through dense brush to come up on the zuzz from the side, where a single lidless foot-wide eye stared blankly at him. Quick as thought, the pulpy body twisted and the beak snapped just short of Retief's knee with a report like a hardshot. Retief scooped up a handful of the tud's gruelly substance and deposited it on the glistening eye, which dissolved, bubbling, into a blackish-purple pit. The zuzz went into a frenzied struggle which tossed the tigress clear. Gertrude landed on her feet and after a few swift licks to smooth her rumpled pelt, stood calmly awaiting Retief's pat. In its struggles, the zuzz had hurled itself squarely onto the greedy surface of the tud, which engulfed it eagerly, spitting out only the horny beak, then contracting to a lumpy sphere which rolled into deep shadow. Giving Gertrude a final pat, Retief took from the breast pocket of his blazer (early late morning; informal, middle three grades, for the use of) the replica fountain pen he had received as *lagniappe* after the signing of the Terran-Yalcan accord in '76, went to the nearest splashed-off gob of the tud's glutinous substance, and sucked up a sample into the pen's bladder.

Meanwhile, Yong had cautiously picked his way around the now quiescent tud to rejoin Retief.

"Now that you've fed it a square meal, it'll lie up all day," the local feline informed his guest. "You know," he added, eyeing Retief obliquely, "I guess in your own way, you Terries ain't so soft, after all. When you dumped that load on old zuzz's eyeball, I wouldn'ta missed that for my next two step-increases. Come on, we got ground to cover." He edged over beside the tigress.

"You OK, kid?" he inquired solicituously. Gertrude replied with a saucy twitch of her ears and a jaw-cracking yawn.

"Sure, play it cool," Yong muttered as he fell back beside Retief. "You know," he confided, "some dames got to act like they're too good for a fellow—but she don't fool me: she's got eyes for me."

"No doubt," Retief replied. "But she's shy—not used to all this excitement."

"I shoulda figured," Yong conceded apologetically. For a few moments they moved along the well-marked trail in silence. "We'll hit the main trail in a couple o' them trices," Yong informed

Retief. "Then a brisk half-hour's walk and we'll be at the Big Market, where I betcha I can show you and the lady here a few sights most foreigners never get to see. But play 'em close to the chest; there's plenty o' Glorbs hangs around the market and some of 'em are government finks, on the lookout for the dodges and all, and lately, there's been a bunch of military personnel. Me, I'm easy-going: I don't like 'em, but I don't bother 'em—long as they don't start on me."

When they reached the intersection with the main trail, Retief resumed his seat astride the big cat, while Gertrude paced alongside, wrinkling her nose at strange odors. Once, a hard-shelled, many-legged creature the size of a small dog leapt at her face, toothed claws cocked; she batted it aside casually. Yong, watching from the corner of his eye, exclaimed in admiration.

"You got to be fast to beat a rulp to the punch," he declared. "That Gertrude is something else," he confided to Retief, who agreed solemnly.

After a fast sprint along the wide trail, Yong slowed and turned his head to counsel Retief:

"Heads up, Terry. We hit the main drag in another hundred feet, and there's likely to be some Glorbs hanging around, looking for trouble." As good as his word, moments later Yong burst into a clearing from which debouched half a dozen well-marked trails. Around the mouth of the widest, half a dozen squat gray Glorbs stood in a tight conversational group. They turned as one, drawing together as Yong skidded to a halt beside them. A terse conversation in the local *bech-de-mer* followed, the Glorbs demanding, Yong interpolating conciliatorily. After a pause, the Vang twisted his head to speak to Retief, who had dismounted:

"These bums claim to be Customs Officers; claim they're looking for smuggled zitz-weed. Prolly lying. They want to search you and Gertrude."

"I won't bother invoking diplomatic immunity," Retief concurred mildly. "But I doubt if Gertie will sit still for any invasion of privacy."

Yong spoke briefly to the Glorbs in the glottal local trade tongue. One of the Glorbs nodded and stepped forward. Retief raised his arms to be patted down efficently. The inspector paused and re-patted Retief's left side, then roughly unzipped the access-slot and, groping over Retief's hip, encountered his 1mm needler, which he unceremoniously jerked from its holster with an exclamation.

"Naughty," Retief commented, and plucked the weapon from the Glorb's grasp. "You said zitz-weed, remember?" The Terran reminded his host. "In any case, the side arm is part of the standard coverall, late early morning, fatigue, middle three grades, for the use of. Just remember your manners, and maybe we won't need to have an Interplanetary Incident."

Yong translated, somewhat garbling the part about the Interplanetary Incident. The excited Glorb retired, rubbing his manipulator members, to confer in heated gabble with his associates.

"You handled that knot-head right," Yong told Retief. "Give these hick cops an ulp and they'll take a yik."

One of the Glorbs went briskly to Gertrude, began his frisk, patting down the tiger's sleek side. She wrinkled her nose and offered a rumbling growl. When the inspector began exploring her neck, she shook him off impatiently, then cuffed him aside, sending him skidding into the underbrush. The other Glorbs rushed forward, and Gertie sent them spinning left and right.

"I ain't sure that was such a good idear, kid," Yong commented to Gertie, as more Glorbs came boiling from the tumbledown barracks off to the right, unlimbering weapons as they closed in, growling sharp commands to each other. As the first one reached Gertie, coming up from behind her, she spun and cuffed him back among his fellows, bowling over half a dozen, who came to their feet drawing guns. Yong uttered a bellow and, with a prodigious leap, placed himself in front of the Terran cat, shielding her from gunfire. The Glorbs halted, and Yong delivered a speech—short, but deadly in tone. As Retief came up beside him, he said:

"They think Gertrude's some kind of off-color Vang. I'm stringing 'em: reminded 'em about the treaty says any Glorb uses one of them fire-guns on a Vang, they get Vang coming at 'em from all directions at once. They'll back off." He edged protectively close to Gertrude, who ambled away unconcernedly.

As Yong had predicted, the excited locals holstered their weapons and withdrew into huddles, all talking at once. Other Glorbs were poking their lumpy heads from the doorways of the long buildings at the far side of the marketplace, only to be shooed back inside by those in authority. One of the stumpy locals confronting Yong barked at the big feline in his stacatto tongue. Yong turned to Retief.

"This clown says he heard about how the Minister was assaulted when he went to pay his respects to the damned foreigners," he translated. "Now he claims to see why.

"There's something going on here, Retief," the Vang added quietly. "There are too many armed troops here. I think they're planning something tricky, and we stumbled into it. No wonder they're so touchy."

"Where's their boss?" Retief asked. Yong pointed to a small, but somewhat more sturdily built hut at the end of the row of barracks. "That's headquarters," he told Retief. "I don't see any rank on them bums, so the colonel's probably in there, on the phone."

"Suppose we pay a courtesy call?" Retief suggested.

"The colonel wouldn't like that a bit," Yong replied. "Let's go."

As Retief, Yong at his side, approached the pivoting panel serving as entry to the small blockhouse, it rotated abruptly, and a small, rather furtive individual, wrapped in a dowdy black ankle-length cloak with umbrella-like ribs, darted through the narrow opening and halted abruptly, confronted by the tall Terran and his cat-like companion.

Retief sniffed, then said in Groaci, "To be surprised to find *you* here, litter-mate of drones."

"To have no idea what you're saying," the stranger replied breathlessly in the same language. "Did you call me a litter-mate of drones?"

"I could have," Retief acknowledged, in Terran. "But we don't understand Groaci Court Dialect, remember?"

"Outrageous!" the small newcomer hissed and started past Yong, who snorted and pinned the fellow flat on his back with a casual swipe of one mighty forepaw. "Smells worse'n a Terry," the big cat commented. "No offense."

"I think you're a little outside your territory, Col. Shinth," Retief pointed out to the struggling captive. "And if you're trying to operate under cover, you'd better lay off those licorice-flavored dope-sticks. Outside of a few degenerates in the Customs and Excise Service, you're the only Groaci I know who smokes them. Dead giveaway."

"Drat your confounded nosy habits!" Shinth hissed as Yong removed his forepaw from the alien's narrow chest. The Groaci hopped up at once, wrapped himself in his tattered cloak and punctured dignity, and turned away. Retief halted him with one outstretched arm. Yong watched incuriously.

"Before you go," Retief said to Shinth, "Let's have a little chat about what's going on here."

Shinth responded by attempting to duck, but was promptly knocked down by Yong, who stood over the frail-looking alien, baring his teeth.

"I'd hate to have to bite you, chum," the constable said mildly. "You'd probably poison me. But if my pal Retief wants to talk to you, you'll have to stick around." He turned to Retief. "You know this little bug?" he asked, yawning.

"He used to be the Groaci Military Attache at Boneyard V," Retief replied.

Shinth hissed and sputtered, twining and untwining his five stemmed eyes with dizzying effect. Yong stepped back and Retief lifted the outraged Groaci to his feet, handed him back his dope-stick.

"Why the concentration of Glorb troops, here in this backwoods market?" Retief asked the Groaci. "And what are *you* doing here, conferring with the high command? Hardly the place for a peace-loving Groaci diplomat." As the spindly alien remained silent except for continued muttering, Retief gave him a slight shake, dislodging several of his jeweled top-three-grade eye-shields. "Come on Shinth, give," Retief urged.

"Retief?" the Groaci burst out. "Surely you, as a fellow diplomat, can't expect me to divulge information prejudicial to the security of the Groacian state?" Hastily, Shinth retrieved and adjusted his eye-shields. "Outrageous!" he commented. "Unhand me at once, Retief; you are aware of course that this assault will be the object of an Official Inquiry! I daresay even your truculent Terry AE and MP will see to it your already glacial advance in rank will be severly curtailed!"

"The security of Groac, eh?" Retief queried. "You must be up to something bigger than usual. What is it, Shinth? Cooking up a spontaneous demonstration against Terran interference in Glorbian internal affairs?"

"Nothing so banal," Shinth replied cooly, as if he were now on secure ground. "Step aside now, there's a good fellow, and perhaps I shall find it in my vascular pump to forget this affair."

"You say that if anyone knew what you're doing here, it would threaten the Security of Groac, eh?" Retief inquired rhetorically.

"Nothing of the sort!" the colonel objected, speaking perfect Terran now. "I was merely out for a stroll, noticed the charming town here, and dropped in to cement relations at the grass-roots level."

"This spot is surrounded by Big Black Bog on three and a half sides," Yong commented. "The only trail in is the one we took. Troops had to be airlifted in. Maybe we better go inside and ask General Mub personal what's cooking."

"What?" Colonel Shinth spoke up in a shocked tone. "Burst in on the General in the midst of his logistical planning? You wouldn't dare!"

"That did it," Yong commented, brushing the excited Groaci aside. Without hesitating, he slid sinuously through the half-open door. At once, hoarse Glorb voices could be heard raised in expostulation; then the doorway disgorged a grayish-skinned Glorb trooper who rolled to a stop at Retief's feet.

"Help!" the excited soldier yelled as Retief put a foot on his face to hold him in place.

"Stay a while," Retief suggested gently. "I'm here to get the details on General Mub's plans."

"Oh, you're one of those alien advisors, Groacs, or whatever. We had word one of you nosy Parkers was dropping in. Trooper Blub reporting sir." The stubby Glorb attempted a snappy salute from the supine position.

"It is precisely *I* who am the nosy Parker," Shinth interrupted excitedly, pushing between Retief and the Glorb, whom the Terran had permitted to rise.

"Now, Trooper Blub," Shinth went on, "you may conduct me to the presence of the General."

"Fruits and nuts," Blub replied in a disrespectful tone. "You don't look nothing like a Groaci, like this gent here." Blub eased closer to indicate his correct alignment, foreign big-shot wise.

"You would confer the mantle of Groacihood on this notorious mere Terran?" the outraged attache hissed in a tone sufficiently high-pitched to fetch a small burrowing creature from its nearby den to investigate. Shinth kicked a lump of dirt at the inquisitive creature, sending it scurrying for its hole.

"Hey, fella," the trooper objected, "don't go kicking no clods at the General's pet dirt-frog!" He hurried over to lean close and make comforting sounds. Looking up at Retiref, he explained: "When Tootsie here gets in a bad mood, the old boy goes into a towering tizzy his own self."

"A tizzy which, however, diminishes to insignificance by comparision with that occasioned by the absence of his orderly when the old devil needs a refill in his humidor!" An enraged Glorb voice roared from the doorway.

"Oh, General, sir!" Blub cried in a delighted tone as he scrambled to his feet and hastily dusted at the mud and grass stains on his pinkish-gray uniform. "Just communing with dear little Tootsie a minute was all," he alibied lamely. "Feller likes to be sure the little darlin is cosy and all."

"You'd be well advised, Trooper Last Class Blub," the General pointed out, "to concern yourself first with the cosiness of your immediate supervisor, Corps commander, and immeasurable superior in the person of myself!"

"Say," Yong commented to Retief admiringly. "He sounds like one of the Ambassadore's like I heard sounding off back at the port."

"He has the gift of ego," Retief agreed. "He could go far in the Corps."

"This here," a not noticably chastened Blub said eagerly as he hurried forward to reestablish his usefulness as liaison between the General and reality, "is that Groaci advisor, Mr., ... ah, what was that name again, sir?"

"Retief!" Shinth yelled in his feeble voice.

"Grab him!" General Mub snapped, pointing at the excited Groaci. "I've been tipped," he added, "that an alien of that name might well attempt mischief here. General Hish himself rang up only a moment ago to let me know the fellow had been sighted at the port by an alert field-man named Thif."

"You're making a serious blunder, you incompetent blimp!" Shinth yelled over Blub's shoulder as the latter slipped the cuffs on him.

" 'Incompetent blimp,' " the General repeated. "Make a note of that, Blub. Where did the noisy little freak come from, anyways?"

"Beats me, General sir," Blub admitted. "He come up and started trying to make trouble just when I was about to announce this Groaci VIP here." The trooper proudly indicated his protege, Retief.

"Must be one of those Terry miscreants Hish told me about," the General deduced. "Hish said they harbored a vicious prejudice against selfless Groacian bureaucrats, as he so eloquently put it. Better lock him up in Number Three," the General concluded briskly, then turned to Retief. "And now, sir, perhaps we can get down to matters of substance." He motioned Retief, accompanied by Yong, ahead, into the dimly lit interior of the headquarter hutment, where half a dozen lumpy Glorb officers, with their colorful rank badges, sat huddled around a knee-high table on which were laid out charts of increasing scale, the final one a close-up photo-montage of the patch of desert allocated to the alien vessels, and the amphitheatre soon to be the scene of the Pan-Galactic Pageant. Retief leaned over it to study closely the fine photographic detail.

"Units all in place just hull-down," the General pointed out complacently, "all in accordance with regs, right down to the prepared press dispatches: Terry Bandits Raid Galactic Glamor Get-together!"

"We're getting close to M-minute," Retief hazarded. "All set to jump off on signal?"

"Sure," General Mub confirmed. "Now that the Whonk entry has arrived, we've got a full bag. My boys are raring to go. The smoke bomb's ready and waiting for the word."

"And what *is* the word?" Retief asked casually.

" 'Y'Yivshish'," the General supplied promptly. "Right? Am I on my carpals, or what?"

"I see the Groaci advisor was so gracious as to provide the term," Retief commented, "along with the rest of the scheme."

"Right, Lord ... uh ... what was that handle again, Your Lordship?" Mub inquired obsequiously.

"Shhh," Retief cautioned. "You might have a security leak here, you know, General."

"In that case, he's in trouble," Yong commented to Retief in a hoarse whisper. "Looks like the infernal Glorbs are up to their cauliflower ears in something that could get the whole planet in hot water." He mosied over to study the charts, casually dislodging a Glorb three-pipper, who complained loudly in his own dialect, then switched to Groaci, which he spoke with a barbaric accent:

"To have tooken my last insult from an uncouth Vang flatfoot!" he screeched. "You just wait a couple days, chum, and you and your whole barbaric tribe will be sitting behind wire looking out at the glorious triumph of Glorb destiny!"

"Would you like to go into a little detail, Colonel Crudbum?" Yong suggested as he pinned the noisy officer with one mighty paw, while yawning cavernously.

"It's all but accomplished!" the prostrate Glorb yelled. "And you'll be awful sorry you mishandled a field-grade officer of Great Glorb!"

"This don't look good, pal," Yong commented to Retief. "This sucker is too fiesty by half." He gave the struggling colonel a dismissing shove and watched closely as the fellow got to his feet.

"The Glorb have always been small-timers," the big cat pointed out. "This time they're pulling something outa their league. Must be they got some big ideas from you Groaci." He winked, giving his usually good-natured face a sinister cast which, Retief reflected, boded little good for any who might attempt to betray the Vang.

"Here," General Mub interrupted busily. "It is hardly your responsibility, Constable, to intrude in state affairs. Kindly limit your officiousness to seeking out and neutralizing these pesky Terries, if any more should venture into the area."

"What's cooking, General?" Yong countered, pointedly ignoring the military big-wig's demand. "Sounds like the Glorb army's getting ready to do something foolish."

"It is the army not of the Glorb alone," the officer came back. "I'll remind you that it is the defense force of the entire planet and thus Glorbian, not just Glorbish, and is recognized as such by a major Galactic power!"

"You mean your pals the Groaci," Yong commented indifferently. "Sure, I know they set you boys up as head tribe here, but don't let 'em sucker you into some dumb adventure you can only lose. No space fleet, remember? You piss off Terra, for example, and you'll be looking up at a solid layer of dreadnaughts englobing the planet. Against that, noisy speeches won't make much of a dent."

"Aha, but let them attempt to land!" Mub came back, unchastened. "They'll encounter not only the advanced technology of Glorb, but the ferocity of the world's lesser life-forms! If I but unloose a thousand tud against their infantry, they'll rue the day—"

"Sure," Yong agreed readily. "I guess I forgot how big an appetite the old tuds have got, at that. I just hope the Terries don't give 'em a bellyache." The big cat winked again at Retief, then retired to a corner to snooze. Mub rustled pages on his desk and gave Retief a quizzical look.

"Now, as to general outlines," he stated hurriedly, "I am of course fully briefed. Up to the point where we sieze the hostages, my duty is clear. But so far, my advisor hasn't divulged the details of our demands."

"Oh, the usual trade concessions," Retief suggested casually, "including exclusive rights to various remunerative markets, of course, plus various protective embargoes, letters of marque to protect your trade lanes, adequate developmental grants, options on a few dozen virgin worlds—that should do for openers," he concluded. "Always remember Groac's status as Most Favored Nation, eh? Would you care to add anything?"

"That sounds adequate," Mub agreed blandly, "for openers only, of course, as Your Excellency suggests. But how about one of those snazzy Thousand-Tonne VIP boats as my personal transport, 'Glorb Number One', OK? And I'll need a Bugatti *Royale* replica for ground travel, armored in an inconspicuous way, and mounting a brace of infinite repeaters for crowd control."

"The General is modest," Retief answered. "And just where do you intend to impound the Galactic beauties after you've taken them hostage? I'll need to review your security arrangements, of course."

"To be sure," Mub agreed expressionlessly. "There's a cave I know of, back in the desert. Nothing fancy, but good enough for a couple of weeks. We could put in some cots, or hot mud boxes, or whatever, and a port-o-let, and cater the whole thing. Just need a couple near-sighted limited-duty troopers to stand guard over 'em, so they don't wander off in the desert and get lost."

As Mub was concluding his remarks, there was a stir at the entrance, and a small, spindle-legged stranger, closely wrapped in a puce cloak thrust past the protesting sentry to confront the Glorb general.

"To see here, General," he whispered. "To have heard report of atrocities directed at one of my staff, a general officer, Shinth by name—"

"Hey!" Mub cut off the recrimination, "it's one

o' them Terries! Grab him, boys, and don't worry about bending him a little!"

At once, a brace of the nearest Glorb sprang into action, seizing the slightly built newcomer by both arms, tearing away his cloak in the process, while the object of their attention hissed indignantly.

"See?" General Mub cried. "I tole you! Them five wiggly eyes is a dead giveaway. Don't let him pull nothing, now. Say, fellow, just who are you, anyways?"

The Groaci, having been spun about, was now face to face with Retief. His eyes went rigid, then wilted, indicating Total Incredulity (41-b). "Retief!" he yelled.

"No, you can't fool me on that one," Mub dismissed the shout. "I got this Retief locked up in my number three dungeon. You'll hafta do beter'n that. Anyways, I know this Retief to be a 'miscreant o' the worst stripe,' I think Hish said. Now, who are you?"

"To be none other than that same Broodmaster Hish whose name you invoked so lightly but now," the Groaci whispered.

"You, Hish?" Mub scoffed. "You're a Terry, I know the type. Got a nerve at that, walking in here. Got some scheme to release this Retief, I guess."

"To perdition with Retief!" Hish shrilled, pointing at the tall Terran. "There stands Retief, as bold as a brass Hoogan idol! Arrest him forthwith! Clap him in irons this instant! I insist!"

"You're in no position to do no insisting, bub," Mub pointed out. "Now spill it: what did you plan to do? What's the idea busting in here while I and my distinguished guest, the Groacian Advisor-in-Chief are tryna have a little chin-chin? Hah?'' The General gestured peremptorily to a guard.

"Number four," he ordered. "And better double-padlock it. This one's the tricky type."

"To rue the day!" Hish keened. "To kneel before a Tribunal of summary expediency and beg forgiveness for this moment!"

"Oh, don't tear yourself up, fella," Mub replied in a tone which implied Expansive Magnanimty (244-b). "You hadda job to do; you gave it a try—but you run up against Major General Mub, DAC, FBY, and flunked out. I'll even put in a good word for your brass at the trial."

"To be not I, but you, dolt," Hish yelled, "who is to stand at the bar of practicality!" Then he was dragged away, still struggling, until the hollow *bonk*! of a spear-butt against his cranial plates silenced him.

"General," Retief said quietly in the hush following the pseudo-Terran's departure. "You forgot to mention just when you plan to utter the signal."

"Oh, sorry about that, your Lordship," Mub replied briskly. "Just coming to that, actually. Let's see . . . how about daybreak? Catch 'em with their sentries just doing the changing of the guard routine. Hit 'em fast and off again in a couple o' them trices I hear the Constable here talking about."

"That sounds just a trifle impulsive, General," Retief told the officer. "Not to me, of course, knowing your deliberative nature, but to the Board of Inquiry."

"Me? I don't need to worry about no Board," Mub dismissed the thought. "I got half them suckers on the payoff roll, and the other half are in on the scheme up to their vibrational nodules."

"Not the planetary board," Retief corrected. "The Galactic Board. You'll get a free trip to Alpha Centauri to attend—quite an experience, if you don't let a set of VIP irons bother you too much."

"I done nothing wrong," Mub declared only a trifle uncertainly. "All I done was follow orders and cooperate with you Groaci. Don't forget it was you fellows that sold the Grand Glorb on the idea we could hold up what he called the Galactic community for whatever we want, to give us our, uh, 'rightful status as a Galactic power', or something, was what Hish said."

"Just wait until the Galactic community reads the headlines," Retief proposed. " 'Glorb General Grabs Galactic Glamor Girls'. What about your status then? They'll be coming after you, personally, with ropes, clubs, knives, baseball bats, spears, pellet guns, blasters, flint knives and reformers. Where can you hide?"

"I don't get it," Mub declared, his lumpy gray face looking chalky-pale. "You, the big Groaci advisor tryna throw a scare into me right on the eve o' yer own scheme. It don't figger."

"Merely testing your mettle, General," Retief explained deftly. "I think now I'd best have a word with the spy in Number Three."

"Sure," Mub agreed, seeming relieved at the change of subject. "Hey sergeant—you with the dumb look," he clarified, gesturing to a heavier-than-average Glorb. "Escort this here noble-being over Number Three, leave him interview the Terry."

6

Number Three was a natural cave hollowed ages ago in the soft limestone of a cliff-face by long-vanished waters. Its entrance was barred with stout two-inch rods, against which Shinth slumped disconsolately, all five eyes drooping listlessly. One snapped to the alert as Retief came up.

"Foul evening, vile Soft One," he spat half-heartedly. "You'll rue the day you impersonated a noble Groacian, your reactionary schemes to promote."

"No doubt, Broodmaster," Retief conceded gracefully. "But I plan to do all my ruing later on, not right now. As for you," Retief switched to the Groaci court dialect. "To give some thought to how you can get yourself—and Groac—out of the trap you've built for yourselves. 'Groaci Grab Galactic Glamor Gals,'" he recited. "To fear Groaci prestige will sink to an all-time low when word gets out."

"Word won't get out!" Shinth hissed. "Not even you, vile wrecker and noxious persecutor of selfless Groacian bureaucrats, would sink so low as to snitch, not that we actually know anything about Mub's mad scheme."

"Tell me all about Mub's mad scheme," Retief directed the excited Broodmaster. "He gave me only the broad outlines. I'd like you to fill in the details."

"Would you not!" Shinth spat. "To have never trusted that blabbermouth Mub! The fool will be the first to know the wrath of outraged Groacihood, one I get sprung from this lousy cell."

"That may be quite some time," Retief pointed out. "According to Sergeant Flup here, the glab-worm comes out of the recesses of his den to feed every seventy-two hours. It's been about seventy and a half, so if you've got your handy escape kit with you, it's time to get it inflated."

"Would stand by and watch a fellow being-of-the-Galaxy die horribly?" Shinth quavered. "Allow a fellow diplomat to disappear into the maw of the fearsome glab-worm? To be a bit surprised, Retief. To have not believed even you could sink to the level of these barbaric natives!"

"Hey!" Sergeant Flup interrupted. "Who you calling barbaric, Terry?"

"And who are *you* calling a vile Terry?" Shinth retorted.

"You was the one said that," Flup reminded his captive. "I heard you my ownself say you were that Retief the advisors warned his Nibs about!"

"No I didn't," Shinth denied. "It's all one of those grotesque misunderstandings."

"What's Grote got to do with it?" the sergeant challenged. "I hear that's a nice, peaceful planet never done Glorb no harm. And are you saying you lied to the General?"

"By no means, Sergeant." Shinth replied with wounded dignity. "If you but knew what awesome forces you tempt when you impugn the veracity of a Groacian Broodmaster. . . ."

"Wait a minute," Retief put in. "A moment ago you were coming on like a poor, humble functionary, following orders; now suddenly you're playing the Interplanetary VIP angle. You'd better make up your mind before the Sergeant decides to take you out of that nice safe cage and run you off into the jungle, where the tud lurks, and the mump-boar roams in search of prey."

"Good idea, Mr. Advisor," Flup commented as he detached his keys from his wide tump-leather belt. "Just what I had in mind. Uh, you don't think the General will bite my ass, do you?" After a moment he added thoughtfully: "Still, it's been chewed before, and there's still plenty of good sweet ass left."

"Time grows short, fellow!" Shinth keened, shaking a knobby fist.

"Too right," Flup admitted as he removed the padlocked panel and stepped back to allow his spindly prisoner to emerge.

"Retief!" Shinth whispered. "You wouldn't really abandon me to the mercies of the fabled tud, would you? Pretty please with sugar on, let a fellow Second Secretary remain safe inside."

"There's still the glab-worm, remember?" Retief replied. "About an hour and a half, I'd say. But you be the judge. After you've written out a full confession, I'll let you choose—or rather this alert noncom will. Right, Flup?"

"You betcha, Mr. Advisor. Anything you say. Cause I know you'll file a good word for me with old Mub."

"Old Mub has already filed some five thousand words on you, none of them good, I fear, Sergeant," the General's voice spoke suddenly from directly behind the NCO, who leaped as if prodded by a spear and alighted explaining, an effort ignored by his superior.

'You'll have to excuse Flup here," Mub said to

Retief. "The poor boob's not playing with a full set of googy-stones. Should of sent him back to Headquarters where it wouldn't be noticed."

Before the situation could deteriorate further, there was a sudden crashing of underbrush and the giant form of Constable Yong arrived in a leap, a narrow-shouldered Terran astride his back, his arms wrapped around the big cat's neck.

"Hiya, chum," the Vang greeted Retief. Magnan, still clinging to his perch, raised his head and weakly cried:

"There you are! I feared you'd been done a mischief when I turned to speak to you and found only that slimy little gossip-monger, Thif, at my elbow. Then I remembered you were on close terms with the, uh, officer here, and when I followed his trail it led me to him, and—"

"Now, Ben," Shinth spoke up from his awkward position in the grasp of Sergeant Flup. "You're a reasonable chap, you'll see to it your associate does nothing prejudicial to Groaci-Terran relations, I'm sure!"

"Of course, Shinth," Magnan concurred soothingly. "But it was uncommonly crude of you to plant Major Fith on us, posing as a reporter. Alas, he was able to divulge only a part of your scheme before he passed—"

"Away?" Shinth blurted, all five eyes vibrating in shock.

"Merely out, Colonel," Magnan reassured the agitated fellow. "But you can rectify the omission. If you hurry, I shall be all the more favorably disposed toward ameliorating the severity of your sentence. Hurry up and Tell All; I have to get the word back in time for Staff Meeting if I'm to score maximum points—ah, abort the mischief, that is."

" 'Tell *All*'," Shinth whispered. "Then you know about . . ." he paused to dash a drop of lachrymal exudation from an eyestalk. "Alas, I am undone," he mourned.

"To be sure," Magnan replied cooly. "Speak up, Colonel. May as well take defeat like a warrior."

"All right, since that wretch Fith has already spilled the legumes, I may as well fill in the details. No court would cry me culpable."

"Start talking," Magnan ordered curtly.

"The Grand War Fleet will be landing at high noon, local, encircling the fairgrounds," Shinth whispered brokenly.

"Ye Gods!" General Mub yelled. "A Terran fleet invading Glorb? Disaster! General Hish assured me nothing of the sort was to be feared!"

"I say, General," Magnan objected tentatively, "Shinth said nothing about a *Terran* fleet. Doubtless it is a Groaci fleet to which he alludes."

"What would Retief know of Groacian treachery?" Mub yelled.

"Actually as a diplomat, he's quite experienced in the field," Magnan assured the agitated patriot. "As am I myself, of course."

"Yes, yes, I suppose your intelligence apparatus has ferreted out many of their fell designs. By the way, what sort of being are you?"

"Surely you jest, General," Magnan suggested. "I am of course, a Deputy Chief of Mission, on temporary assignment to the Pageant."

"Sure, but except for His Lordship here," the

General indicated Retief, "I never saw one like you before. You're not one of them Glimps, are you?"

"By no means, sir," Magnan said soothingly. "Now if you'll excuse me, His Lordship and I must be off; final preparation for the preliminary competition, you know."

"You call an invasion force a preliminary competition?" Mub inquired in his usual yell. "What's next? Genocide?"

"It was the pageant to which I alluded," Magnan corrected the officer. He turned to Retief. "Shall we go? I'd best hurry ahead with the Constable, in the interest of prompt action." He went briskly to the side of Yong, who had stretched out comfortably in a patch of sunlight.

"Nix," the Vang demurred. "I'm sticking with my old pal Retief."

"Oh, very well," Mub agreed. "Hand him over, Sergeant," he directed the non-com who was still gripping Shinth's skinny arm.

"Glad to, sir," Flup said promptly, thrusting the crestfallen Groaci toward Magnan.

"There must be some mistake," Magnan began, recoiling; then his eye was caught by Retief, who shook his head unobstrusively.

"But then I suppose the Constable can accomodate another."

"No sweat," Yong agreed. "But I still ain't going anywhere without Retief."

"How about it, gents?" General Mub said earnestly to Magnan. "Can you fellows get a battle fleet out here to cancel out the one this little beggar's got standing by?"

"But, my dear General," Magnan demurred, "that would be in violation of sacred interplanetary agreements."

"Not if we acted in response to a formal request from the General," Retief pointed out.

"To be sure," Magnan agreed thoughtfully. "So, I'd best hurry back to my office aboardship to draw up the document."

"Nope," Yong put in. "I'll take Retief, nobody else."

"The blank Technical Assistance forms are in my desk drawer, just under the Foreign Office Notes," Magnan told Retief quickly. "Fill one in and hurry back. No typos, remember: the Glorbian Foreign Minister is finicky about using blank forms in the first place."

"Let's all go, except for *him*," Mub suggested with a venomous glance at Yong. "My staff whirly-gig or whatever you call it, is standing by just over the ridge."

"I'll see you there," Yong commented as he turned and bounded away.

Retief unobtrusively stepped closer to Shinth, whom Flup had thrust back into his cell. He handed the Groaci his fountain pen.

"Give the glab-worm a shot of this in the eye, when it come out for lunch," he suggested, "then break it in two and toss it down its throat, and retire to a neutral corner," then he rejoined Magnan and the General.

7

Ten minutes later, in Magnan's office, General Mub signed with a flourish the hastily typed-up form, requesting, or more accurately, demanding the immediate dispatch of technical assistance, complete with trained personnel and full field equipment. "Yep," he commented, "the boys back at HQ will sit up and take notice when they see how I pulled their fat outa the fire this time. I'll have that third star in no time, soon's they see the Groaci fleet slip in to block off the Terries."

"General Mub," Magnan said solemnly, "an unfortunate misunderstanding has somehow arisen. We are not Groaci; that noisy fellow in Number Three is a Groaci, while Retief here and myself are genuine Terrans, ready to save your fat and get you that star."

"What?" Mub yelled. "You mean I got one of Glorb's benefactors in the slammer, and I'm standing here chinning with the notorious Retief? They'll bust me back to buck general—or maybe T-5. Corporal! Lock up this pair of sharpies!" He gestured to a torpid two-striper standing by, who shuffled his feet, but failed to move.

"Pray don't be hasty, General," Magnan urged, backing away. "Consider: whether you call us rose or weed, it is nonetheless the wretch in Number Three who had admitted that it is *his* hostile vessels which are about to invade sacred Glorbian soil."

Mub paused in mid-yell to scratch at his heavy

jaw with a blunt finger. "You got a point there, fella; and frankly I been troubled by one little detail: 'sneaky little five-eyed sticky-fingers' is what Yong used to call the Groaci—and you boys don't look like you got quite that many eyes—and old Retief—or whoever the sucker in Number Three is—has got a whole lot of 'em—maybe even five, like Yong said."

"Good thinking, General!" Magnan congratulated the officer. "Now I must get on the SWIFT transmitter and get those Peace Enforcers in here before M-minute." He hurried across to the alcove filled by the Galactic-Ultimate-Top-Secret-shaped wave interference-front device, and in a moment had transmitted a certified true copy of the agreement to Sector and had elicited a promise of the prompt dispatch of the requested advisory group.

There was a screech from beyond the cabin door, which slammed open to admit Yong, behind whom an excited clerk was dithering. "Oh, Mr. Magnan!" he cried. "I had to show him your office, because—"

"Never mind, Bobby, I quite understand," Magnan said off-handedly as he ducked aside to avoid the Vang's abrupt arrival.

"Sorry I'm late," Yong said, panting slightly from his run. "I run into Gertie and talked the kid into coming back here. Some guys down below took over and escorted her to her quarters. Seemed like she was hungry."

"Nice work, Yong," Retief said, then stepped into the passage, beckoning the constable to follow.

"I need your help, Yong," he told the big cat. "Shinth has his troops poised, ready to move in on signal. So I wonder if perhaps you could round up a few friends to take up position around their detachments and discourage them a little."

"You bet, Retief," Yong agreed enthusiastically. "I'm adjutant of a reserve outfit, and I can have the boys in place in half an hour." With that, the huge carnivore turned and dashed off along the passage.

Magnan emerged from his office, an anxious expression on his narrow features.

"I trust we've done the correct thing, Retief," he muttered behind his hand as General Mub came up. "I'd best advise His Excellency of the status quo at once. General, if you'd be so kind as to accompany me . . . ?" He turned to the morose Glorb who was examining the carpeted deck closely.

"Looks like snarf-weed, cropped close by a tud," he commented. "But it ain't. How'd you get it to grow inside? I could use some of the same strain to plush up my field HQ. By the way," he went on, "it looks like everything's just about set, down below. The old pageant ought to be starting any second now."

"No doubt, General," Magnan agreed, "but I'd be most appreciative if you'd stay by me until after we've informed the Ambassador of our arrangements."

"Don't worry, Mr. Magnan. I don't figger to sneak off and give the signal; now I know the score, I wouldn't say 'Yivshish' if you was to offer me a medal."

"Careful, General," Magnan cautioned. "Don't even whisper the word. Someone might overhear." Mub nodded agreement, and the little party went off in search of Ambassador Grossblunder, finding him surrounded as usual by eager staff members, on the ramp in the shade of the towering vessel.

"Oh, there you are, Ben," the great man greeted his Counselor. "The time has come for you to work your miracle. You may now produce your solution to the contretemps in which I have found myself, due of course to no lack of perspicacity on *my* part. Who could have imagined such barbaric rules would be in effect here? To parade in the nude, indeed! Preposterous. Though it is a bit sticky in regulation full early late afternoon ceremonial attire." Grossblunder plucked at his sodden dicky and mopped his low, grayish forehead with a large floral patterned tissue. "Speak up, Ben," he urged as no response was apparent to his dictum.

"Ah, oh yes, the miracle," Magnan gobbled. "I was just coming to that, Mr. Ambassador. But as I was saying—you may expect the arrival of a squadron of Peace Enforcers at any moment."

"Magnan!" Grossblunder barked. "Have you gone mad? One hint of Terran militarism at this halcyon celebration of friendly inter-being rivalry would shatter the Corps image beyond salvaging." He broke off, muttering to himself. Just then a stir in the crowd which had withdrawn to the vicinity of the judges' stand turned all heads as one.

"La cucaracha! Or possibly caramba!" Grossblunder blurted. "Or whatever it is the Mexicans say to express astonishment."

"Why, I declare," a fragile-looking Second Secretary murmured. "It's a Groaci VIP car! And, why, I shouldn't wonder if that were the Groaci Top Advisor, General Hish himself, alighting!"

"Hish, eh," Grossblunder muttered. "This could

be disaster with a capital *D*, gentlemen." He fixed Magnan with a choleric eye. "No more talk of Terran battle fleets, now, Ben," he commanded sternly. "If Hish should catch the merest hint—I leave to your imagination the entry I should be forced to make in the Egregious Blunder column on your next ER."

"But, sir," Magnan said mechanically, turning to Retief for a cue, then subsiding at the latter's headshake.

"See here," General Mub spoke up. "I'm going over and have a word with that Groaci blunderer! Tryna get Great Glorb mixed up in his double-dealing schemes! And then letting you Terries ace him outa position, too!" He stamped off, still fuming.

"Whatever is the general talking about?" Ambassador Grossblunder demanded of the circum-ambient air, before Magnan fell under his gaze again. "You, Ben, you brought that fellow out here. What's he up to now?"

"I'll just hurry along and see," Magnan volunteered. He set off at a brisk trot, Retief at his side. As they arrived at the long, low Groaci limousine with its three-star flags, Mub was accosting the Groaci Planetary Rep.

"What's the big idea, General?" the Glorb demanded. "I just found out the Terries are onto your Grand Plan for the Realization of Glorb Destiny and all! Now what are you going to do?"

Hish turned as impressively as his five-foot stature and knobby knees above jeweled greaves allowed, stared Mub in the eye. "To modulate your tone, fellow," he hissed in the Groaci court dialect.

"To be aware whom you have the privilege to address? I am Chief Advisor to the Glorb Council of Elders if not Betters. You would call *me* to account?"

"Damn right," Mub replied spiritedly in his own guttural tongue. "You're the one set me up for a Galactic General Court Martial, suckered me into deploying a full division to hit the girlie show while a hundred cameras are grinding. I musta been off my apple to listen to orders like them, even if the Council *did* OK the caper!"

"Quietly, fellow," Hish cautioned, apparently unperturbed, except for the tell-tale tinkle of one zircon eye-shield hitting the pavement in response to a violent twitch of his oculars.

"Mub got to him that time," Magnan commented to Retief behind his hand. "Up until now, I wasn't really sure that even the Groaci would embark on a scheme so reprehensible as that outlined by Shinth."

"Shinth?" Hish echoed in an exasperated tone. "I've been attempting for an hour to contact the scamp to move up M-minute by a quarter-hour. Where is the fellow, drat him? Probably off basking in the limelight somewhere, while I carry on the coolie-labor in his stead!"

"Shinth is confined in the den of a hungry glab-worm, General," Magnan offered. "By now he may well have been ingested."

"Terries!" Hish spat the word like a mouthful of Furthuronian garg. "You think to eavesdrop on high-level consultation between my esteemed colleague, General Mub and myself, eh? To think again, Magnan. I've not forgotten your audicious meddling in Groacian affairs of state on a number of previous occasions! To be warned! And you, too, Retief—yes, I recognize you, sir! Which reminds me that there's a handsome price on your head. Seize him, Mub!"

"Naw, you're all mixed up, General," Mub told the Groacian. "I got this Retief tucked away in my Number Three confinement facility. He'll keep."

"You've blundered, you cretin!" Hish told the Glorb. "I tell you this fellow is that same Retief who has so often meddled in Groacian affairs! Put him in irons at once!"

Mub rasped at his hairless scalp with an untrimmed fingernail. "Well, I dunno, General. I know, there was a little mix-up about who was who, but we got that all squared away—I think. Lessee, the Groaci are the ones with the five eyes—hey! I just remembered *you* got about six eyes your ownself! So if you're really a Groaci, then these here boys are really Terries, and the sucker I got in the lock-up must be a Groaci like he said. Funny he told me he was Retief at first."

"Enough of this yivshish!" Hish hissed.

"Shh!" Mub cautioned belatedly, noticing a number of nondescript Glorb stevedores hovering nearby. But at the word "yivshish" they spun and disappeared into the press. Mub lunged after them, but turned back, frustrated.

"My boys are trained to a fine edge," he half-moaned, half-boasted. "By now, they got the word to their cell-chiefs, and in about ten seconds . . ." he broke off, went to tip-toe to look over the variegated crania of the polyglot crowd to stare toward the distant hills.

"Dust clouds, Retief," Magnan pointed out. "Shinth was leveling with us, for once. What in the world are we to do? Mub's troops are encircling—" he turned to scan the horizon, seeing rising dust at every point.

"Just be calm, Mr. Magnan," Retief counseled. "I think you'll find the situation well in hand."

Now the fringe of the crowd had begun to notice the stir all around the temporary spaceport. After a moment, a lone armored personnel-carrier appeared from the approaching roil of dust, racing directly for the huddle of alien craft parked on the hot desert rock. A cry went up:

"We're under attack! Help!" An excited Varoonian mud-spider in the elaborate straps and bangles of a senior mob-master rushed past, ululating his tribal danger cry. But the approaching half-track, and a dozen others like it now visible in line astern, were wheeling aside, slowing, then going into a huddle as the crowd streamed away from their vicinity. One car backed abruptly and came on more slowly, circling wide, then hanging a hard left to drive directly toward the point where Retief and Magnan waited beside the limousine into which Hish had retreated, muttering sibilantly of nest-fouling drones.

At a distance of fifty feet, the car executed a stylish slalom and slid to a halt with its prow neatly socketed in the sizable dent it had made in the polished flank of the Groacian VIP car. Inside, Hish could be heard to utter a sharp shriek. Then a great pink-and-green pelted creature leapt easily from the driver's seat of the armored vehicle and strolled over to touch noses with Yong, speaking briefly to him in the yowling Vang language.

"Captain Rip here says they got the Glorb tied up tighter'n a belly-button tick," the Constable reported tersely. "What next, fellows?"

"I see no reason now that the pageant shouldn't continue as scheduled," Magnan suggested. "Thanks to you, Constable Yong. How thoughtful of you to so neatly counter the Glorb-Groaci initiative."

"It was Retief's idea," Yong demurred modestly. "Oh," he went on quietly, "is it OK if I call him by his name now?" He was eyeing Hish suspiciously as that official emerged hesitantly from the air-conditioned depths of his Bugatti *Royale* replica.

"Have to look out, Ben," Hish whispered. "That's one of those savage Vang tribesfellows; I've heard all about them. Dangerous savages."

As Magnan opened his mouth to reply, a shrill whistling sound crossed the threshold of audibility and rose to a piercing scream, as a sleek Groaci battlecruiser flashed overhead, executing a showy slow roll.

"To be disastered!" Hish moaned, and sprang back inside his car to grab up his command microphone. "To cancel Plan Jay-Blue at once," he keened. "To report all is discovered! To withdraw outside planetary space and then to disperse on normal routine patrol. To deny everything!"

"Too late, Hish," Magnan called into the dark interior of the car. "About a hundred and fifty newshawks saw that with their own sensory organs. Better rethink your strategy in a hurry."

Hish bounded out once more, his hip-cloak askew, to confront Magnan boldly.

"To have rethought my strategy well in advance, Ben," he whispered. "This is a mere tactical setback. I have worked out a new angle—ah, evolved new policies in consonance with the developing situation, that is, and I am ordering the Groacian Goodwill Fleet to land at once, to restore order."

The PA system crackled and hissed across the now dust-wreathed arena.

"As you were, folks," a hearty voice boomed out. "Just a little aerial display before we begin the main event—the Pan-Galactic Pageant of Pulchritude! Let's return to our seats now, everybody—and let's give the judges a chance to look over entry Number One, a dazzling beauty from Yazoo Twelve!"

There was a bustle as the judges, Yong included, pushed through the milling crowd to the judges' stand.

"They're two-thirds Glorbs, Retief," Magnan pointed out redundantly as a dozen of the squat autocthones pushed officiously to the forefront of the ranked judges.

Magnan turned at a tug at his sleeve, to see Jerry, the code-room clerk, at his elbow, panting from a brisk dash.

"Mr. Ambassador wants to see you on the double, sir," he blurted and dashed away.

"Well, I suppose one must bite on the bullet," the Counselor commented philosophically as he began the trudge back to his moment of reckoning, as armed Groaci scout-boats settled in all across the rocky plain.

"What's this, Ben?" Grossblunder yelled from a distance of twenty feet. "You go across to exchange amenities with my esteemed colleague, Planetary Rep, Lieutenant General Hish, and a moment later the Groaci fleet invades in force! What in the world did you do to rouse his ire in such a dramatic fashion?"

"It's all a mistake, Mr. Ambassador," Magnan explained half-heartedly. "You may have noticed the tanks that were bearing down on us in such a menacing fashion—"

"'May have noticed', Magnan?" the Ambassador yelled. "Do you imagine I'm deaf, blind, and otherwise sensorially deprived? The infernal machines came within a hairsbreadth of running me down where I stood!"

"Except you were high-tailing it for the ship and devil take the hindmost," young Marvin Lacklustre commented a trifle too loudly.

"Ah, I mean they stopped just as Your Excellency was reboarding the ship in order to take effective counter-action," the boy amended with an ingratiating smirk.

"I had just recalled, Marvin," his chief pointed out icily, "that Miss Ripetree was alone and doubtless distraught at the sudden appearance of armed vehicles bearing down in force from all directions. My place at that moment was at her side, of course."

"Spikking Peaches," First Secretary Sitzfleisch put in, "where is she, anyways? The show's about to begin."

"I was coming to that," Grossblunder pointed out cooly. "Now, Ben, tell all of us about your neat solution to the problem of public immodest display."

"Oh, sure, sir," Magnan blurted, "I was just thinking, well, here we are on Glorb, so when in Rome, etc. OK?"

"I fear, Ben your meaning is much too cleverly concealed in that utterance. Better put it a trifle more plainly."

"Naked Terries, male, female, or undecided, are devoid of significance to these aliens, so what the heck! Tell her to get in the spirit of the occasion. After all, surely she has nothing to be ashamed of?"

"You disappoint me, Ben," Grossblunder said in a hushed tone. "I had, quite frankly, expected a more creative proposal from you. And it's not the lustful opinion of those leering dotards on the judge's stand I am concerned with. It is my own reluctance to see my little protege exposed publicly which occasions my distress." He paused to dab at an eye with a monogrammed hanky.

"Gosh, sir, don't cry," Magnan urged. "I've got another idea." He turned to Retief. "Can you get Gertie spruced up in a hurry?"

"Gertie?" Grossblunder echoed. "I don't know whence you evoked this substitute, this shameless doxy willing to strut her stuff in the altogether, but it's unthinkable! Imagine the image on telly screens across the Arm; myself—Career Ambassador Elmer Grossblunder, with a naked wench clinging to my arm in the full glare of sunlight? It's no good, fellows, I'm a ruined man. And Peaches—"

"Peaches what?" a feminine voice called from the open entry port above. All eyes turned to see the titian-haired beauty standing, naked as a Rhoon egg at the top of the stair. "I've been listening to you clowns," Peaches went on, "and I didn't come all this way out here to hide in my budoir while Terra loses to some oversized lobster from Hotcake or some downy caterpillar from Ignatz Nine! I'm game; come on, Poochy, let's hit the runway!"

Before His Excellency could respond, a swirling cloud of dust blanketed the little party of diplomats; when it settled, the ominous gray-blue bulk of a Groaci cruiser bristling with guns was to be seen, still vibrating on its landing-jacks from the violence of the pinpoint landing.

"That's Admiral Foosh's flagship!" Grossblunder croaked during a brief pause in the paroxysm of coughing which had empurpled his squarish face. "All is lost! We are presented with a *fait accompli*! Groac has stolen a march on us! Retief! Do something! I've heard you're resourceful, but I hardly see what you can pull out of your hat this time!"

"How about a squadron of Peace Enforcers, Mr. Ambassador," Retief suggested urbanely.

"And where, sir, do you intend to find this miraculous deliverance?" Grossblunder choked.

"How about right over there?" Retief suggested, pointing.

"And there!" Someone added, pointing in another direction.

"And there!"

"Ah, right on schedule, just as I'd planned," Grossblunder commented cooly. "Now on to the main business of the day: the defense of Terra's womanhood from unfair competition by peacocks and snakes and what have you. Peaches, my dear," he called. "Do let's be off! The judges are waiting!"

Peaches, slim and perfumed, linked arms with her sponsor and they went to the ENTER end of the walkway before the stand and, waiting a moment for the exit of a silken butterfly-like being from remote Gulberkian, proceeded, arm in arm under the critical scrutiny of the variegated judges.

8

Half an hour later, relaxing in the lounge aboardship, Grossblunder told the visiting fleet officers:

"Lucky you chaps happened along. I suppose Admiral Zinsh surrendered without firing a shot when he realized he'd been outmaneuvered."

"Not quite, Mr. Ambassador," a lean gray-haired Rear Admiral demurred. "Their main force was standing by off-planet in battle array. I got my units around his flanks without being noticed, and when he sent his armed scouts down to make the grandstand play, I put one across the bows of his flagship."

"Neatly done," Grossblunder commented. "I wonder where Jerry is with the announcement—not that I'm worried: the ovation they gave Miss Ripetree was sufficient evidence. Even the Glorbian judges showed some enthusiasm for the first time." He fingered a prominant wart on his chin with one hand and drummed the squarish fingers of the other on the polished surface of an end table. Then he paused, sat erect and said:

"Hark! I think I hear Jerry coming now." Even as he spoke, the excited lad burst into the long low-ceilinged room and without pause sang out:

"Terra wins, Mr. A! And—I mean, but—holy macaroni, the Chief Adjudicator is here, he insisted, so

I brought him up to make the presentation personally." He turned, made ushering motions to the open door behind him, and a short, stubby grayish figure wrapped in a formal toga stumped in, almost buried under a vast horseshoe of pink and white blossoms.

"Wait! I'll get Peaches at once!" Grossblunder offered, rising as if to avoid the cameras busily clicking behind the Adjudicator.

"Pray don't bother," the Glorb official grated. "You don't want any peripheral personnel to share the spotlight, nor do we, dear sir or madam as the case may be."

"Of course! I mean, of course not!" Grossblunder babbled, attempting to skirt the importunate Glorb. "I'll just—" he ducked, but not in time. The vast floral arrangement descended about his neck, nearly felling him.

"But—but—I don't understand!" he yelped, brushing a dangling Barrovian jelly-blossom from before his mottled face.

"*Too* charming!" Adjudicator Blug cooed. "Just a few more, fellows, close up," he commanded the photographers and trideo crews over his shoulder, before moving in to place a square gray hand on Grossblunder's shoulder. "You were the *only* entrant we even considered," he told Grossblunder in a confidential tone. "We all admired your shapely bulk, of course, and the delicate tints of your complexion, but, candidly, it was the subtlety of your wart distribution pattern that swayed old Fug to cast the deciding ballot. Congratulations, Your Excellency! Now all the Galaxy will applaud Glorb aesthetic sensibility and taste displayed for all to see, putting an end, one hopes, to the nasty talk, of which I've had report, of Glorb insensitivity and preoccupation with the crass."

"No doubt, my dear Mr. Adjudicator," Grossblunder burbled. "But I still—I mean, Miss Ripetree expects. How about it I quietly pass the word on to her, on the Q.T. She'd appreciate it a lot, I know, and my duties, that is, if Sector gets a good look—see here, you confounded idiot, I didn't let Miss Ripetree parade naked in front of thousands just for nothing! I must refuse the honor, though I *do* appreciate it. Don't think me unaware of the honor. But after all, it is to Terra that the crown truly belongs—" Grossblunder paused to extricate his ear from the questing tendrils of a Squamese tickler vine—"so, if you'll allow me, I shall appoint Miss Ripetree as my representative to accept the accolades and all, while I get on with my paperwork." So saying, the Ambassador managed to free himself from the hundred pound horseshoe and duck aside from Fug's embrace. He grabbed a half-full champagne glass from the nearest table and yelled:

"Gentlemen, a toast! To Terra in her hour of victory! Now, Ben, go get Peaches—quietly, you understand! Not a hint of the trifling misunderstanding." He broke off to drink deeply as did they all.

epilog

Three hours before ETA Sector, Retief tapped and entered Magnan's spartan but immaculate quarters, holding in his hands a pink-and-yellow spotted kitten the size of a full-grown bobcat, with green stripes across its back.

"Gertie's fine," Retief said. "So are all nine of her family," he added.

Magnan gaped, then grinned and reached out gingerly to take the cuddly baby.

"Good lord!" he muttered. "And we thought they were fighting!"

Book

TWO

RETIEF'S RANSOM

"Monsters?" said First Secretary Magnan of the Terrestrial delegation to the planetary Peace Conference at Lumbaga. "Where?" He gazed searchingly around the crowded bazaar, thronged with gaily garbed pedestrians. A nine-foot, orange-skinned local jostled past humming a tune through a nose set in the middle of his forehead; a three-legged native with pink and purple spots haggled vigorously with a stallkeeper distinguished by a red- and green-striped epidermis, seven eyes arranged in random fashion on a lumpy head further adorned with a handsome spread of mismatched antlers.

"I see no monsters," Magnan said stuffily. "Only ordinary Lumbagans. I fear you've been listening to rumors, my dear colonel."

"I'm not talking about these fellows," the military attaché muttered, "I'm referring to the recurring reports of meat-eating magicians, carnivorous cadavers, and ferocious freaks swarming from the swamps."

"Nonsense." Magnan dismissed the thought, pausing to admire a merchant's display of chest wigs, plastic trideos tuned loudly to competing channels, prosthetic tentacles (the all-purpose appendage, suitable for sports or formal wear), native mudwork, and murky carboys of mummified glimp eggs for the luxury trade. "I concede that only six years ago the locals were little better than Neolithic savages; but today, thanks to the enlightened policies of the *Corps diplomatique terrestrienne*, they're already well into their Medieval period."

"An acute observation," Second Secretary Retief acknowledged. "Too bad it's so hard to distinguish between Neolithic savagery and the Medieval variety."

"The problem," Colonel Warbutton said, "is that no two of these ruddy natives look alike! Everyone on the planet's a member of a minority of one—and none of the minorities can stand the sight of another!"

"Pish-tush, Colonel," Magnan chided. "I confess that what with the multiplicity of native racial strains the problem of prejudice does pose something of a riddle for our Togetherness Teams, but I'm sure we'll soon turn up a solution satisfactory to Sector HQ."

"I'm hardly the chap to spook easily," Colonel Warbutton persisted. "A few riots in front of the embassy are nothing to get excited about, and the mud-and-ragweeding of the odd diplomat is par for the course. But when they run ads in the daily paper offering bounties for alien heads in good condition, it's time to start barricading the chancery."

"Mere campaign rhetoric," Magnan dismissed the objection. "After all, when a people as diverse as the Lumbagans—with their hallowed traditions of mutual genocide—set out to choose a ruler acceptable to all, there's bound to be a modicum of unrest among dissident elements."

"Especially when the dissident elements outnumber the population," Retief agreed. "I have a feeling that Ambassador Pouncetrifle's decision to sponsor a planetary government was a trifle overzealous."

"A gross understatement," Colonel Warbutton grunted. "Inasmuch as no two Lumbagans can agree on so much as the correct time, I suspect they'll have some difficulty in agreeing on who's going to tell them what to do."

"Your remarks reflect scant confidence in the process of democracy, as implemented by Corps peace enforcers," Magnan said rather sharply. "You'd do well to recall that firepower outweighs flowerpower, and a vote in the hand is worth two in the offing."

"But what more can we do?" the colonel inquired plaintively. "We've already fired our big guns, pacificationwise: saturation leaflet bombing, nonstop armistice propoals, uni-, bi-, and multilateral cease-fires, interlocking demilitarized zones—the works. And they go right on headhunting—to say nothing of leg-, arm-, and haunch-hunting!" Warbutton's remark was interrupted by the impact of a clay pot against the wall three feet from his head, accompanied by a sharp rise in the decibel output of the crowd.

"Maybe we'd better start back," Retief said, "unless we want to get a closer view of the Saturday riot than usual."

"Ridiculous, Retief," the first secretary said a trifle uneasily. "Merely a display of high spirits. My analysis of the trends, local unrestwise, indicates today will be utterly peaceful."

Retief glanced across the cobbles toward the low, irregular buildings at the far side of the plaza, between which greenish sunlight glinted on a stretch of open sea dotted with sails, and gleamed chartreuse and orange on the adjacent island of the equatorial archipelago which constituted the sole land masses of the world.

"You may be right," he said, "but there seem to be a remarkable number of spears, spikes, pitchforks, swords, and carving knives in evidence."

"Purely decorative, Retief. In spite of splendid progress toward civilization, the locals seem to feel more comfy with a symbolic weapon in hand."

"No doubt—but there's a note in the crowd noises that reminds me of a beehive just after it's been poked with a stick."

"They're merely taking a childlike pleasure in their bargaining, Retief. Heavens, I've heard shriller haggling in Macy's." Magnan glanced up severely at his junior. "It's hardly like you to display such timidity, Retief. I suggest you buck up now; I don't intend to return until I've secured the beaded tea cozy I promised Aunt Ninny—"

"Duck!" Retief snapped, and swept Magnan aside as a broad-headed assegai clanged against the rough-hewn stone wall behind them. He caught it on the rebound, grabbed Magnan's arm and thrust him into a doorway as, with a mass screech, the mob surging through the narrow way erupted into violence. Robed locals of wildly varied skin coloration and wart distribution brandished suddenly produced weapons in hands numbering from one to six, and charged each other with bloodcurdling yells. Glass shattered nearby; smoke boiled from an overturned toasted-nidnut cart. A tall, blue-faced Lumbagan with four staring eyes, three pendulous ears, and a mouth capable of encompassing a tripleburger in one gulp rushed toward the Terrans, swinging up a five-foot steelwood cutlass edged with broken glass. Retief dropped the spear-point to chest level and grounded the butt against the plank door behind him. The alien braked, too late; the spearhead took him square in the midriff. Magnan made a squeaking noise as the victim dropped his sword and grasped the shaft of the spear with three of four hands, and with a powerful surge, withdrew it.

"Hey, you loused up a perfectly good duodenum that time or I miss my guess, Terry," the warty local said in a rather barbaric dialect of the local tongue, fingering the bloodless entry wound. "What's the idea? The word was, you Terries don't fight back."

"Sorry, fellow," Retief said, "Sometimes the word gets distorted in transmission. How about passing the new version along to your compatriots; it may save wear and tear all around."

"Yeah, I'll do that." The alien turned and was swept away by the crowd.

"I can't think what went wrong with my analysis," Magnan wailed as a brass-tipped arrow chipped the lintel above him. "I must have misjudged the intensity of the xenophobic coefficient—or possibly read the seasonal hostility index from the wrong column!"

"Get the door open!" Warbutton yelled behind Retief as he parried a thrust by a passerby pausing to take a slash at the target of opportunity.

"But that would be illegal entry!"

"Getting killed in public without a death permit is a felony punishable by decapitation plus a year in the local Bastille, according to the local penal code," Retief pointed out. "Take your choice."

There were rattling sounds behind Retief, followed by the creak of rusty hinges. At that moment, a large Lumbagan burst from the crowd, whipped a rusty but effective-looking power gun from under his doublet, took aim at Retief's head—

A small local sprang at the gunner, entangling the latter's legs in several of his own, and with a hearty shove sent him sprawling while the shot burned harmlessly across the pavement. With a yell of fury, the fallen assassin leaped up. Retief felt the draft on his back from the open door behind him.

"This way," he called in the local patois; the diminutive Lumbagan dived past him through the opening; Retief jumped through behind him, slammed the heavy panel. Missiles clattered against it as he shot the massive bolt. Angry fists hammered, angry voices screeched threats. Magnan uttered a yelp as he noted the presence of the alien.

"Help! One of them got in!"

"He's with us," Retief said. "Thanks for the assist, Mr. . . . ?"

"Ignarp's the handle. Glad to oblige, Terry. Some of the boys got no use for Terries, but what do those slobs know? A bunch of Blue-spots and Four-eyes and Shaggy-feet and Wart-heads—"

"Corps policy frowns on the use of racial epithets, Mr. Ignarp," Magnan remonstrated. "Besides which," he added surveying the Lumbagan, "unless I'm very much mistaken you seem to have a number of warts of your own."

"Oh, yeah; I forgot. I just picked those up on sale last week."

"It must be confusing," Magnan said sympathetically. "With so many minorities to choose from, I suppose one hardly knows whom to discriminate against."

"Yeah—you Terries have got the best system; just check a couple minor details like how many eyes or what color spots a guy's got, and you know who your friends are. A lot easier than trying to pick 'em one at a time."

"What made you pick us?" Retief asked.

"I got a soft spot in my head for foreigners," the local said. "Come on, I'll show you the way out of here." He waved them toward the dark, stone-floored passage leading back into the gloomy recesses of the monolithic structure.

"Well, how lucky you happened along, Mr. Ignarp," Colonel Warbutton said, falling in behind their guide. "By the way, where are we going?"

"You Terries are housed right in the Castle complex, along with the other foreigners, right? You're practically there now."

"Heavens, I hope we're not late for the Joint Staff meeting." Magnan said, glancing at his thumb watch. "Who'd have thought when we set out for a short constitutional we'd end threading a maze with a pack of rabid racists at our figurative heels?"

"Think of the impact on the ambassador when you give your eye-witness report," Retief encouraged his superior.

"That's a thought," Magnan agreed. "Ah—just what was it I eye-witnessed?"

"The initiation of the Spring Hostility Rites," the local called over his shoulder. "The boys certainly started things off with a bang."

"The spring rites?" Warbutton queried. "I was under the impression the Winter Mayhem Festival was still on."

"So it is; along with the Ritual of Revolution, the Symbolic Sacrament of Savagery, and o' course the Perennial Violence Cycle. With a crowded schedule, we get a certain amount of overlap."

"Why—the situation is deteriorating into total anarchy!" Magnan gasped.

"Not so, Terry," their guide demurred. "We got rules. Like we always give warning before we change sides."

"What sort of warning?" Magnan queried.

"Well, a kick in the right spot usually gets the message across," the Lumbagan confided. "But we're not particular. A sharp blow on the head will do in a pinch."

"Or a spear between the ankles?" Retief suggested.

"I hope Gumrong sees it that way. He's not a bad fellow; in fact he was my sidekick and loyal comrade-in-arms. But he holds a slot as my mortal hereditary enemy for the rites—so naturally when he jumped you Terries, I stepped in. Lucky you got that door open, or my component parts would be strewn all over the jungle by now, rooting for acorns."

"Which side are *they* on?" Warbutton inquired dazedly.

"Luckily, Lumbagan vegetable life is neutral," Retief said. "Otherwise the prospects for planetary pacification would be even dimmer than they are."

"They couldn't be," Magnan groaned. "How in the world are we going to bring racial tolerance to a world whose only recreation is mutual mass murder?"

"If you come up with the answer to that one, Mr. Magnan, I predict a sharp upward turn in your career prospects," Retief commented.

"Watch your step, gents," the Lumbagan said, indicating a narrow stone stair leading down into pitch darkness. "Just a little farther and there we are."

As Magnan hesitated, Retief stepped past him.

"You must be a little confused, Ignarp," he said. "Mr. Magnan doesn't have time right now to explore any abandoned mine shafts."

"Who's leading this parade, you or me, Terry?" the Lumbagan said truculently. "I'm the guy that just saved your necks, remember?"

"Just between us," Retief said, "Why did you decoy us here?"

Magnan gasped.

"Wh—where'd you get an idea like that?" The Lumbagan edged sideways, but was restrained by Retief's quick grab.

"Hey—leggo my neck," he yelped. "I already told you—"

"Uh-huh. But I happen to know Spring Rites don't start for another two days. Somebody went to a lot of trouble to set up the whole charade, including the conveniently unlocked door. Why, Ignarp?"

"No fair, Retief," the local grunted. "I heard you

Terries didn't know a mob killing from a quiet little domestic knifing—"

"Some of these impressions die hard." Retief gave the local's collar another half-twist. "Come on, give, Ignarp."

"Retief," Magnan demurred, "are you sure? After all, if anyone had wanted to do us an injury they could have done it as well in the street. . . ."

"Wrong," the Lumbagan contradicted. "This was a hush-hush deal. And besides, the orders were to bring you in whole."

"You admit your duplicity?" Warbutton barked.

"With your chum's knuckles digging into my medulla oblongata, I got no choice," Ignarp said aggrievedly.

"Whose orders?"

"The ones that hired me," Ignarp muttered. "They wanted a Terry in good condition, that's all I can tell you. I'm just a legman—"

"Hold it," Retief said. From the dark stairwell came faint sounds as of stealthy feet approaching.

"We'll have to defer our talk until later, Ignarp," Retief said. "Lead the way out of here—and this time get it right."

"I might as well; if the boys see me with your thumb under my ear, my rep as a slick conniver is shot anyway. Come on. . . ." He led the Terrans back along the passage, took a branching corridor—hardly more than a damp-walled tunnel cut through the massive masonry pile—and in five minutes halted at the foot of a narrow stone stair leading upward.

"It comes out in the embassy commissary," he said glumly. "Just don't let on I told you about the gap in your security. There's a couple dozen families living high on imported caviar and pâté who'd hate to go back to pulverized nidnuts and dehydrated frinkfruit."

"Stealing from embassy stores?" Magnan gasped.

"Relax," the local advised. "It's costing you a lot less than if we applied for disaster-area status and welfare handouts. As we see it a self-respecting life-form ought to make its own way."

"What shall we do with the beggar?" Warbutton said. "No good turning him over to the local constabulary. Pity we can't do him in out of hand, but that sort of thing doesn't look at all good when the yellow press gets hold of it."

"Lemme go now, pal," Ignarp said. "I admit it was a lousy idea. And to clinch the deal, I'll throw in a tip for free: Look out when Summer Slaughter time comes rolling around. I'm assigned to a Terry-Go-Home team, and those babies play rough."

"Come along, Retief," Magnan said, starting up the stairs. "There's no point in escaping death at the hands of a mob only to face an irate Chief of Mission."

Retief released his grip on the Lumbagan. "We'll call it even for now, Ignarp. Go back and tell our employers that we Terries like a chance to RSVP our invitations."

"You foreigners are full of surprises," the local muttered, and darted away.

"Here, Retief," Warbutton remonstrated, "we should have held the blighter up by the heels until he'd divulged all the details of the conspiracy."

"I have a feeling he'll talk more freely on his home ground," Retief said, and glanced at the finger-marked card he had lifted from the Lumbagan's coat pocket. "The Stake and Kidney Tavern, number twelve Dacoit Street," he read.

"I know the spot," Warbutton said. "An unsavory dive across from the scalpfields where the hair is short."

"It's a date," Retief said.

2

Magnan and Retief were among the last to take seats at the long table in the conference room, netting a baleful glance from the protuberant eye of Ambassador Pouncetrifle, seated at the head of the table beside Jith, his diminutive Groacian opposite number and Joint Chairman of the Lumbagan Peace Commission.

"Now, if we're *quite* ready," his Excellency began in an ominous tone, "I—"

"A moment, if you please, Harvey," Jith spoke up in his breathy whisper. "It happens to be my turn to chair the meeting, so if you don't mind—"

"What's this, one of your little jokes?" Pouncetrifle barked. "Most amusing, Mr. Ambassador. Now, as I was saying—"

"Just hand me the gavel, there's a good chap, and we'll get on with the meeting." Jith plucked the microphone from before the Terran dignitary. "Fellow beings—" he started.

"Look here, Jith." the Terran said sharply, "you know perfectly well you took precedence in the elevator this morning—and at breakfast, I distinctly noted the bearer handing you your menu before so much as whisking the crumbs off my chair—"

"Doesn't count," Jith cut in tersely, and keyed the microphone. "This afternoon, I should like to review our progress in bringing racial equality to Lumbaga." His amplified voice crackled through the room.

"—to say nothing of your subtle maneuver in bribing the chief of the motor pool to repaint your parking space upwind of mine!" Pouncetrifle's remonstrance rose above the PA system.

"And in bringing the blessings of noncombatant status to the unhappy natives of this benighted world," Jith continued, "no offense to our native guests intended, of course." The Groaci inclined three of his five eyestalks in a perfunctory salute to the latter—a pair of observers squatting silently on a bench by the far wall, both bulky, multilimbed, and heavily swathed in beaded robes. They returned the gesture with stony expressions.

"Now, the past six years during which the Interplanetary Peace Tribunal has exercised its good offices in the search for an avenue of racial rapprochement have not been unmarked by progress," Pouncetrifle stated, leaning across to address the microphone. "To date, we've completed forty-two VIP villas for Class One personnel and above, a hundred-table billiardium, and a forty-bed fun house—"

"Frivolities aside," Jith breathed, recommandeering the mike, "I direct your attention to the recent consecration of a hundred-stall cybernetic confessional, featuring coin-operated holy sand dispensers, a scourgomat capable of processing one gross of penitents per hour, and a most ingenious mechanized collection plate, employing 1000-gauss magnets—"

"On the substantive side," Pouncetrifle's voice boomed out amid a vicious feedback howl as he ripped the mike from his rival's grasp, "pacification efforts proceed apace. In reply to certain critics I can report that close statistical analyses by departmental teams skilled in the detection of obscure phenomena report that the percentage of casualties among unemployed frume-leaf gatherers between the ages of eighteen and forty-nine during the daylight hours in alternate months are down a big, big .0046 percent over a similar period last year."

Jith ducked under Pouncetrifle's arm to clutch the microphone.

"While it's quite true that the basis of the racial conflicts here on Lumbaga have not yet been isolated," he stated breathily, "nor have the precise ideological battle lines been delimited, nor the values involved definitely identified, some progress has been made in the study of native beadwork, a circumstance which lends substance to the hope that in the near future—say the next half-dozen years—we may meet with limited success in determining who is fighting whom—or should I say whom is fighting who—if not why."

"Come to the point," the assistant military attaché muttered. "What it boils down to is that with all these rival cliques, factions, races, mobs, unions, congregations, bands, platoons, crews, and clans constantly involved in squabbles, bickerings, pitched battles, bombings, disagreements, feuds, wrangles, wars, altercations, misunderstandings, ruptures, brawls, rows, sit-ins, shoot-ins, and assorted Donnybrooks, with the participants changing sides at irregular intervals according to no known scheme, our chances of unifying the planet under a single flag are on a par with the likelihood of my making Light Colonel by Voom Festival."

"Alas, I fear we're actually losing ground," the Groaci functionary seated beside him whispered in tones of deepest pessimism. "Not content with strewing each other's members in the public ways, the aborigines now widen the scope of their hostilities to include us selfless dilpomats. Only yesterday I was savaged by a seeing-eye leg—"

"Heavens, what about me?" Magnan cut in. "Only minutes ago I was forced to deal sharply with a chap intent on an audacious diplomat-napping."

"You didn't lend substance to any potential charges of Terran intellectual brutality, I trust, Magnan?" a sharp-eyed cultural attaché said.

"Naturally not," Warbutton spoke up. "I was present, luckily, and smoothed the incident over."

"Pah!" the Groaci whispered. "There are plots afoot here, I feel it in my cartilaginous members!"

"Poppycock," Warbutton snorted. "The natives may appear to detest our internal integuments, but down deep they like us."

"About six feet down, preferably," someone muttered.

"Now, before we can set about establishing one-world rule on Lumbaga," Pouncetrifle cut through the chatter, the smooth flow of his diction somewhat marred by the silent scuffle in which he was engaged for possession of the floor, "it's clear that until we devise some means of discriminating—pray pardon the expression—between the wildlife and the population, certain problems will inevitably crop up in categorization of life forms as to vermin, livestock, and constituents. I now call on Mr. Lunchbun, our xenoecologist, for a brief report on the complexities of Lumbagan biology." The ambassador favored his Grocian colleague with a frosty smile and subsided. From his place near the foot of the table, a sad-faced chap with thinning hair rose, rattled papers, and cleared his throat.

"As his Excellency so discerningly pointed out," he began in a nasal drone, "the ecological situation here on Lumbaga is hardly susceptible to analysis by conventional means. To begin with, we've so far identified over two hundred thousand distinct phyla of basic wild life running loose on the islands, a circumstance which has sent our ecological computer into catatonic withdrawal—"

"Yes, yes, Mr. Lunchbun," Jith prompted impatiently. "If you have nothing further to report—"

". . . we deduce from paleontological evidence," Lunchbun bored on, "that life has spontaneously arisen from the primordial Lumbagan mud on at least a hundred thousand separate occasions—"

"Fascinating, no doubt," Jith said sibilantly. "Now to other matters, such as provisions for a rest and recreational camp for Groaci ladies and their lovable grubs—"

"While all of the surviving life forms are mutually infertile," Lunchbun droned on, "—in fact, reproduction in the conventional sense is not practiced by Lumbagan life—it seems that symbiotic relationships provide the necessary proliferation of ecological niche-holders necessary for the full exploitation of the environment—"

"Yes, yes, quite so," Jith piped faintly. "Now as for my proposal for a gift to the Lumbagan masses of a Bolshoi-type ballet theatre—"

"Now, as for the VH—vital hierarchy, a term referring to the ascending order of complexity of competing and cooperating species—it appears we're faced here with a regular gradation from the mindless free-living gall bladder and/or medulla oblongata through the *pneumopteryx*, or flying lung, the night-blooming liver, or *Hepaticus noctens*—"

"Kindly speak either Terran or Groaci," a representative of the latter species whispered irritably, "as a courtesy to those of us who are not specialists in arcane linguistic lore."

"—to the subcultural forms such as the Gliding Leg, *Pedis volens*, and the Bounding Rib Cage, *Os leapifrons*—"

"Splendid," Pouncetrifle said heartily, "I'm sure we all enjoyed Mr. Lunchbun's most lucid rundown on the subject on which he has just presented his briefing. Now, the next item on the agenda—"

"To continue," Lunchbun cut through the rising conversation level, "I've recently achieved a breakthrough, classificationwise." He turned to pull down a wall chart. "The basic building blocks of Lumbagan life, which I've designated here with Chinese ideographs for convenience, are capable of a large but finite number of cross-combinations, indicated by Egyptian hieroglyphics, which compounded forms in turn are capable of further linkages to create still more complex entities, shown on the accompanying schematic by Greek letters, Norse runes, and the letters A thru Q inclusive. The chart represents schematically the theoretical relationships of biological subgroups and groups within the hyper- or super-groups, in light of the presumed intergroup taboo structure, the affinity-schemes implicit in observed pro- and counter-indications social-mobilitywise, and the mutual interdependency pattern as deduced from a careful sifting of rumors from the interior. Naturally, it's only approximate."

"Yes, yes, we all know the woods are full of tongues, elbows, and less mentionable members," Pouncetrifle prompted the speaker. "Get to the point, man!"

"Well, I'm skipping over the most fascinating part—but as it happens, Mr. Ambassador, I have a few slides for you this afternoon," Lunchbun said hastily. "Freddy . . . ?" He signaled to a local employee hidden in the wings; the lights dimmed and a pair of vivid trideo images flickered into existence above the ornamental fungus centerpiece adorning the long board. One of the beings represented was a seven-foot creature with an oversized head crowded with sensory appendages in no particular arrangement, surmounting a cluster of arms of varying lengths, which sprang directly from a flattened pelvic girdle to which were attached three long, skinny legs, each ending in a pair of multitoed feet, the whole encased in a warty hide of a mottled purplish hue. The other was some four feet in height, with a lumpy head adorned by antlers, fangs, tusks, eyestalks, and a bushy magenta crest matching a ruff springing from the base of a long, limber neck. The remainder of the creature consisted largely of a penduluous, leathery paunch of a peculiarly objectionable yellowish shade, featuring stubby wings, tentacles, pincers, and a clump of noodlelike appendages presumably designed for locomotion.

"Here we have lab mock-ups of a pair of hypothetical composites, embodying what appear to be the most popular elements of what I term the ABCD and WXYZ forms," Lunchbun stated in a proprietary tone.

"On the whole," Colonel Warbutton commented, "I think the chap on the left has the more wholesome look about him. True, he's gone a bit overboard frequency-of-occurrencewise, but those *are* recognizable arms, legs, and the like—"

"I assume the simulacrum on the right represents the higher form," Ambassador Jith spoke up, "inasmuch as it has tastefully selected handsome stalked oculars, efficient grasping chelae, and a most soothing pigmentation, reminiscent of my own."

"Hold it right there," a reedy voice interrupted the proceedings. One of the local observers was on his feet—six in number—waving several arms. "I object! You foreigners are profaning the arcane mysteries by exhibiting undraped bodies without throwing in some redeeming entertainment value. What do those fellows do? Dance? Sing? Nonstop pray? Juggle zingfruit? No! They just stand there!"

"Why, how remarkable," Magnan whispered to Retief. "I didn't know the observers spoke Terran. Heavens, I wonder if we've uttered any indiscretions, racial-prejudicewise. . . ."

"They're full of surprises," Retief agreed. "Not the least of which is the fact that they've stayed awake through Lunchbun's lecture."

"Curious," Magnan mused. "I would have sworn that yesterday the one with the six feet had three eyes and a half a dozen snoof-organs; today he's down to two of the latter and only one of the former."

"Now, now, ah, sir or madam," Pouncetrifle was soothing the aroused local, "I'm sure no offense to your local mores was intended. I'll see that it doesn't happen again—"

"Don't do that, sport," the Lumbagan said in a more expansive tone, producing a tambourine from beneath his robes. "Just drop a little something in the old collection box, and on with the show."

"Why, yes, of course, I suppose a small contribution to a worthy charity would be quite in order," the ambassador agreed hastily.

"Small, nothing, sport! A couple thousand standard creds would be about right—and don't try to tell me how to spend it. I'm not in business for my health. And while I've got the floor, maybe I can interest some of you gents, Terry and Five-Eyes alike, in a snappy line of musical spud peelers for which I happen to be sole agent in this end of the archipelago—"

"What's this? Mercantile endeavor in the midst of solemn diplomatic proceedings?" Ambassador Jith whispered. "And a competing line, at that!"

"Look here—you can't conduct yourself as a peddler," Pouncetrifle said sternly.

"Why not? Anything shameful about honest merchandising, sport?"

"You were accredited here as an official observer, not a purveyor of novelty items!"

"Nix, sport. That was another fellow entirely—or almost entirely; I picked up a nice used clavicle from him on the way out."

"Where did he go?"

"He had to get back home and see to his liver and lights, you know how it is."

"He was in need of surgery?" Pouncetrifle gasped.

"Are you kidding? The guy runs a small giblet ranch two islands over."

"Then—what are *you* doing here?"

"I came in to get out of the cold wind. Why?"

"What about your, ah, the other one?" Pouncetrifle demanded, indicating the second local, who had not stirred during the exchange.

"Him? That's my sidekick, name of Difnog. I kind of look out for him, you know, since he lost his wits."

"In an accident?" the press attaché inquired with morbid interest, craning his neck for a better look at the victim.

"Nope, in a game of nine-handed *splung*. Difnog was a shrewd player, but he was outclassed; he only had seven hands at a time."

"Well, I'm sure that's all very interesting. Mr., er—"

"Gnudf. Yeah, but I got to be going. If you'll hand over the cash, I might still be able to make it down to the body shop before closing time."

"The effrontery of the fellow," Magnan sniffed as the ambassador and the budget-and-fiscal officer went into a huddle. "It's a well-established principle that the CDT only gives handouts to *bona fide* enemies."

"Maybe he's hoping to qualify," Retief suggested.

"It's a status much sought after, of course," Magnan conceded. "But a seasoned diplomat like Pouncetrifle will require proof of authentic hostility, not mere aspiration to the role."

"Maybe Gnudf can establish that he was part of the gang that broke all the windows out the Information Service Library yesterday."

"Nonsense, Retief, that was merely an expression of youthful impatience with established social forms."

"What about the mob that invaded the chancery at gunpoint last week and threw the classified files out the window along with the code clerk?"

"A student prank, nothing more."

"And I suppose the fellows who slipped the stink bombs into the ambassador's kitchen during the banquet were actually only expressing legitimate minority aspirations."

"Doubtless—although the matter nearly got out of hand. The ambassador didn't wish to offend the cook by complaining of what he assumed was the aroma of native cookery, and the guests were equally hesitant to appear critical of the ambassadorial cuisine. We might have all stifled in silence if Ambassador Jith hadn't chosen to take it as a direct affront to the Groacian state."

"Golly, I wish I'd been there," the assistant military attaché commented. "Old Jith didn't care for the smell, eh?"

"On the contrary, it seems that the effluvium of burning hot-water bottles closely resembles that of sacred Groacian incense. Pouncetrifle had to promise to book a troop of Groaci tirual grimacers for the next culturefest before he could placate him."

"I see your point, Mr. Magnan," Retief conceded. "It's not easy to qualify for enemy status these days."

"Precisely. It's one of the hopeful signs I like to point out to those who complain that our culture is going downhill."

The B-and-F officer having departed with the two locals to work out a settlement, the ambassador gaveled the meeting back to order.

"Gentlemen," he said firmly, "my predecessors waged pacification on Lumbaga for six years with no visible result. The native passion for mutual mayhem rages unabated. The confounded locals appear to *like* to fight! Now, then, it's vital at this juncture in my career—vital, that is, to the success of our mission—that we produce a breakthrough, racial-tolerancewise, without further delay. Naturally, I have a vastly effective plan all ready for implementation, but still, I'd be willing to listen to suggestions from the floor. Now, who's first?"

"I propose saturation bombing of the entire planet," a Groaci attaché proposed in a crisp whisper, "followed by mop-up squads armed with flame-throwers, fragmentation grenades, and other pesticides."

"Why—how brutal!" Magnan blurted.

"But effective," the Groaci pointed out. "One cannot deny: No population—no popular unrest!"

"Heavens," Magnan confided to Retief, "it wouldn't do to say so for the record, but one must concede there is a certain directness about Groaci methods."

"Possibly someone can offer a less spectacular alternative," Pouncetrifle said grimly. "Perhaps one designed to preserve an electorate for the new world government to govern!"

"Ah—what about a contest, sir?" Magnan piped up. "Cash prizes for snappy integration jingles, say."

"*I* know," the assistant military attaché cried, "cash rewards for defectors, deserters, scabs, AWOLS, and turncoats!"

"What about straight cash grants to all who'll come and stand in line for them?" the senior economic attaché proposed grumpily. "If they're standing in line they can't be out participating in raids."

"Splendid notion, Godfrey," Colonel Warbutton spoke up. "We can stall them along until we have the majority of the able-bodied personnel queued up. Then—a lightning swoop, and we round up all the troublemakers at a stroke!"

"Don't we run the risk of accidentally scooping up a percentage of innocent noncombatants?" the press attaché said doubtfully.

"You can't break eggs without dropping a few on the floor, or however the old saying goes," Warbutton stated curtly. "In any event, since the majority of the population are activists, part-time guerillas, undercover commandos, and/or weekend warriors, the risk is statistically negligible."

"But—what do we do with them, once we've clapped them in all concentration camps?"

"Pension 'em off," Warbutton stated firmly.

"There appears, gentlemen," Pouncetrifle cut in coldly, "to be an emphasis on the materialistic in your proposals. While I recognize that massive handouts—monetary aid to the deserving, that is to say—have long been a staple of Terran policy, I feel in this instance an approach on a loftier level is in order."

"Oh-oh," the commercial attaché muttered. "That sounds like budget-cut to me."

"Gentlemen. . . ." The chief of the Terran delegation looked bleakly along the table. "Unless we achieve a discernible advance toward planetary unification within the next thirty days, I suspect a number of promising diplomatic careers will be nipped in the bud."

"Frankly, Mr. Ambassador," Magnan spoke up, "unless the local anti-Terran prejudices can be overcome in the near future, we may be nipped before we can be fired. Why, only today—"

"Anti-Terran prejudice? Nonsense, Magnan! Mere rumor! I've already pointed out how popular we Terrestrials are—"

With a loud crash, the window on the ambassadorial left burst inward, scattering a shower of glass chips over the table, while a paper-wrapped brick thudded to the floor. An eager vice-consul retrieved the latter.

"Why—it's a message," he exclaimed. "It says: A GOOD TERRY IS A DEAD TERRY!"

"You see?" Pouncetrifle said heartily. "Only a dear friend would feel free to perpetrate such a broad practical joke. And now"—he rose hastily—"we'll adjourn and make ready for tonight's reception."

"Good idea," Warbutton said sourly as the meeting broke up. "Before our unknown prankster decides to lob a grenade through and really bring down the house."

3

Standing before the mirror in his apartment in the Terran wing, Retief flicked a speck of dust from the chrome-plated lapel of his celery-top-green, midevening, hyperformal cutaway and checked the effect in the rippled surface.

"Wow, Mr. Retief, *quel* splendor," his valet commented with an envious sigh. "Jeeze, youse don't happen to have an old suit like this one you don't need any more, I guess?"

Retief surveyed the five-foot figure of the local youth, vaguely humanoid except for the unusual number and variety of eyes, ears, and snoof-organs adorning his cranium, plus the circumstance that his shoulders seemed to spring directly from his hips without the intervention of a torso.

"Not precisely, Fnud," the diplomat replied, opening the closet door. "But how about a banana-yellow, demi-informal jumpsuit, appropriate for croquet, mah jong, and ouija board sessions during the hours twelve noon to three pee em inclusive?"

"Gangbusters, Mr. Retief," Fnud fondled the gleaming garment. "I'll get my tailor to stitch the sleeves right onto the waistband, and then watch me shine at the neighborhood booze-and-knife bust tonight!" He snapped two of the nine fingers on his right hand. "Say—why don't you drop around, Mr. Retief? Plenty of straight grain formaldehyde and bloodshed—all the makings of a memorable night on the town. What do you say?"

"Sorry, Fnud. The joint ambassadors are staging the annual Victory Ball tonight, and I'll have to be there to keep an eye on the silverware. Maybe next week."

"It's a date." Fnud studied his employer's six-foot three-inch physique, wagging his asymmetrical head admiringly. "You know, that's kind of a neat arrangement you Terries use at that, Mr. Retief. A nifty idea, having just the two of everything, like eyes and ears and all. But how come only one nose?"

"Just for contrast. You can overdo a good thing, you know."

"Yeah. You know, a nose ain't a bad idea at that. Maybe I'll invest in one when I get my next step increase. What does a deluxe job like the ambassador's run?"

"I see you have an eye for a noble organ, Fnud. I'd say the cost in brandy alone would be well up into three figures."

"I guess it's outa my reach then. Oh, well—I'll settle for a more modest shnozz and maybe install a spare kidney. A fellow can't have too many kidneys, they say."

The valet seemed suddenly to recollect himself. "But Jeez, Mr. Retief, I don't guess you got time to waste talking about my development program. The shindig starts in a few minutes, and I'm due in the kitchen."

"You go ahead, Fnud. I'll make it on time."

When the door had closed behind the local, Retief opened the casement window and lifted a potted jelly-flower from the planting box on the sill, extracted from beneath it a flat 2mm needler which he tucked under his gold satin cummerbund. As he turned away, something caught his eye, dangling just beyond the window. It was a heavy-gauge rope ladder, swaying slightly in the breeze. At that moment there was a soft sound from the direction of the hall door, as of stealthy fingers examining the latch. Retief turned swiftly to the open closet, lifted a formal black coverall from the rod and crossed the room to hang the garment from the curtain rail above the open window. He switched off the light and stepped silently behind the bathroom door as the outer door swung open soundlessly.

A small, spindle-legged Groaci in a drab-colored hip cloak and plain eye shields slipped into the room, pushed the door shut, and headed directly for the closet. He was halfway there when the wind stirred the empty suit hanging in the window. The intruder snatched a bulky power gun from his tunic and aimed it at the garment.

"So—to have mistakenly judged your chambers to be unoccupied, Soft One," the alien hissed in his native tongue. "To place your manual extremities above your organ cluster and to prepare to go quietly!"

The hanging garment stirred. The Groaci jumped backward. "One more move, Soft One, and *jsssp!* to join your forebears in the Happy Burrowing Ground!"

The suit seemed to edge sideways as the breeze thrust at it.

"To make no move to escape!" the Groaci keened. "To turn slowly and mount the ladder thoughtfully provided by a trusted lackey. . . ." The alien's faint voice faded out as he apparently noted something amiss with the supposed target. "Retief . . . ?" he whispered, advancing cautiously. A yard from the window, he uttered a hiss of annoyance and lowered the gun.

"Not bad technique, Lilth," Retief said, emerging from concealment, the needler leveled at the Groaci. "Except that your draw was a little on the slow side—"

With a soft cry, the startled intruder whirled, leaped to the window, thrust aside the hanging coverall and lunged, checked himself too late. For a moment, he teetered on the sill; then with a despairing cry he toppled outward and dropped from view. Retief arrived at the window in time to observe the splashdown in the moat five stories below, marked by an imposing column of stagnant water and fruit rinds fountaining upward. The rope ladder, he noted, was gone.

"Too bad," he murmured. "It's getting so you just can't trust a lackey anymore."

There was a stealthy rap at the door; Retief went to it, swung it open. The visage of the Groaci counselor appeared, all five eyes canted alertly to scan the interior of the room.

"Neatly executed, Lilth," he started—and froze at the sight of Retief, casually puffing a dope stick alight.

"Evening, Nish," the Terran greeted his informal caller. "Looking for your code clerk? I'm afraid he just stepped out."

"You? What—that is, how—I mean to say—murderer!" Nish rushed to the window to stare down in dismay at his *landsman* floundering among the imported carp. "Mayhem! A wanton attack on the person of a diplomatic member of His Groacian Excellency's staff! Seize the miscreant!"

A number of persons, both Terran and Groaci, attracted by the cries of the deputy chief of the Groaci Mission, were now thrusting their heads into Retief's apartment. The choleric features of the Terran counsellor, Career Minister Biteworse, appeared amid the press.

"What seems to be the trouble here?" the plump senior officer demanded in a penetrating nasal tenor.

"I demand the instant arrest of this . . . this ruffian!" Nish whispered, his feeble voice shaking with emotion.

"Why, er, certainly," Biteworse agreed. "That is to say, ah, what's he done this time?"

"This time he's gone too far! His reputation for the flaunting of the niceties of diplomatic usage is notorious—but the defenestration of my colleague, junior rank notwithstanding, is the final anvil!"

"You mean—he threw someone out the window?" Biteworse looked disconcerted.

"Even now the unhappy chap sinks for the third time!" Nish declaimed.

"Hadn't we better, er, throw him a rope?" Colonel Warbutton suggested from the window, craning to observe the still-struggling figure far below.

"Don't seek to alleviate the gravity of the offense by ill-timed salvage efforts!" Nish hissed. "Clap the criminal in irons! In fact, Biteworse, I suggest you declare your entire staff under arrest until a properly constituted Groaci Board of Inquiry has sifted the matter to the bottom!"

"Now, now, let's not be hasty," Biteworse demurred. "Why don't you just settle for Retief for now, and hold off on the mass incarceration until our respective chiefs of mission have had time to review the matter—"

"No quibbling! I'll settle for half the Terran Mission in durance vile and the remainder stripped of diplomatic privilege and confined to quarters!"

"Why, that's generous of you, Nish." Biteworse pursed his lips judiciously. "But I'm not prepared to go farther than Retief plus a couple of third secretaries, and the revoking of snack-bar privileges for all personnel below Class Three rank—"

"Before you commit yourself, sir," Retief spoke up casually, "I'd like to point out that Mr. Nish seems to be laboring under a false impression."

"What?" The Groaci whirled, his throat sac vibrating in expression of total indignation. "You suggest that the spectacle of my underling even now perishing in the moat is a nonobjective phenomenon?"

"Oh, he's down there, all right," Retief confirmed. "But he couldn't have fallen from *this* window, as I'm sure you'll agree."

"Indeed? And why could he not?"

"It's my apartment. And my *Do Not Disturb* sign is lit. So, obviously, Lilth couldn't have been in my room—unless, of course, you'd like to stipulate that he was guilty of trespass, unauthorized entry, burglary, and a number of other irregularities."

"Why—the very idea," Nish said weakly.

"Clearly a simple case of mistaken identity," Biteworse announced briskly. "Now, if it had been Retief who fell, it would be logical to assume he had effected egress through this window. . . ." His voice trailed off. "By the way, Nish—just how did it happen that you were on the spot so soon after Lilth was pushed—fell, that is—out of, ah, some other window, I mean to say?"

"I but nipped up to borrow a book," the discomfited Groaci snapped.

"Indeed?" Biteworse purred, back in command. "I wasn't aware Terran literature was a fancy of yours, my dear Nish. You must drop by and browse over my modest collection some evening—when you're not engaged in, ah, other duties, here in the Terry wing."

"Meanwhile, don't forget your book," Retief said, offering a fat volume titled *How To Tell Your Friends from Your Enemies with Virtual Ninety-Percent Accuracy*.

"Bah!" Nish muttered, spurning the proffered tome. "We'll all be late for the gala." He shouldered his way through the crowd.

"Just between us, Retief," Second Secretary Magnan inquired confidentially, after the others had left, "What was that little sneak Lilth after?"

"I didn't get a chance to ask him," Retief said. "However, he left this as a momento of his visit." He held up a small disk-shaped object dangling from a strap of imitation alligator hide. "I found it by the window."

"It looks like an ordinary Mickey Mouse watch," Magnan said doubtfully. "However, I assume from your enigmatic expression it's something more arcane. Dare I ask what?"

"That's what I propose to find out, Mr. Magnan, at the first opportunity."

4

"I don't like it, Retief," Magnan said behind his hand, half an hour later, surveying the gala crowd of Terran and alien diplomats thronging the ballroom from his position near the hundred-gallon punchbowl, cut from a single crystal of red quartz mined in the interior.

"It could stand a little more gin," Retief agreed judiciously.

"Not the punch—the atmosphere!" Magnan corrected. "And I don't refer to the air conditioning; I mean the ominous feeling that something dreadful is about to happen."

"Relax, Mr. Magnan," Retief said soothingly. "The ambassador won't be making his speech for half an hour yet."

"Kindly spare me your ill-timed japes, Retief! As you know, I'm extremely sensitive to extrasensory vibrations of all sorts—a trick I fancy I inherited from my Aunt Prudelia—"

"That *is* a neat trick," Retief acknowledged, raising his glass *en passant* to a well-shaped stenographer waltzing past in the grip of Colonel Warbutton.

"Retief! Kindly attend to my remarks! After all, a diplomat learns to rely on his hunches—"

"A telling point, Mr. Magnan," Retief said, and deposited his glass on a passing tray. "And I have a hunch Miss Braswell would be grateful for a few civilian anecdotes, after two and a half waltzes' worth of military reminiscences."

"Quite possibly," Magnan said icily. "However,

I suggest you defer your mission of mercy until we've dealt with the more substantive problem of incipient skulduggery in the air!"

"If you're referring to the fact that Ambassador Nith has been in a huddle with his military attaché for the past twenty minutes, I agree it bodes no good for joint peacemaking efforts," Retief conceded.

"It's not only that—I've observed that Counselor Lilth seems to be exceptionally clubby with the Bogan military observer."

"So he does. While Ambassador Pouncetrifle has been cornered for the past forty minutes by three of our guests from the Dames Auxiliary for Militant Pacifism."

"I doubt that the dowagers have any fell intent," Magnan said. "However, that sneaky little Groaci cultural attaché—Fink, or Sneak or whatever his name is—"

"Snink; he seems unusually absorbed in whatever it is that Counselor Biteworse is holding forth on. He's had him backed in among the potted frogfronds for the past half hour."

"Ever since the arrival of the provisional Minister of Illegal Activities, to be precise," Magnan pointed out. "And at the same time, the *pro tem* Chief of Police has been huddling with Captain Thilth—even among the Groaci, not one whom one would care to entrust with assisting one's *grand-mère* across the street."

"Not if she were carrying more than jelly-bean money," Retief concurred. "All of which suggests that there are plans afoot that have nothing to do with the tranquillity of Lumbaga."

"In that case, how can you stand there ogling

the female clerical help?" Magnan demanded indignantly. "It's perfectly obvious that the Groaci and their toadies are up to no good!"

"Very probably, Mr. Magnan. However, if we stand here with our heads together, looking gloomy, they're likely to deduce that we're onto them—"

"And a good thing, too! The very idea, plotting right under our noses!"

"Better there than in some place less easy to observe," Retief suggested.

"The gall of the scoundrels! Come, Retief—let's report our suspicions to His Excellency at once—"

"I suggest we wait a few more minutes, Mr. Magnan. There are a pair of Groaci administrative aides edging past the Marine guards over by the French doors; let's give them time to get in the clear."

"Whatever for?" Magnan gasped. "So they can rifle the chancery safe?"

"We won't let them get that far. But it would be interesting to know what they've got in mind."

"But—what if they plant a bomb—or set fire to the building—or insinuate a set of falsified documents into the voucher files?"

"The last item is pretty scary," Retief conceded. "Still, maybe we can stop them before any real damage is done—" He broke off as the drapes twitched shut behind the aliens whom he had been observing. "Shall we trail along and see what they're up to, Mr. Magnan?"

"Well—we really ought to refer the matter to the appropriate authorities ... still, they'd hardly dare anything really drastic right here in the complex—and it *would* be rather a coup to lay

them by the heels unassisted." Magnan twitched
the multiple lapels of his grapejuice-colored, early
midevening, hyperformal cut-away into line, assumed a stern expression, and followed Retief as
he made his way through the crowd.

On the terrace, they caught a glimpse of their
quarry just disappearing over the balustrade into
the shrubbery below.

"Just as I thought!" Magnan gasped. "And there's
a *Keep Off the Grass* sign in plain view! I'll report
them at once, and—"

"Wait." Retief motioned Magnan back. There
were sounds of threshing in the bushes, then soft
footfalls along a flagstoned path. Suddenly a bril-
liant beam of greenish light sprang up, shining
vertically up through the foliage. It blinked once,
twice, three times. There was a pause; then the
signal was repeated.

"The plot thickens," Retief said softly as Magnan
clutched his arm. "Let's see what's next."

Again they heard footfalls, this time approaching. The shrubbery rustled. A pale Groaci visage
appeared over the balustrade. A moment later the
two aliens had regained the terrace and were saun-
tering casually back toward the French doors, puffing dope sticks in an insouciant manner.

"Why, the very idea," Magnan whispered from
the shadow of the pilaster where he and Retief
were concealed. "They're rejoining the party just
as though nothing at all had happened!"

"You'd hardly expect them to skulk back in just
because they skulked out," Retief pointed out. "Also,
nothing much *has* happened—yet."

"You mean—you think there'll be more?"

"I suspect that what we saw was a modulated light signaler. They could have conveyed an unabridged set of Corps regulations in the time they had."

"But—whatever would they want with a set of CDT regs?"

"A figure of speech, Mr. Magnan—" Retief broke off as a faint *Bee-beep!* sounded from his wrist. He turned back his cuff; the tiny figure of Mickey was glowing softly in the dark; his arms whirled against the disc, semaphoring frantically.

"Come in, Lilth!" a tiny, harsh voice rasped in badly accented Lumbagan. "Why haven't you reported in as scheduled?"

Retief brought the device close to his face. "Alas," he whispered, in a passable imitation of the Groaci's breathy tones, "I was detained by certain unscheduled natatorial exertions—"

"You've been advised how important split-second timing is! Where are you now?"

"On the south terrace, catching a breath of revivifying night air from the rigors of the receiving line," Retief hissed.

"Cretin! To the roof at once! It's now M-minute minus four! Get going!"

"Roger and out," Retief breathed.

"Just a minute! You're not Lilth!" The glow died from the watch face. Mickey's hands came to rest at twenty fifty-six.

"It was useful while it lasted," Retief said, and tossed the deactivated communicator aside. "Let's go, Mr. Magnan. It looks like we're running late for a hot date."

Two and a half minutes later, after a dizzying

run up a tight spiral stair cut into the thick stone of the keep walls, Retief and Magnan stepped silently out onto the complex roof. The bright pink light of the two moons cast double shadows across the rough, tarred planks.

"Looks like we're first on the scene," Retief noted. "Let's pick an inconspicuous spot and wait for developments."

"Retief," Magnan gasped, breathing hard from his exertions. "What in the world do you suppose. . . ?"

"This afternoon someone hired Ignarp to gather us in. Later on, Lilth seemed to have the same idea. Somebody seems to have an urgent desire to own a Terry."

"But—if that's true—aren't we playing into their hands?"

"Sometimes it's the only way to get a look at the other fellow's cards."

"But what if they catch us here! I suggest we go back at once and file a written report—"

"Too late now," Retief said softly as the door through which they had emerged was thrust rudely open. A short, plump figure emerged, sputtering, closely accompanied by a trio of hefty individuals in floppy hats and trailing hemlines.

"Why—it's the ambassador—and the ladies from DAMP!" Magnan chirped. "Gracious, what a relief—" As he started to step out, Retief pulled him back.

"One more sound out of you, Terry, and we deliver you in do-it-yourself-kit form," one of Pouncetrifle's escorts barked at the Chief of Mission in the native tongue.

"Why—they're not DAMP members at all!" Magnan whispered. "They're not even ladies! In fact"—he gulped as one of the trio tossed aside a voluminous frock and followed it with the hat—"they're not even human!"

"Sit tight, Mr. Magnan," Retief said, "the party's not complete yet. . . ."

Overhead a soft *whap-whap-whap* became audible, grew swiftly louder. A dark shadow floated across the lesser moon; dust swirled up as a small copter settled gently in at the far side of the roof.

"No navigation lights!" Magnan blurted. "That's a violation of the provisional traffic code!"

As the bogus pacifists hustled the ambassador toward the copter there was a clatter from the door, accompanied by a clink of medals. Colonel Warbutton appeared, turned back to assist a slighter figure through.

"Remarkable view from up here, my dear," the military attaché said expansively. "Just savor a lungful of that fresh air!"

"It smells like turbo fumes to me," Miss Braswell's voice replied. "But I thought you said we were going up to your office for some emergency dictation. . . ." Her voice trailed off into a yelp as two dark shapes loomed suddenly beside her and her escort.

"Here, what's the meaning of this!" Warbutton boomed, struggling in the grip of what appeared to be a portly matron. "Are you ladies out of your minds? Attacking a military man is no way to wage pacifism!"

"It's an ambush," a Lumbagan voice yelled. "Over the side with the both of 'em!"

"Don't shoot, Retief!" Magnan blurted as Retief

stood and snapped his needler into his hand. "You'll hit His Excellency!"

As the kidnappers thrust Warbutton toward the parapet, Retief jumped toward the lone alien man-handling the ambassador toward the copter. The ersatz dowager whirled to intercept him; he palmed the gun and rammed a right hook into the local's midsection, grabbed the ambassador's arm and spun him toward the open door. One of Warbutton's captors whirled with a yell and dived after the escaping dignitary, only to trip over Magnan's outthrust foot. Warbutton wrenched himself from the grasp of the other, dived for the door, bulldoz-ing Miss Braswell aside to the embrace of the first of the three thugs, now back on his feet; he lifted her, sprang toward the parapet as the second Lumbagan caught Warbutton's ankle, bringing the military man down with a resounding crash. Retief reached the parapet in the same instant that Miss Braswell's captor, with a hearty heave, tossed her over the side. He dived, caught her hand as she fell, her weight dragging him half across the para-pet. Instantly, horny hands seized his ankles, lifted, and shoved. As he went over, Retief grabbed for the coping, hooked his fingers over the edge. With a bone-wrenching shock, he was brought up short, the girl dangling below him. The Lumbagan ap-peared above him, fist raised to smash at his fin-gers: then Magnan's narrow features were visible over the alien's shoulder as he brought an elevator shoe down on the local's skull.

As the Lumbagan crumpled, Retief pulled him-self up, hauling Miss Braswell over the parapet beside him, to see the other two Lumbagans wrestling Warbutton toward the copter. He charged them, hurled one aside—and collided with Warbutton as the colonel tore free and dashed for freedom.

"Help!" Warbutton yelled, grappling Retief. "I demand protection!"

Retief thrust him aside, lunged for the copter as it lifted suddenly, rotors beating furiously. He was too late; the machine rose swiftly, bore away to the west across the dark rooftops. As he turned back, the two still-present Lumbagans plunged through the door a scant inch in advance of Warbutton. Retief caught the colonel by the collar and dragged him back, too late. The fugitives were gone.

"I'll have you court-martialed for this, you whippersnapper!" Warbutton yelled.

"Oh, Mr. Retief, you were wonderful!" Miss Braswell sighed, and sagged against him.

"I'd have nabbed the lot of them if you hadn't interfered with my pursuit just now!" Warbutton ranted. "Actually, I've been well aware of the ruffians' plans for some weeks now!"

"In that case, maybe you know where they're taking him," Retief cut in.

"Taking who?" the colonel snorted.

"Magnan," Retief said. "They got him."

5

"Out of the question, Mr. Retief," Ambassador Pouncetrifle snorted, yanking his rumpled lapels into line. "No one leaves the embassy until the present crisis is past! Having lost one diplomat, through no fault of my own, I have no intention of blotting my copybook further!"

"Why, even while I was manning the barricades on the roof," Warbutton stated indignantly, "a *coup*, by the way, which would have succeeded brilliantly but for the interference of Retief—even as I manned the barricades, I say, a mob of irresponsibles invaded the courtyard and pelted the chancery's north facade with overripe frinkfruit!"

"It would be as much as our lives were worth to sally forth in the midst of the disorders," an Information Service man spoke up. "I say let's acknowledge the failure of the mission get busy concocting an alibi—"

"Conducting an analysis in depth of the unforeseen factors necessitating a rethinking of Corps policy anent the timetable for Lumbagan unification, I presume you mean," Biteworse amended. "Make a note of that phrase, Miss Braswell. It will do nicely as a title for my report."

"I'll handle the report end, Fenwick," Pouncetrifle snapped. "I hereby assign you the chairmanship of a task force to turn up evidence proving me blameless in the fiasco."

"I think you're all mean," Miss Braswell spoke up, netting shocked stares from the great men present. "Poor Mr. Magnan was just marvelous when he conked that big, ugly brute over the head—"

"He assaulted Colonel Warbutton?" Pouncetrifle barked. "Obviously the man's in the pay of the enemy!"

"How perfectly silly!" Miss Braswell exclaimed. "Those big bullies dragged him into that copter and took off while Mr. Retief was trying to unglue the colonel from his neck! He—"

"That will do, Miss Braswell!" Pouncetrifle barked. "The situation is deteriorating hourly, gentlemen." He turned a choleric gaze on his staff. "And if Mr. Retief's to be believed, the Groaci are back of the skulduggery, as usual—"

"Don't believe a word of it," Warbutton snapped. "The fellow's making a transparent attempt to cover up—"

"Be that as it may, Colonel—I decree no further contact with our Groaci colleagues. Also, no contact with Lumbagans. In addition, no contact with offworld representatives of any stripe!"

"W-will it be all right if I cable Sector?" the communications officer inquired diffidently. "Just to keep them informed?"

"Better not," Warbutton said. "We don't know how far the rot has spread."

"I'm not certain I'd go *that* far," Pouncetrifle said sternly. "However, I see no point in unduly alarming the department with premature reports which my critics might distort so as to imply some culpability on my part. We'll wait for cheerier tidings."

"B-but if the embassy is surrounded by hostile mobs . . . and under air attack by native commandos . . . and threatened from within by fifth columnists . . . and we can't even tell anyone . . . how in the world are we going to get any cheery tidings—to say nothing of getting ourselves out of this pickle?" the political officer queried.

"We'll employ a wait-and-see strategey," Pouncetrifle decreed. "We'll retire to the air-raid shelters and wait a few days, and see if they'll go away. Possibly not the most dynamic program open to us"—he forestalled objections with a plump palm— "but one hallowed by centuries of bureaucratic tradition. Now. . . ." He favored the assembled staff with a frosty twinkle. "I've decided to advance the schedule for the checkers tournament so as to fully occupy our time underground. And as an added fillip, I personally will make available to the winner an autographed photo of myself admiring my plastic doily collection for a modest charge barely covering expenses." He fixed Retief with an icy glare. "And as for you, sir—you may regard yourself as under close house arrest pending a full investigation by Colonel Warbutton into your conduct during the raid."

"The old meany," Miss Braswell commiserated with Retief after the meeting had dispersed. "He's going to let poor Mr. Magnan fend for himself without lifting one of his pudgy little fingers to help him—and blaming it all on you!"

"His Excellency is a bit distraught at the moment," Retief soothed the girl. "I suspect he'll revise this morning's pronouncements in his dispatch to Sector after this is all over."

"But—what good will that do Mr. Magnan?"

"I agree something needs to be done in the meantime to lend substance to his retrospections. Actually, I have one or two errands to run in that connection. Will you convey my regrets to the checker team?"

"But—he put you under house arrest! Doesn't that mean you can't leave the complex?"

"Not quite; it just gives him grounds to disavow me in case things don't work out."

"You mean—he *expects* you to go AWOL?"

"Let's just say he's prepared to risk it."

"But you—you're risking your life, going out there! You can hear the mob howling around the front entrance!"

"I'll use another route to avoid the autograph fans."

"Mr. Retief—take care," Miss Braswell whispered; she kissed him quickly on the cheek and fled.

Five minutes later, wrapped in a dark cloak, Retief opened the hidden door behind the dumbwaiter and descended into the catacombs.

6

Dacoit Street was deserted. The yells of the demonstrators gathered before the grand entrance to the Castle complex were a dull surf-roar here. The shops were shuttered and dark; scattered brickbats and broken spears attested to the activities of the day, but only a few candy wrappers and old newspapers blowing across the oily cobbles lent movement to the scene, pitch dark but for a weak glow from a spluttering flambeau at the next corner.

Retief made his way unmolested through the

narrow ways; five minutes' brisk walk brought him to a corner half a block from a rough-hewn door under a swinging signboard adorned with a lumpy purplish shape pierced by a pointed length of wood. Yellow light leaked from a small leaded-glass window. As Retief took up his post under the spreading branches of a music tree, a gust stirred the leaves, evoking a rippling arpeggio of crystalline sound that mingled mournfully with the fluting of the night wind.

A small wild creature resembling a disembodied blue eyeball with tiny bird feet hopped along a twig overhead, goggling at the Terran with an appearance of intentness heightened by the absence of an eyelid. A second free-lance ocular appeared, peeping from among glassy, needle-shaped leaves. Nearer at hand, another variety of the local fauna—this one a convoluted three-inch ellipsoid bearing a remarkable resemblance to an oversized ear—perched in a froomble bush, pivoting slowly from left to right and back again as if tuning in on a faint sound in the distance.

"You boys ought to get together with a nose and form a corporation," Retief murmured. "You'd be a dynamite vaudeville act."

Both eyeballs whipped out of sight; the ear jerked and began to crawl hastily down the stem. A faint footfall sounded from the direction of the nearby alley mouth. Retief faded back against the bole of the ancient tree and eased his 2mm gun into his hand. A furtive five-foot figure wrapped in an ankle-length djellaba emerged into view.

"Ignarp," Retief called softly. The newcomer jumped and emitted a sharp yelp.

"Galloping gastropods!" he hissed. "You nearly scared me out of my epidermis!" He advanced another step to peer closely at Retief with three large, watery eyes not unlike those concealed in the foliage above.

"Aren't you the Terry I did the big favor for this afternoon?" he queried. "Frankly, all you foreigners look alike to me."

"An accusation I can't level against you, Ignarp," Retief said. "Didn't you have four eyes and a purple hide this afternoon?"

"Yeah; I stopped by my place for a shower and change." Ignarp gave his rattling sigh. "I didn't know it was going to be such a rough evening. What are you doing out in the streets? The rallying cry of the mob is 'Get Terry.' "

"It does seem the incidence of violence is escalating since the peace talks have been under way. Any idea why?"

"We got a few ideas—but maybe it's not time to spill 'em."

"Who's 'we'?"

"I guess it won't hurt to tell you; I'm a member of an undercover organization known as the Goody Redistribution Action Bunch. But why pump me? I'm just an average citizen, trying to get along—"

"Don't kid me, Ignarp. Conditions have changed since this afternoon. They got Magnan."

"Why, the lousy, sneaky, double-crossing—"

"Don't take it so hard; you can still earn a nice fee. Just tell me who hired you and why."

"Well—that sounds like a gracious offer. But let's get out of sight. I've got the feeling unfriendly eyes are upon us."

"After you, Ignarp."

"Come on," he said. "The Stake and Kidney's a discreet bistro, if not too clean. All the regulars will be out rioting, so we'll have a modicum of privacy."

The local led the way past the shuttered fronts of darkened shops to the heavy door, rapped a complicated tattoo, shifting from one of his six large feet to another and casting worried glances along the avenue until the door rattled and swung inward with a lugubrious creak. An undersized cranium adorned with an odd assortment of sensory organs poked out at belt level to look the callers up and down.

"For Greep's sake, Fudsot, let us in before the City Guard sees us," Ignarp hissed. "This Terry's got diplomatic immunity, but those dupes of the power structure would like nothing better than to rearrange my internal components along more conventional lines."

Grumbling, the landlord ushered them down three crooked steps into a long, low-ceilinged room smelling of fried zintx patties and sour wine. He locked the door behind them, and indicated a five-legged table in the corner.

"Too conspicuous," Ignarp demurred. "How about the back room?"

"That'll run you an extra five xots."

"Five xots? You're as bad as the entrenched exploiters!"

"Except they'd charge you ten—and then report you. Pay up or get out, and you and your offworld chum. It's all the same to me."

"OK. OK. The Bunch will get around to you, you

tool of the establishment!" Ignarp extracted a small-mouthed purse from beneath his voluminous robes and handed over a triangular coin of green plastic. Fudsot subjected it to close examination under what seemed to be an olfactory organ before using a six-inch key to unlock the small door at the back.

"It's all yours, gents," he grunted. "For the next half hour, anyways. After that it'll cost you another five xots."

"Bring us wine," Ignarp ordered as he dusted off a three-legged stool.

"Sure. Four xots for a quarter-zub o' the house brew. Six xots for bottled-in-bond. And I can give you a special deal on some aged Pepsi; I happened to get aholt of a small consignment through a special contact down south. Five xots the flask, uncut."

"Smuggler," Ignarp snapped. "Profiteer! Robber! We'll take the Pepsi—in sealed bottles, mind you!"

"Sure—whatta you think I am, one o' those chiselers?"

Ignarp waited in glowering silence until the landlord had delivered the refreshments and withdrawn.

"That's what we're up against," he said gloomily. "You'd think Fudsot would be a loyal supporter of the movement—but no, he's out for the fast xot!"

"What's this movement all about?" Retief asked.

"I should think it was obvious," Ignarp said sharply. "Even a foreigner can see that the entire planet's in the grip of an elite corps of self-serving reactionaries!"

"Curious," Retief said, puffing a Chanel dope stick alight. "I had the impression that anarchy was complete. In fact, that's why we Terries are here—"

"I know all about your so-called Peace Commission, Retief. You Terries and those main-chance Groaci are all spinning your wheels. Sure, we fight a lot—we have ever since the dawn of recorded history, six years ago. And even before, if the old tribal legends mean anything. And that's jake—except lately it's taken a nasty turn. The old system of you break my back, I'll break yours, is falling apart!"

"Uh huh." Retief sampled his drink. "And where does your Bunch come into the picture?"

"We've formed a third force to combat the special privilege groups. Of course, we're just getting started—only thirteen members at present—but we won't stop until the gross inequities of the system have been corrected!"

"You intend to divide up the wealth, an equal share for everyone?"

"You think we're out of our brainpans? We'll keep the loot for ourselves, naturally!"

"That's your idea of an equitable arrangement?" Retief inquired mildly.

"Of couse not!" Ignarp looked puzzled. "It's just simple, old-fashioned greed, the noblest of emotions."

"Sounds like a highly realistic program," Retief said. "And what about the rest of the population?"

"We're planning on selling them into slavery, naturally. And say—maybe you Terries would like a slice of the action!"

"What makes you think so?"

"Well—aside from the fact that the mob is out to get both of us—I've heard you Terries get your jollies out of taking things away from the original owners and handing them over to new management. I could never figure out why, but we members of GRAB are perfectly willing to get in on the redistribution."

"That's a fair assessment of our foreign-aid policy, Ignarp; but sometimes it's a little difficult to determine who the deserving parties are."

"Simple enough: Possession is *prima facie* evidence of moral leprosy; have-nots are pure in heart by definition."

"But if we hand the planet over to you fellows, then *you'll* be the haves—"

"That's different," Ignarp stated crisply. "Now, when can we expect the first consignment of guns, tanks, bombers, zip guns, poisoned bodkins, and the rest?"

"Well, there may be a few administrative delays, Ignarp. Even a bureaucrat as dedicated to the spread of enlightenment as Ambassador Pouncetrifle may have some difficulty picturing a baker's dozen of malcontents as the authentic inheritors of the mantle of planetary dictatorship."

"I had an idea you might try to stall," Ignarp said accusingly. "Fortunately, we have a telling ideological point in reserve." He leaned toward Retief confidentially. "The situation," he stated solemnly, "has a very nasty—are you ready?—racial angle."

"Tell me about it."

"You don't sound very excited." Ignarp said in

tones reflecting disappointment. "I heard all a fellow had to do was mention the word and you Terries automatically started writing checks."

"A mild exaggeration. In any event, the syndrome hardly applies to Lumbaga. You fellows don't have any races."

"Hey, what kind of a crack is that?"

"I've noticed," Retief said, "that the eyeballs and lower lips hopping around in the underbrush don't look much different than the ones you and your fellow citizens employ in your daily activities—"

"Now, hold it right there, Retief! I don't like the turn the conversation's taking—"

"In fact," Retief went on unperturbed, "it seems that the higher forms of Lumbagan life are all evolved from the lower forms by combination—"

"Don't come preaching your godless evolutionary doctrines around here!" Ignarp snapped.

"Don't worry, I'm just making it up as I go along," Retief said soothingly. "If my theory is correct, you, for example, represent the end product of a whole series of combinations—"

"Let's not get personal, Terry!"

"Just getting a few facts straight, Ignarp, no offense intended. Tell me, how old are you?"

"That's none of your blasted business, Retief!"

"I thought you wanted Terran backing in your scheme to take over the world."

"Yeah, that's right, but—"

"Then it's my business."

"Well ... I don't know exactly," Ignarp muttered. "But the best theories give a figure around a quarter of a million. That's average, of course.

After all, by the time you go back a couple of centuries, things get kind of vague." The Lumbagan looked embarrassed, as attested by the purplish tinge mounting his wattles.

"I think I understand," Retief said. "When a Lumbagan has a bad heart or a broken arm, he trades the injured member in on a new one. In time, he's completely replaced. Is that it?"

"That covers most of it," Ignarp said hastily. "Now, back to practical politics—"

"So in effect, a Lumbagan never dies. The question is, how does he get started?"

"Cripes, Retief, is nothing sacred to you foreigners?"

"My interest is purely scientific, Ignarp."

"This racy conversation gets me all stirred up," the local said. "However, I guess it's for the cause. You've got it right as it goes, but there's a few points you missed. Like the fact that the Singletons—you know, the free-living eyeballs and pituitary glands and the like—can only get together in bunches of up to ten. An ear might team up with a tentacle for mutual security, you know, and then later add on an esophagus—strictly by instinct, natch. Not all these teams work out, of course. Evolutionary dead ends, you might say. They break up again, no hard feelings, and maybe later the different parts join another accretion. In the end, after a few million years, you get quite a large number of working accretions swinging through the jungle or creeping around in the underbrush, as happy as clams. So OK. A tenner Singleton can't add any more free units—but what *can* happen is that two Singletons can link up to form a Dubb. Got it?"

"I'm trying, Ignarp. Pray continue."

"Right. Now, that's not the end of the trail. Two well-established Dubbs can get together, and make up a Trip. Now, a Trip's a pretty complicated life-form; most of 'em don't work out, but with up to forty basic units to play around with, you *can* come up with some pretty successful combos. But Trips are a lot rarer than Dubbs, naturally."

"Naturally. And I suppose two congenial Trips can join forces, to continue the process?"

"Right! And when that happens, you get a Quad." Ignard looked at Retief expectantly.

"And two Quads can combine to make a still more complicated creature?"

"Huh? Where'd you get an obscene idea like that!" Ignarp looked shocked, an effect achieved by rotating his eyeballs rapidly. "A four-decker is the ultimate produce of evolution—a Lumbagan—like me!"

"I won't say it's clear, Ignarp, but it's not quite as opaque as it was. But you still haven't explained why you Lumbagans spend so much time disassembling each other—or just how you decide who's against whom."

"That's where the racial angle comes in. Now it's perfectly natural and wholesome when everybody is out to get everybody else; but when discrimination rears its ugly head—that's different. And even that wouldn't bother me," Ignarp added, "except I happen to be a member of the persecuted minority."

"A minority usually implies at least two people

with a few characteristics in common," Retief
pointed out. "Since every Lumbagan is unique—"

"Except my kind," Ignarp said gloomily. "Somehow, due to a component nobody's isolated yet,
we've got something nobody else has got."

"A disability?"

"Heck, no, Retief! They'd forgive us that! We're
vastly superior, that's what gravels 'em! Just a
hint of our special skill, and the witch-hunt is
on!"

"And just what is this trait that gives you the
advantage—"

"Aha! That's our big secret! You see—"

There was a sudden sound of disturbance in the
outer room: a dull clatter, a yelp, a thump that
rattled the cups on the table. Something crashed
against the door hard enough to splinter wood.

"I might have known," Ignarp cried, leaping up.
"Sold out by the vested interests!"

Retief came to his feet, looking around the small,
dim-lit room. The only visible opening was a small
ventilator grill.

"So long, Retief!" Ignarp yelled. "I'll be in
touch. . . ."

With a rending crash, the door burst inward.
The creature which bounded through the opening
was seven feet tall, with sour yellowish skin
blotched with black and purple. Three gaunt, bris-
tly, knob-kneed legs terminating in broad rubbery
webbed feet made up two thirds of its height. Four
left and two right arms of graduated lengths sprang
from the hunched shoulders, protected by a cara-
pace resembling the shell of a turtle adorned with
twisted spikes. Atop a short, thick, tendon-corded

neck rested a pointed head given over largely to a foot-wide, purple-lipped mouth crowded with needlelike fangs, below a pair of wide-set eyes the size of tennis balls, a bloodshot yellowish white except for the off-centered metallic black pupils. A thick, powerful prehensile tail ending in a three-fingered hand waved a gnarled steelwood club aloft.

With a bellow, the monstrosity charged. Retief spun the table into its path, ducked a wild swing as the giant crashed into the obstacle with a plank-splintering impact. At the open door he turned; the intruder was threshing its way clear of the remains of the boards, but the GRAB member there was no sign. Retief had time only to notice that the grill was missing from the register before the monster tossed aside a shattered timber and leaped toward him. Retief stepped through and slammed the door, dropping the heavy bar in place as the armored alien crashed against it.

In the gloom of the outer room, the squat figure of the landlord was dimly visible, scrambling for cover. Retief reached him in two strides, caught the back of his coarse-weave tunic, lifted him to tippy-toes.

"A slight double cross, eh, Fudsot? Who paid you?" he inquired genially, as the door behind him resounded to the berserker's blows.

"Leave me go, Terry, or I'll see to it you're broken down into surgical spares—"

"What was the idea? Were you out to get me, or was it Ignarp you were after—or both?"

"You know so much—you tell me," Fudsot grunted.

"But Ignarp fooled you," Retief said. "He separated into subassemblies of a convenient size and went out the ventilator, right?"

"You Terries aren't supposed to know about that," Fudsot muttered. "A lousy fate, even for a trouble-maker like Ignarp."

"So that's the last of Ignarp, eh?"

"As Ignarp, yeah. His sweetbreads and tonsils are back where they started ages ago—free-living Freebies looking around for a partner to start up a new tenner." Fudsot wagged his head mournfully.

"A sad end for a social reformer of his zeal," Retief said. "Still, there's much to be said for the carefree life of a lone adenoid. I'll be on my way now, Fudsot, but before I go—just what was that that broke up our drinking party? I've gotten accus-tomed to a certain pleasing variety in the local citizenry, but that chap was in an entirely new category."

"I heard rumors, but—" Fudsot broke off.

"But what?"

"But it would be bad for my health to spread 'em. How's about getting him outa my back room now, Terry? I got to set the place to rights for the pre-dawn dustup crowd."

"No thanks, I can't use him."

"You mean—you're leaving that monstrosity on my hands?"

"Certainly. Mind if I use the back entrance?"

"No! That's where . . . I mean, there isn't one," the landlord finished sullenly.

"That's where they're waiting to make the pickup, eh? Thanks for the tip." Retief pushed through a greasy door behind the bar, crossed a kitchen reek-ing of stale fat, slipped out into a narrow alleyway decorated with neglected garbage containers. There was a soft rustling from a dense patch of shadow. A small, spindle-legged figure swathed in a dark cloak stepped forth. From the folds of the garment a gloved grasping member protruded, gripping a small power gun.

"So—success attends my efforts! The moose has taken the bait, and sprung the trap!"

"Mouse, I think you mean, Wilth," Retief corrected. "What brings you out in the damp night air?"

"Drat," the Groaci hissed. "Who informed you of my identity?"

"Don't you remember? The ambassador introduced us last week, at the Mother-in-Law's Day Pepsi bust."

"I refer to the treacher who betrayed my disguise."

"Oh, he's the same fellow who's standing behind you now with a crater gun aimed at your dorsal suture."

Wilth stared violently, causing one of his government-issue eye shields to clatter to the cobbles. "Undone!" he keened, as Retief stepped forward to relieve him of his weapon. "Unhappy Wilth! I rue the day the mound burst to expose me to the harsh external world!"

"By the way, what did you have in mind doing with this?" Retief inquired, aiming the gun negligently at its former owner.

"My instructions—I assure you, my dear Retief, nothing personal was intended—were to intimidate you with the firearm, thereby causing you to accompany me to a designated place for an uninhibited interview with a Most Highly Placed Person."

"Most highly placed in the Groaci hierarchy, I assume?"

"But of course. Do you imagine I'm in the habit of trepanning fellow diplomats—even Soft Ones—for the convenience of members of lesser races?"

"I shouldn't have asked. And what was to be the subject of this conference?"

"Do you further imagine I am privy to the machinations of MHPP's?" Wilth glanced nervously behind him. "As a courtesy to a colleague, would you kindly instruct your toady to point his piece elsewhere...." His faint voice faded. "Wh-where is the creature?"

"He couldn't make it," Retief said. "Liquor inventory, you know—but the intention was there. Now—"

"Hoaxed!" Wilth whistled. "Hoodwinked by vile Terran duplicity!"

"Don't take it so hard, Wilth. No harm done; it's always a rewarding experience to make the acquaintance of an MHPP of whatever persuasion. I'll go with you."

"You'll ... ah ... accompany me to the rendezvous as planned?" Wilth goggled all five eyestalks at Retief.

"Why not? The evening is still young." Retief snapped open the butt of the power gun and removed the energy cell, handed the disarmed weapon back to the Groaci.

"Why, this is quite decent of you, Retief," Wilth whispered breathlessly. "What a pity all Groaci-

Terran relations can't be conducted in the same spirit of amity."

"They are, Wilth, they are," Retief said soothingly. "Shall we go? I wouldn't like to keep the MHPP waiting."

"Good notion. But no tricks, Retief. I trusted you once, to my sorrow. . . ."

"Don't worry, Wilth. I wouldn't want to miss an opportunity to hobnob with the great."

"I wasn't aware you were a climber, Retief," Wilth said as he motioned the Terran ahead.
"Luckily your social aspirations coincide with my own plans for career advancement, to our mutual advantage. Straight ahead; I'll follow with the gun, for the sake of appearances."

It was a brisk ten-minute walk through the tortuously winding streets—hardly more than tunnels threading through the monumental jumble of Lumbagan architecture. Wilth halted at a small but massive door set in a deeply recessed niche, pounded stealthily on the dark panels. Weak grayish light leaked out as the door opened. A Groaci in the uniform of a peacekeeper peered out.

"Inside, Soft One," Wilth ordered curtly. Retief preceded his putative captor along a cramped passage papered in a pattern of puce and mustard lozenges to a highly varnished bile-green door that reflected the watery glow of the ceiling dimstrip. The guard rapped. At a faint response, he thrust the door wide and motioned Retief through.

A Groaci in jeweled eye shields was seated behind a wide desk. He waved a negligent three-fingered hand at Retief, indicating a stool.

"Any difficulties?" he inquired of his underling in Terran.

"Your Excellency would be amazed at how easy it was," Wilth replied glumly. "I was even astonished myself."

"To not accept the legends of Terry invincibility," the senior alien snapped, switching to the Groacian tongue, "lest you predispose yourself to quail in the breech!" He turned three eyes on Retief while holding the glare of the other two on Wilth. "I," he announced, "am Hivemaster Shlush. You, I believe, are the fellow Retief?"

"A pleasure, Your Excellency." Retief acknowledged his identity with a nod and seated himself.

"You," Shlush continued ominously, "are not unknown to me by repute."

"I'm flattered."

"Don't be," Shlush hissed. "Your name, Soft One, is a byword for the Terran duplicity and meddling that have plagued Groaci foreign policy since the first intimations of our manifest Galactic destiny!"

"That's a rather uncharitable description of Corps policy, Hivemaster," Retief commented. "By the way, what brings you here? I don't recall seeing your name on the last embassy list—"

"Not to pry into matters of no concern to foreigners!" Shlush hissed.

"In fact," Retief went on, "I seem to recall that you were rather suddenly retired to civilian life after that fiasco on Grabnark IV—"

Shlush jabbed a digit at Retief, all five eyes canted alertly in his guest's direction now. "Your role in the humbling of the great is not forgotten, Retief! But now the era of Terry domination comes to an end! No more will we Groaci suffer graciously the intolerable interposition of foreigners between ourselves and the objects of our desires!"

"Go on." Retief puffed a cigar to life, blew aromatic smoke across the desk.

"You," Shlush hissed, "have the honor of being the first Terry to learn the fate of all inferiors who seek to impede the path of Groaci expansion!"

"I hope I prove worthy of the distinction," Retief said pleasantly.

"Ah, you have done so long since, my Retief—on the first occasion when you laid violent hands on the person of an Exalted One! And as soon as certain specialty devices I have caused to be installed in the vaults beneath my present humble quarters reach operating rpm, you shall reap your reward!"

"In the meantime," Retief suggested mildly, "I take it you'd like to have a little talk."

"Indeed yes," Shlush whispered. "How perceptive of you, Retief."

"Not at all," the Terran demurred. "Wilth told me."

"To have babbled of state secrets, littermate of drones?" The hivemaster hissed the question at his underling.

"Whom, I, Excellency? Why, to have but hinted he'd best be on his metacarpals—"

"To commit another indiscretion, and to find yourself trussed by the poleces alongside the Soft One!" Shlush turned back to Retief. "But I'm slighting my hostly obligations," he said smoothly. "Would you care for a little something while we chat?"

"Brandy, thanks," Retief said comfortably.

"You," Shlush addressed the guard still hovering by the door. "To fetch brandy at once. Black Bacchus will do."

"To congratulate Your Excellency on Your Excellency's taste," the peacekeeper hissed unctuously. "But to wonder if Your Excellency would amplify Your Excellency's instructions to include data as to where I'm supposed to fetch it from."

"The usual source, hivefellow of defectives!"

"To do as commanded, Exalted One—but don't you inkthay the errytay ightmay recognize the abellay?"

"To assume you have itway enough to ourpay it in the itchenkay!" Shlush favored Retief with the Groaci equivalent of a sour smile. "I've instructed the fellow to serve our refreshments in a VIP decanter reserved for important guests," he translated.

"I'm sensible of the honor," Retief said. "Now, what was it you wanted to tell me?"

"Tell you? My dear Terry, you fail to grasp the full implications of the situation. It is *you* who are going to tell *me!*"

"What would you like to know first?" Retief said promptly.

"You may begin with full details of secret Terran armament schemes, overall invasion strategy, D-day tactical plans, and close-support logistical arrangements," Shlush said crisply.

"I can cover that in a very few words," Retief said. "There aren't any."

"Pah! You expect me to believe that an organization of the sophistication of the CDT intends to play it by ear?"

"Play what by ear?" Retief inquired interestedly.

"The take-over. What else?"

"The take-over?" Retief tipped an inch of cigar ash onto Shlush's polished desk top. "What of?"

"Of this plague spot known as Lumbaga, naturally!"

"Who's taking it over?" Retief inquired interestedly.

"We are! That is to say, *you* are! I mean to say, of course, having gotten wind of the perfidious schemes laid by you treacherous Soft Ones under the cynical guise of pretended participation in bogus peace talks, we Groaci have naturally been compelled to take appropriate steps to safeguard the endangered lives, property, and sacred self-determination of the indigenous autochthones."

"Remarkable," Retief said. "And I suppose that to properly protect the Lumbagans, it will be necessary for Groac to temporarily garrison a few troops here. And perhaps to take over a certain number of islands for official use. And possibly to requisition a modest percentage of the planetary production and manpower for the fight against foreign exploitation. And a reasonable tax levy to support a portion of the expense of this selfless action is to be expected."

"I see you have a grasp of the realities of interplanetary do-goodism," Shlush acknowledged. "Now, as beings of the world, why not just give me a brief rundown on your own development plans? Don't bother going into detail; I have specialists on my staff who'll assist you later in dredging up the odd unremembered trifle from the depths of the subconscious. For now, just limit your exposition to the high points."

"You're too shrewd for me, Hivemaster," Retief conceded. "Did you think up this scheme yourself?"

"Ah-ah," Shlush chided his prisoner. "No prying, Retief. Not that it matters, of course, inasmuch as you'll soon be occupying a shallow excavation under the dungeon floor—but it's bad form tipping one's opponents off to the details of one's operations, particularly as I have no time to waste. Now—"

"On a tight schedule, eh? Tell me, Hivemaster, is Ambassador Jith in on the plan?"

"Jith is a dependable civil servant of considerable seniority," Shlush said smoothly. "It was deemed unwise to burden him with excessive detail regarding operations outside the sphere of his immediate concerns."

"Just who *is* your boss in this operation, Shlush?"

"Ah-ah—mustn't pry, Retief," the Groaci wagged an admonitory digit at the Terran. "Suffice it to say he's a most unusual chap, a virtual super-Groaci of most uncompromising kidney, not the sort, as he himself declares, to stand idly by while Groac is cheated of her Lumbagan patrimony! You'll meet him soon enough."

"Let me see," Retief mused aloud. "As I recall, it was a Terry tramp captain who first put Lumbaga on the star maps. He stayed long enough to peddle a few gross of glass beads and take on a cargo of salted glimp eggs; oddly enough, his report made no mention of the natives' warlike tendencies."

"Doubtless he fortuitously happened along between massacres," Shlush said tersely. "But—"

"The next time Lumbaga cropped up in an official dispatch, ten years later, was on the occasion of a run-in between a Terry survey crew and a Groaci gunboat. It appears your people were well-established here by then."

"Yes, yes—and naturally enough, they took appropriate action to discourage unauthorized tourism. Now—"

"Shooting up an unarmed survey craft was the wrong way to go about it, I'm afraid," Retief said philosophically. "Our sociological teams couldn't pass up a challenge like that. They came swarming in—with suitable escorts of Peace Enforcers, of course—to ferret out the unhappy incidents in the collective Groaci childhood that were responsible for your aggressions, and—"

"I well recall the incident; an unexampled instance of Groaci restraint in the face of Terran provocation—"

". . . and found a planetwide riot in progress," Retief continued. "They also turned up the fact that your boys were running a rather dubious traffic in hearts, lungs, and other negotiable commodities—"

"Specimens destined for Groaci zoos," Shlush snapped. "Our Groacian interest in exotic wildlife is well-known—"

"—which raised certain questions among the coarse-minded. There was even a theory afoot that you were disassembling the natives, shipping them out as Freebies, and putting them back together for use in the sand mines."

"A baseless allegation! Besides which, the practice was at once discontinued out of deference to the prejudices of the unenlightened."

"A far-sighted move, in view of the number of guns lined up on you at the time. The Interplanetary Tribunal for the Curtailment of Hostilities moved in then, and war has raged ever since."

"I am not in need of a toenail sketch of recent Lumbagan history!" Shlush hissed. "The manifold of iniquities of the CDT are well known to me!" The excited hivemaster broke off as the door opened abruptly.

"To forgive this intrusion, Exalted One," the underling who had gone to fetch brandy hissed. "But—"

"To better have an explanation of surpassing eloquence," Shlush screeched, "or to dangle inverted from a torture frame ere tiffin time!"

"The best, Excellency," the unfortunate fellow whispered, advancing into the room, closely followed by a hulking Lumbagan with a single eye, three legs, an immense grin, and a large, primitive needle gun in his fist.

"To shoot him down!" Shlush hissed in his native tongue to Wilth, who stood frozen against the wall.

"To . . . to . . . have apparently forgotten to load my piece," the latter whispered, and let the impotent weapon fall with a clatter.

"Which one of you aliens is the head Groaci around here?" the newcomer demanded.

Wilth's eyestalks tilted toward his chief. The latter scrunched back in his chair, eyeing the aimed pistol. "Ah—why do you ask?" he inquired cautiously.

"On account of there's a big shot that wants to see him," the Lumbagan stated, studying the four foreigners in turn.

"Better hurry; I don't know what assorted innards are bringing in the open market, but it will be less if they're full of steel splinters."

"Merely a, er, social call, I assume?" Shlush said hopefully.

"Assume whatever you like—only snap it up. The big boy don't like to be kept waiting." The caller glanced at the Dale Evans watch strapped to his lower left wrist. "Anyway, I change sides in half an hour, and I don't like unfinished business hanging around."

"Well, I suppose one must observe the amenities," Shlush said with a certain lack of conviction, rising slowly.

"It's all right, Shlush," Retief spoke up. "It's noble of you to cover for me, but we can't fool this fellow. I'll go quietly."

"Ha! Trying to pull a fast one, hah?" The Lumbagan pointed the gun at the hivemaster's head and squinted his lone eye along the barrel. "I've got a good mind to plug you for that. But to heck with it. I got to make my own loads for this popper, so why waste one?" He motioned with the bulky weapon at Retief.

"Let's go, big boy." He paused. "Hey, you aliens all look alike to me, but it seems like you got a little different look to you, somehow." He studied Retief, comparing him with Wilth and the guard with quick-side-glances.

"Two legs," he muttered. "One torso, one head—

ah! Got it! *They* got five eyes each, and *you* only got two, kind of sunk-in ones. How come?"

"Birth defect," Retief said.

"Oh, excuse me all to heck, pal. No offense. OK, pick 'em up. We got a brisk walk ahead, and the streets are full of footpads."

7

Two of Lumbaga's small pink moons were in the sky when Retief and his captor, after traversing a passage hollowed in the thick walls of the pile housing secret Groaci Headquarters, emerged into the street.

"This seems to be my night for meeting the local civic leaders," Retief commented as they turned west, toward the waterfront. "Who is it you're taking me to?"

"You'll find out," his guide said shortly, swiveling his asymmetrical head from side to side so as to bring his single eye to bear first on one side of the route ahead, then the other. "If anybody jumps us, it's every guy for hisself," he notified the Terran.

"You expecting to be attacked?" Retief inquired easily.

The alien nodded. "Naturally," he said glumly. "Why should tonight be any different than any other time?"

"I understand street battles are the Lumbagan national pastime," Retief commented. "You sound a little unenthusiastic."

"Oh, a little rumble now and then, a friendly fight in a bar, a neighborly clash in the alley, sure.

I'm as normal as the next guy. But the pace is getting me down. Frankly, Mr.—what was that handle again?"

"Retief."

"I'm Gloot. Like I was saying, Retief, between you and me I'd as lief take a break—a long break—from the fray. I got enough lumps to last me, you know? And there's plenty others feel the same."

"Then why do you go on squabbling?"

"That's kind of hard to explain, to a foreigner. I'm just sashaying along, minding my own business, and all of sudden—zop! The old fighting frenzy hits me, you know what I mean?"

"I'm striving to grasp it," Retief said. "By the way, does that gun work?"

Gloot looked at the heavy pistol. "Sure. Don't worry, the first guy that jumps us will be out shopping in the morning for a new navel and a few other accessories." He shook his head mournfully. "Unfortunately, I can't say the same for the second guy."

"Single shot, eh? How's your aim?"

"Well, I ain't bragging, but I usually hit what I shoot at."

"Five xots you can't hit that sign," Retief challenged, pointing to a board swinging in the wind ahead.

"You kidding? I could drill it dead center with one eye closed—at least I could up to last week when I misplaced my best eye."

"Phooey. I heard you Lumbagans couldn't shoot your way out of a greenhouse."

"Oh, yeah?" Gloot brought the gun up, took his stance, squeezed. . . .

The *Boom!* echoed along the canyonlike street like a bomb burst. As the reverberations faded, a voice somewhere ahead shouted an angry inquiry; a door slammed. Feet clattered, approaching from both directions.

"Now look what you made me go and do!" Gloot wailed. "Come on, let's get out of here!" He turned and galloped back the way they had come, ducked down an intersecting alley as a party of mismatched vigilantes in red cloaks surged into view around a turn.

"There they go!" a hoarse voice yelled. "Get the disturbance-creating rascals!"

Retief followed the sprinting Lumbagan along the noisome way, skidded to a stop as the other's dark bulk loomed ahead.

"Up there!" Gloot croaked. "Make it quick!"

Retief found the rungs of a ladder mounting the rough masonry wall; he went up it swiftly, negotiated an overhanging cornice, pulled himself up on a slanted roof of curled tiles. A moment later Gloot scrambled up beside him. Seconds later, their pursuers blundered past below in full cry.

"Wow, that was close," Gloot breathed as silence descended again. "Those boys are the City Guard. They don't mess around."

"Permanent cadre?" Retief asked.

"Right. Eight on, eight off. Of course, most of 'em got off-duty jobs with the major mobs; but when shift times arrives they fall in for duty, even if the mob happens to be in the middle of a shoot-out with the guard at the time."

"That could be a trifle confusing."

"Yeah, but they got ground rules. When the whistle blows, there's a five-minute time-out while the cops and robbers change sides."

"A civilized system," Retief conceded.

"I guess the coast is clear—but—" Gloot looked at his watch and uttered a coarse expletive. "Now looky what you made me do, Retief! I've run over shift-end! And I would of scored a nice bonus if I would of brought you in in one major piece!"

"You could explain you were unavoidably detained—"

"What—and hand a negotiable piece of merchandise like you over to the bums I used to be teamed up with? Besides, if they saw me now they'd set on me in a trice!"

"Don't your former associates change sides at the same time you do?"

"Sure—but they go their way, I go mine. I got to agree, it's enough to confuse a foreigner. Heck, even I get mixed up sometimes." Gloot sighed as he crawled up the sloping roof to scan the view beyond. "Seems like things are getting kind of out of hand," he said sadly. "A fellow can't hardly keep track of his own affiliations these days."

"What about us aliens?" Retief asked. "How do we fit into the hostility pattern?"

"You don't. My grabbing you was strictly business. Now that I've changed sides, all bets are off. It was nice meeting you, Retief. Frankly, I'd heard you Groaci were kind of creepy little characters, but you seem like a pretty good sport. Well, cheers. I've got to try to make it down to the port now without getting my sweetbreads scrambled. Timeout's almost over, and I'll be fair game."

"Who are you taking me to, Gloot?"

"Some bum over on Groo-groo Island. Why?"

"I'd like to meet him."

"No dice. I got a previous engagement. I'm part of a harbor hijack crew now and we've got a big heist scheduled."

"Suppose I go with you?"

"Sorry, I got no time to show tourists the sights," Gloot rose and started over the ridgepole; as he did, three figures in the red cloak of the City Guard appeared, clambering over the parapet opposite.

"There they are!" a muffled voice barked. "Get 'em!" Without hesitation, Gloot charged downslope, dealt one of the three a terrific buffet on the side of the head, sending him sprawling; but before he could regain his balance, the other two cops had grappled him and wrestled him toward the edge. Thus occupied, they failed to notice Retief until he had secured a firm grip on both capes, and with a vigorous pull, tumbled their owners backward. Recovering quickly, Gloot upended the nearer guardsman over the parapet. The last of the three dived for Retief, met a knee under the jaw, and collapsed in a limp heap.

"Say," Gloot said, breathing hard, "that was real friendly of you, Retief."

"Or unfriendly, depending on the viewpoint," Retief pointed out.

"Right. And from my viewpoint right now you came through like a champ. Well, so long, Retief. See you across the barricades." Gloot swung over the side of the roof; Retief followed him to the ground, clambering down the rough-laid masonry to the dark street below.

"Maybe you'll reconsider that invitation to come along and meet your friends," he suggested.

"Nope. We've got a full crew already."

"Just as a diplomatic observer," Retief reassured the local. "Naturally, I couldn't participate in anything violent."

Gloot shook his head. "Those boys upstairs are going to be kind of irritated when they come to. Us hijackers have got enough troubles without taking on a foreigner, with or without a police record. If I was you, I'd kind of drop out of sight for a few hours."

"Good idea. Aboard your boat would be a good place to be inconspicuous."

Gloot lifted his gun from its holster and thumbed back the hammer. "I ain't going to have to get rough, I hope?" he said, rather sadly.

"Not with that," Retief said. "Single-shot, remember?"

"Oh, barfberries," Gloot exclaimed, eyeing the bulky weapon in irritation. "I should of known you didn't gull me into shooting it off for nothing." He studied Retief appraisingly. "I don't feel like tangling with you, not after the way you handled those bums on the roof. And besides, I'm short an arm right now, on account of a chum asked me to lend him a hand and forgot to return it. Why not just go your way and I'll go mine."

"I want to know who's been trying to kidnap me, Gloot. You can still take me along to this big shot, and demand a nice ransom for me."

"Hey—the idea ain't without merit. . . ." Gloot said with cautious enthusiasm. "But don't look for any favors. The boys play rough, and this is their night to chew stones and spit gravel."

"I'll try to stay out of harm's way."

"A sixty-foot pirate sloop's kind of a funny place for that," Gloot said. "But—that's your problem, not mine—just so you stay alive long enough for me to collect."

8

An odor of ripe seafood and rotting wood rose from the lateen-rigged junk wallowing half sunk at the sagging wharf. A bulky Lumbagan with the usual random placement of facial features stepped out of the shadows to bar Gloot's way as he approached.

"Hi, Snult," the latter called in guarded tones. "This here is Retief. He came along to get an alien's-eye view of the operation."

"Yeah?" Snult replied without detectable enthusiasm. He barked a command over his shoulder; two large locals with exceptional triceps development stepped forward.

"Dump this spy in the drink," Snult grunted, pointing to Retief. "And then hang Gloot to the yardarm for half an hour for reporting in late." He turned his back and sauntered off. The two bully-boys advanced, reaching for Retief in a businesslike way. He leaned aside, caught the proffered arm of the nearer and gave it a half twist, causing its owner to spin around and bow from the waist, at which point an accurately placed foot propelled the unfortunate chap off the pier. The second enforcer lunged, met a chop to the neck, followed by a set of stiffened fingers to the midriff. As he doubled over, Retief turned him gently by the elbow and assisted him over the side, where his splash mingled with that of his partner. Ten feet away, Snult paused.

"Quick work," he said over his shoulder. "But . . . *two* splashes. . . ?"

Gloot stepped to his departing chief, seized him by the back of the neck and unceremoniously pitched him into the water.

"Three," he corrected, and thrust out a large, six-fingered hand to Retief. "The cruise is off to a good start. We've been needing a change of administration around here. Come on, let's hoist anchor before a platoon of cops come pelting down the dock looking for you." He swaggered down the gangplank bawling orders.

There were a few questions from the crew who, however, quickly adjusted to the change in management, assisted by a number of sharp blows from a belaying pin wielded by the new captain. In a matter of minutes the ancient vessel had cast off and was threading her way out across the gargabe-strewn waters of the bay.

"The target for tonight is a shipment of *foof* bark," Gloot advised his guest as they relaxed on the high poop deck at the stern an hour later, quaffing large mugs of native ale and admiring the view of the moonlit jungle isle past which they were sailing. "It comes from Delerion, another few islands to the west. Potent stuff, too. A pinch of *foof* in your hookah and you're cruising at fifty thousand feet without oxygen."

"Dope traffic, eh? Is that legal?"

"No law on the high seas," Gloot said. "And damn little on land. I guess you'd call the *foof* trade semilegit. They pay taxes—if the free-lance customs boys are sharp enough to collect 'em. And they place a few bribes here and there. However, they overlooked the good ship *Peccadillo* and her merry crew, which makes 'em fair game." He peered across the oily ripples. "She ought to be rounding the point of that next island and weathering right into our trap any minute now."

"You seem to know a lot about the opposition's movements," Retief commented.

"I ought to—I heard all about it last week when I was a *foof*-gatherer."

"I didn't know you Lumbagans changed islands as well as affiliations."

"I was a prisoner of war down there. I managed an escape during the changing of the guard. By the way, keep a few sharp eyes out for a low-slung boat with a big carbon arc light on deck. Inter-island Police. They're supposed to be up at the other end of the line now, but you never can tell."

"I can see you've done your homework, Gloot."

"Sure; I got the schedules down pat last time I was on the force."

"Don't these rapid changes of allegiance get confusing?" Retief inquired. "I'd think you'd run the risk of accidentally shooting yourself under the impression you were on the opposite side."

"I guess you can get used to anything," Gloot said philosophically.

"There's Groo-groo coming up on the starboard

bow," Retief said. "Isn't it about time to start tacking in?"

Gloot yawned. "Later, maybe," he said. "I decided maybe it's too much trouble trying to ransom you. I prefer life on the briny deep to floundering around in the creepers—" He was interrupted by a shout from the masthead; jumping up, he aimed a spyglass toward a dimly seen shape gliding closer across the dark water.

"Oh-oh—get set. That looks like ... yep—it's them! Hey, Blump!" Gloot sprang to the companionway. "Hard aport! And keep it quiet!"

As the unwieldy craft came sluggishly about, a dazzling yard-wide shaft of smoky blue light lanced across the water, etching the privateer's crew in chalky white against the velvet black of shadows.

"Heave to, you bilge scum!" an amplified voice bellowed from the direction of the light, "before I put a solid shot into your waterline!"

"We're in trouble," Gloot rapped. "That's old Funge on the bullhorn; I'd know his voice anywhere. One of the best pirate captains around, when he's working the other side of the street."

"Do we strike, Cap'n?" a crewman cried from amidships.

"Remind me to keelhaul you when this is over!" Gloot roared. "Strike nothing! Swing our stern chaser around and run it out over the port rail!" He charged across the deck, sharply canted by the abrupt maneuver in which the elderly tub was engaged, as the sailors dragged the small wheeled cannon into position.

"Load with cannister; double-charge!" he yelled. "Get a firepot up here! Hold her steady on a coarse

of one-eight-oh, and stand by to come about fast!"
He turned to Retief who was standing nearby,
observing the preparations for action.

"Better get below, Mister," he snapped. "This is
no place for noncombatants!"

"If you don't mind, I'll stick around on deck.
And if I may make a suggestion, it might be a good
idea to steer for shore."

"For shore? You must be hysterical with panic!
Everybody knows Groo-groo is swarming with car-
nivores that are all stomach and teeth, with just
enough legs to let 'em leap on their prey from
forty feet away."

"In that case, I hope you're a strong swimmer."

"Don't worry, Retief, those revenue agents are
lousy shots—" Gloot's reassurances were interrupted by a flash and a *Boom!* and the whistling
passage of a projectile that sailed high overhead to
raise a column of water a hundred yards to starboard.

"I see what you mean," Retief said. "Neverthe-
less, I think you're about to lose your command."
He pointed with his cigar at the water sluicing
across the buckled planks of the deck. "We're
sinking."

As he spoke, cries rose from the crew, who suddenly found themselves ankle-deep in seawater.
Gloot groaned.

"I guess I took that last corner too fast; she's
opened her seams!"

A breaker rolled across the desk. A crewman,
swept off his feet, went under with a despairing
cry. As the vessel wallowed, the waters surged,
rushed back across the half-submerged planking,

swirling around Retief's shins. The crewman was no longer in evidence; instead, a swarm of disassociated parts splashed in the brine, as the Lumbagan's formerly independent components resumed their free-swimming status, making instictively for shore.

"Well, so long, Retief," Gloot cried. "Maybe our various limbs and organs will meet up again in some future arrangement—" he broke off. "Ah—sorry, I forgot your hookup is a one-time deal. Tough lines, Retief. Take a last look around, here we go. . . ."

"Let's swim for it, it's not far."

"Well, I guess you could do that if you want to prolong the process. As for me, I'd as soon get it over with—"

"And miss finding out if the superstitions are true? Come on, Gloot, last one ashore's an amputated leg." Retief dived over the side. He stroked hard against the suction created by the sinking hulk, surfaced in time to see the tip of the mast descend slowly from sight amid a vigorous boiling of water strewn with flotsam from the ill-fated *Peccadillo*. Multitudes of Singletons which had formerly constituted the privateer's complement churned the waves, heading instictively for shore. A ragged cheer went up from the revenue cutter.

Gloot bobbed up a few yards away. "She was my first command," he said sadly. "I guess maybe she was put together a little too much like us Lumbagans."

"A melancholy moment," Retief acknowledged. He shrugged out of his jacket, pulled off his shoes and thrust them into his side pockets and set off at an easy crawl, Gloot dog-paddling beside him. It was a cool evening, but the water was pleasantly warm, mildly saline. Groo-groo congealed from the darkness ahead, resolving itself into a cluster of rhubarb-shaped trees above a pale streak which widened into a curving beach. They rode the breakers in, grounding on coarse coral sand, and waded in through tidal pools to shore. Ahead dark jungle loomed, impenetrable in the dim light of the moons, now obscured by ragged clouds.

The Lumbagan tested the wind, all ears angled to attitudes of total alertness.

"Hear something?" Retief asked.

"Yeah," the Lumbagan breathed. "Kind of a stealthy slosh."

"That's just the water running out of your boots," Retief pointed out.

"Huh? Oh, yeah."

The lesser moon emerged from behind the clouds. Retief scanned the beach, noted a small keg half-buried in the pink sand, the word RUM stenciled on the end.

"At least we won't want for basic supplies," he commented as he extricated the container. "You're about to sample Terry booze, Gloot."

"Not bad," the local commented five minutes later, after the puncheon had been broached with a lump of coral and the contents sampled. "It kind of burns, but my stomach kinds of likes it. In fact"—he paused to hiccup—"I like it all over. Actually, I just suddenly realized life is just a bowl of bloopberries, now that my vision has improved—"

"I see you're one of those affectionate drunks," Retief said as Gloot flung an arm about his shoulders. "Better take it easy, Gloot. You may need all your faculties intact for the evening ahead."

"Take it easy? I only had one li'l old swallow. And what's scheduled for the evening? Fun? Gaiety? Wine, song, and crossword puzzles?"

"More of a cross-track puzzle," Retief corrected. "Look." He pointed to a three-toed footprint deeply impressed in the sand.

Gloot studied the impressions. "Ha! I've got it!" he caroled. "Terries—just like my old buddy Shlush!"

"I doubt it," Retief said. "Aside from the fact that they're eighteen inches long—"

"So they're *big* Terries!" Gloot held a large, flat hand over his head. "This high!" He glanced up at the hand and seemed to sober abruptly. "*This* high?"

"That's a little high for a Terry, especially the kind you have in mind," Retief said. He followed the tracks, which led up across the wet sand to the edge of the forest.

"Let's go find the big Terries and have a li'l party," Gloot proposed cheerfully. "All palsies together."

"I understood you didn't care for Terries, Gloot."

"That was then," Gloot cried gaily. "This is now. Terries are my pals, the Groaci are my pals—everybody's my pals, even this little fellow," he added as a small free-flying pineal gland fluttered about his head. "Kootchie-koo—ain't it cute, Retief?" he added as it landed on his head.

"A most appealing organ," Retief agreed. "But I think you'd better lower your voice."

"What for? Somebody snoozing?" Gloot stood, weaving slightly. "Tell the little guys with the hammers to go away," he mumbled, groping at his scalp; there was a sudden flutter as the visitor departed hurriedly. Gloot sat down hard on the sand.

"Tell 'em to turn off the sireens and the bright lights," he moaned, "and take the stewed gym shoes out of my mouth. . . ."

"Congratulations, Gloot," Retief said. "I think you broke the galactic speed record for hangovers."

"Wha? Oh, it's you, Retief. Lucky you happened along. I just been set upon by a strong-arm mob and worked over with lead pipes. Which way'd they go?" Gloot staggered to his feet.

"You were too much for them," Retief reassured his companion. "They fled in various directions."

"Yah, the yellowbellies," Gloot muttered. "Oh, my skull."

"Where on the island does this big shot hang out?" Retief asked.

"Beats me. I was to of been met on the beach."

"Let's take a look around," Retief suggested, studying the looming woods above them. "You check that way"—he pointed to the south—"and I'll have a look up here."

Gloot grunted assent and moved off. Retief followed the curve of the shore for a distance of a hundred yards before the beach narrowed and was pinched out by a rocky ridge extending down from the forest-clad slope above. There were no tracks, no empty beer bottles, no signs of animate life. He returned to the starting point. Gloot was nowhere in sight. He followed the Lumbagan's bootprints as they wove unsteadily across the sand, then turned toward the nearest tongue of forest. Directly under a stout branch extending from the mass of foliage, the trail ended. Above, barely visible among the obscuring leaves, was the freshly cut end of a coarsely woven rope.

9

Retief studied the ground. Other footprints were visible here, but Gloot's were not among them. The marks leading away from the spot, he noted, were deeply impressed in the sand, as if the owners had been burdened by a heavy weight—presumably that of the Lumbagan.

Retief started off along the clearly marked spoor leading up into the deep woods. The darkness here was almost total. Creatures of the night creaked, chirred, and wailed in the treetops. An intermintent wind made groaning sounds among the boughs. Nearer at hand, something creaked faintly. Retief halted, faded back against the knobby-barked bole of a giant tree.

A minute passed in silence. Just ahead, a small figure emerged cautiously from the underbrush; a curiously truncated Lumbagan, advancing in a stealthy crouch. Gripping a stout club in a cluster of fists, the native advanced cautiously, peering under bushes and behind trees as he came. Retief silently circled the sheltering trunk, stepped out behind the stranger and cleared his throat. With a thin yell, the native sprang straight into the air and struck the ground running, but with a quick grab Retief snared him by the garland of teeth encircling his neck.

"I'm looking for a friend of mine," Retief said in the native tongue. "I don't suppose you've seen him."

"Him monster like you?" the terrified captive squeaked, hooking a finger under his necklace to ease the strain.

"Another type of monster entirely," Retief said; he gave a succinct description of his traveling companion.

"Negative, Sahib. Tribe belong me not nab monster fitting that description. By the way, how about letting go ceremonial collar before I suffer embarrassment of bite own head off."

"You'd be more comfortable if you'd stop tugging," Retief pointed out.

"Against instinct not try get away from monster," the native explained.

"Curious; a moment ago I had the distinct impression you were trying to get closer to me."

"Iron maiden on other foot now. You eat now, or save for snack?"

"I'll wait, thanks. Is your village near here?"

"Usually don't stop to chat with stranger," the captive muttered, "but in this case looks like best bet to increase longevity. Monster right, I citizen of modest town half mile up trail."

"I'd like to pay it a visit. How about acting as guide?"

"I got choice in matter?"

"Certainly," Retief said. "You can either lead me there or take the consequences."

"Most likely lead monster there *and* take consequences. Chief Boobooboo not like stranger poking around."

"In that case you can introduce me. Retief's the name. What's yours?"

"Zoof; but probably change to Mud, once chief get eyeful of humiliating circumstances attending surprise visit."

"Actually, Zoof, it's not absolutely necessary that I lead you there by the neck, if you'll promise not to run out on me."

"Got funny feeling monster run faster than me anyway. OK, it's deal. I lead you to village; when you get there, you look over menu, maybe pick choicer specimen."

"It's a promise." Retief said. "Nice teeth," he added as he disengaged his hand from the necklace. "Local product?"

"Nope, fancy imported, guaranteed solid plastic." Zoof started through the dense woods, Retief close behind. "No catchum real tooth these days. Life in woods going to hell in handcart. Monsters ruin hunting, lucky made deal with Five-eyes monster for steady supply grits and gravy."

"The Five-eyes you refer to wouldn't by any chance be Groaci?"

"Could be. Shiny-leg city slicker, same big like me, all time whisper, like offer deal on hot canoe."

"That's Ambassador Jith to the life. But I wasn't aware his interests extended this far back into the brush."

"Sure, small monster go everywhere, do everything. All time ride giant bird, make stink, noise, pile up stone, while big monster trample underbrush, rig net, hunt, eat—"

"What do these big monsters look like?" Retief inquired.

"Take look in mirror sometime, see for self."

"They're Terrans—like me?"

Zoof twisted his head to study Retief. "Nope, not exact same, maybe. Not so much eyes. Some got more. Some two time so big like you, tear head off, eat one bite—"

"Have you seen the monsters yourself?"

"You bet; see you, see Five-eyes, hear plenty rumor fill in gaps in information."

"Are there any Groaci at your village now?"

"We find out," Zoof said. "Home town just ahead." He led the way another fifty feet and halted.

"Well, what monster think of place?"

Retief studied the gloomy forest around him, insofar as he could see in no way different from the previous half mile of woods.

"It's unspoiled, I'll say that for it," he commented. "Is this Main Street?"

"Monster kidding? Is snazzy residential section, plenty tight zoning, you bet. Come on, we find chief and boys over at favorite hangout, Old Log."

"A bar?"

"Nope, just swell place root for grubs."

"I take it the Grubs aren't a ball team?"

"More of hors d'oeuvre," Zoof corrected. He led the way through a dense stand of forest patriarchs, emerged in a small, open glade where half a dozen Lumbagans, differing wildly in detail, wandered apparently aimlessly, gazing at the ground. With a sharp cry, one pounced, came up with a wriggling creature which he thrust into a sack at his waist.

"My grasp of Lumbagan zoology is somewhat hazy," Retief said. "How do these grubs fit into the general biological picture?"

"Play essential role," Zoof replied. "Grub grow up be kidney, jawbone, kneecap, you name it."

"So much for future generations. Still, it's no worse than eating grass, I suppose."

"Not eat 'em," Zoof corrected. "Collect, sell to skinny-leg monster, get plenty Colonel Sanders fried chicken and other exotic chow, you bet."

The grub hunters had interrupted their search to stare inhospitably at Retief.

"Hey, Chief," Zoof greeted his leader, "this monster name Retief, express desire meet jungle big shot. Retief, shake grasping member of Chief Boobooboo, son of Chief Booboo, son of chief Boob."

"Grandpa name Boo, not Boob," the chief corrected sternly. "Why you want me, monster? Zoof not look tender?"

"Actually I was looking for a friend—"

"Hmm, neat switch. Usual custom eat enemy, but after all, why be prejudice? Eat chum too, get varied diet." Boobooboo looked appraisingly at Zoof.

"As it happens, I've already eaten," Retief said. "The friend I'm looking for seems to have been involved in an incident involving a rope."

"Monster bark up wrong flagpole," the chief stated. "Unsophisticated aborigine unequal to technical challenge of make rope."

"Any idea who might have snared him?"

"Sure."

"Possibly you'd confide in me."

"Why?"

"I don't suppose the simple desire to do a good turn would be sufficient motivation?"

"Not *that* unsophisticated," Boobooboo said flatly.

"Good time remember ancient folk wisdom embodied in old tribal saying: What's In It For Me?"

"What about a firm promise of a year's supply of pizza pies?"

"Not much nourishment in promise," the Chief pointed out. "Got better idea. . . ." Boobooboo lowered his voice. "Know where big supply eatables located; you help collect, maybe I get bighearted and tell all."

"I think I'd prefer a more definite commitment," Retief said. "Strike out the 'maybe' and we might be able to get together."

"Sure; just stuck 'maybe' in so have something to concede."

"I see I'm dealing with a pro," Retief acknowledged "*En passant*, where is this food supply located?"

"Half mile that direction." The chief pointed. "Enough chow for whole tribe from now to next St. Swithin's Day."

"I take it you've actually seen the groceries for yourself?"

"Sure, same time deliver."

"I see: you plan to hijack the supplies you've been selling to the Groaci."

"Hijack loaded word. Just say decide to share wealth with underprivileged. Monsters got wealth, we got underprivilege."

"At the present rate, Chief, I predict your supply of unsophistication won't last out the winter. But why do you need my help? You have enough troops to stage a raid on your own."

"Monster not get big picture. Skinny-legs spoilsport hide comestibles away inside magic cave, patrol perimeter with plenty fearsome monster, tear a simple tribesman apart with two hands while hunt fleas with rest."

"And you think I can penetrate this fortress?"

"Maybe not; but better you than me and boys; we just simple pastoral types; hunt, fish, steal, not go in for heavy work."

"On the whole, Chief Boobooboo, the proposition doesn't sound overwhelmingly attractive."

"I figure maybe you feel that way; so save snapper for end: you come here ask about missing buddy? Monster in luck; get economical combination deal. Kidnapped pal same place victuals. Get two for price of one."

"I think," Retief said, "I've been outmaneuvered."

A quarter of an hour later, Retief and Chief Boobooboo, attended by Zoof and the bulk of the truncated tribesmen, stood in the shelter of a giant mumble tree, the soft mutterings of its foliage covering the sound of their conversation.

"Straight ahead, can't miss it," Boobooboo was saying. "But watch snares; you get caught same way absent chum, deal off."

"Understood, Chief. And you'll keep your people posted in position to create a diversion in the event I have to leave the vicinity in haste."

"Correct; we stand by, catch any wandering grub come galloping past."

"It's been a pleasure dealing with you, Chief. If you ever decide to give up the rural way of life, drop me a line. The Corps could use your talents instructing a course of naïveté."

"Thanks, Retief. Keep offer in mind in case present caper not pan out."

The forest was silent as Retief made his way along the dimly marked trail, but for a stealthy rustling in the undergrowth which ceased when he halted, began again when he went on. He had covered perhaps a hundred and fifty yards when he rounded an abrupt turn and was face to face with twelve feet of tusked nightmare.

10

For a moment Retief stood unmoving, studying the monstrosity looming gigantic ten feet away. Its bleary, pinkish eyes, three in number, stared unwinking at him from a lumpy face equipped with tufted whiskers placed at random around a vast, loose-lipped mouth and a scattering of gaping nostrils. From its massive shoulders, immense arms hung almost to the ground; three bowed legs supported the weight of a powerfully muscled torso. The big fellow's generous pedal extremities were housed in gigantic sneakers with round black reinforcing patches over the anklebones. A long tail curled up over one clavicle, ending in a seven-fingered hand with which the creature was exploring the interior of a large, pointed ear. Other hands gripped a naked two-edged sword at least nine feet in length.

Retief took a hand-rolled Jorgenson's cigar from an inside pocket, puffed it alight, blew out pale violet smoke.

"Nice night," he said.

The monster drew a deep breath. "AHHHrrrg-hhh!" it bellowed.

"Sorry," Retief said, "I didn't quite catch that remark."

"AHHHrrrghhh!" the creature repeated.

Retief shook his head. "You're still not getting through."

"Ahhrrgh?"

"You do it well," Retief said. "Exceptionally nice timbre. Real feeling."

"You really like it?" the giant said in a surprisingly high-pitched voice. "Gee, thanks a lot."

"I don't know when I've seen it done better. But is that all there is?"

"You mean it ain't enough?"

"I'm perfectly satisfied," Retief assured his new acquaintance. "I just wanted to be sure there wasn't an encore."

"I practiced it plenty," the oversized Lumbagan said. "I wouldn't of wanted to of did it wrong."

"Certainly not. By the way, what does it mean?"

"How to I know? Who tells me anything? I'm just old Smelch, which everybody pushes me around on account of I'm easygoing, you know?"

"I think I met a relative of yours in town, Smelch. Unfortunately I had to rush away before we really had a chance to chat."

"Yeah? Well, I heard a few of the boys was to of been took for a glom at the bright lights. But not me. No such luck."

"You don't happen to know who's been down for a barefoot stroll on the shore do you, Smelch?" the Terran inquired casually. "A party with three-toed feet."

"Three? Lessee." Smelch's tail-mounted hand scratched at his mottled scalp with a sound reminiscent of a spade striking marl. "That's be more'n one, and less than nine, right?"

"You're narrowing the field," Retief said encouragingly.

"If I just knew how many nine was, I'd be in business," Smelch muttered. "That ain't nothing like say, six, fer example?"

"Close, but no dope stick. Skip that point, Smelch, I didn't mean to get technical. Were you waiting for anything special when I came along?"

"You bet: my relief."

"When's he due?"

"Well, lessee: I come out here awhile back, and been here for quite a time, so what does that leave? Say—half a hour?"

"More like a jiffy and a half, give or take a few shakes of a lamb's tail. What's up at the top of the trail?"

"That's what nobody ain't supposed to know."

"Why not?"

"On account of it's like a secret, see?"

"I'm beginning to get a glimmering. Who says it's a secret?"

Smelch's fingernail abraded his chin with a loud roaching sound.

"That's supposed to be another secret." Smelch's features rearranged themselves in what might have been a puzzled frown. "What I can't figure is—if it's a secret, how come you know about it?"

"Word gets around," Retief said reassuringly. "OK if I go up and have a look?"

"Maybe you ought to identify yourself first. Not that I don't trust you, but you know how it is."

"Certainly. I'm Retief, Smelch." He shook the

hand at the end of the tail, which returned the grip firmly.

"Sorry about the routine, Retief, but these days a guy can't be too careful."

"What about?"

Smelch blinked all three eyes in rotation, a vertiginous effect.

"I get it," he said, "that's what you call a joke, right? I'm nuts about jokes; only the trouble is usually nobody tells me about 'em in time to laugh."

"It's a problem that often plagues ambassadors, Smelch. But don't worry; I'll be sure to tip you off in advance next time."

"Gee, you're a all-right guy, Retief, even if you are kind of a runt and all, no offense."

The sound of heavy feet came from uptrail; a squat, five-foot figure lumbered into view, as solidly built as Smelch but less beautiful, his various arms, legs, and ears having been arranged with a fine disregard for standard patterns. One of his five hands gripped a fifteen-foot harpoon; his four eyes, on six-inch stalks, goggled atop a flattened skull which gave the appearance of having been matured inside a hot-water bottle.

"About time, Flunt," Smelch greeted the newcomer. "You're a shake and a half late."

"Spare me any carping criticisms," Flunt replied in a tone of long-suffering weariness. "I've just come from an interview with that bossy little—" He broke off, looking Retief up and down. "Well, you might at least offer an introduction," he said sharply to Smelch, extending a hand to the diplomat. "I'm Flunt. Pardon my appearance—"

He indicated two uncombed fringes of purplish-blue filaments springing from just below his cheek-bones. "But I just washed my hide and I can't do a thing with it."

"Not at all," Retief said ambiguously, giving Flunt's feet a quick glance: they were bare, and remarkably human-looking. "My name's Retief."

"Goodness, I hope I'm not interrupting anything," Flunt said, looking questioningly from one to the other.

"Not at all, Smelch and I were just passing the time of night. Interesting little island, Flunt. See many strangers here?"

"Gracious, I hope not. I'm supposed to do dreadful things if I do—" Flunt broke off, gave Retief a startled look. "Ah, *you* aren't by any chance a stranger . . . ?"

"Are you kidding?" Smelch spoke up. "He's Retief, like I told you."

"Just so you're sure. Little Sir Nasty-nice wouldn't like it a bit if outsiders sneaked a peek at his precious whatever-it-is. Really, for this job one needs eyes in the back of one's head!"

"Yeah," Smelch said. "Lucky you got 'em."

"Flunt, do you know anyone with three-toed feet in these parts?" Retief asked.

"Three-toed feet? Hmmm. They're a bit passé this season, of course—but I think I've seen a few around. Why?" His voice lowered confidentially. "If you're interested in picking up half a dozen at a bargain price, I think I may be able to put you onto a good thing."

"I might be," Retief said. "When could I meet the owners?"

"Oh, I don't think you'd like that," Flunt said soberly. "No, I don't think you'd like that at all, at all. And neither would little Mr. Sticky-fingers, now that I reflect on it. Actually, I shouldn't have mentioned the matter. My blunder. Forget I said anything about it."

"Come on, Retief," Smelch said loudly. "Me and you'll just take a little ankle up the trail, which I'll point out the points of interest and like that." He gave the Terran an elaborate three-eyed wink.

"Capital idea, Smelch," Retief agreed.

"Look here, Smelch," Flunt said nervously, "you're not going to go sneaking around you-know-where and getting you-know-who all upset about you-know-what?"

"I do?" Smelch looked pleased.

"Maybe you don't; it's been dinned into your head hourly all your life, but then you've only been around for a week. . . ." Flunt turned to Retief.

"I hate to sound finicky, Retief, but if this um-myday tries to ipslay you into, well, anyplace you shouldn't eebay, well . . . one has one's job to do." He fingered the barbed head of his harpoon meaningfully.

"I can give you a definite tentative hypothetical assurance on that," Retief said crisply. "But don't hold me to it."

"Well, in that case. . . ." Retief felt Flunt's eyes on him as he and Smelch moved up the trail toward whatever lay above.

II

For the first hundred yards, nothing untoward disturbed the silence of the forest at night—nothing other than the normal quota of chirps, squeaks, and scuttlings that attested to the activities of the ahundant wildlife of the region. Then, without warning, a gigantic shape charged from the underbrush. Smelch, in the lead, late in swinging his broad-headed spear around, took the brunt of the charge solidly against his chest. His explosive grunt was almost drowned in the sound of the collision, not unlike that of an enraged rhino charging a Good Humor wagon. The antagonists surged to and fro, trampling shrubbery, shaking trees, grunting like beached walruses. Suddenly the stranger bent his knees, rammed his head into Smelch's midriff, and rose, Smelch spread-eagled across his shoulders. He pivoted sharply, went into a dizzying twirl, and hurled the unfortunate victim from him to hurtle into the undergrowth, snapping off a medium-sized tree in the process. The victor paused only long enough to beat out a rapid tattoo on his chest and wait until a brief coughing fit passed before whirling on Retief. The Terran sidestepped the dimly seen monster's first rush, which carried the latter well into the thicket beside the path. As he threshed about there, roaring, Smelch reemerged from the opposite side of the route, shaking his head and muttering. The stranger came crashing back onto the scene only to be met by two lefts and a right haymaker that halted him in his tracks.

"Sorry about that, Retief," Smelch said contritely, as his antagonist toppled like a felled oak. "But the mug got my dander up, which he shouldn't ought to come out leading with his chin anyways."

"A neat one-two-three," Retief commented, blowing a plume of smoke toward the fallen fighter. "Let's take a closer look." He parted the brush to look down at the casualty who lay sprawled on his back, out cold. The ten-foot-tall figure was remarkably conservative for a Lumbagan, he thought: only two legs and arms, a single narrow head with close-set paired eyes, a lone nose and mouth, an unimpressive chin. The feet, clearly outlined inside rawhide buskins, featured five toes each, matching the hands' ten fingers.

"What's the matter?" Smelch said. "You know the mug?"

"No, but he bears a certain resemblance to a colleague of mine."

"Jeez, the poor guy. Well, beauty ain't everything. Anyways, here's your chance to pick up a set of dogs at a steal, if you know what I mean." He rammed an elbow toward Retief's ribs, a comradely gesture capable of collapsing a lung had it landed.

"I think I'll pass up the opportunity this time," Retief said, stepping forward to investigate a strand of barbed wire vaguely discernible in the gloom. It was one of three, he discovered, running parallel to the trail, firmly attached to stout posts.

"Retief, we better blow," Smelch said. "Like Flunt said, nobody but nobody don't want to poke his noses and stuff in too close around you-know-where."

"Actually, I don't think I do," Retief corrected his massive acquaintance. "Know where, I mean."

"Good," Smelch said in a relieved tone. "You're safer that way."

"Not afraid, are you?"

"Yeah." Smelch nodded his head vigorously. "I hear they got ways of making a guy regret the day his left leg met up with his right."

"Who says so?"

"Everybody, Retief! All the boys been warned to stay clear, once they was outside. . . ."

"You mean you've been inside?"

"Sure." Smelch looked puzzled, an expression involving a rapid twitching of his ears. "How could I of not been?"

"Flunt's been there too?"

"Natch. You don't figure the moomy-bird brung him, do you? That's a little joke, Retief. I know you know the moomy-bird didn't bring him."

"How about this fellow?" Retief indicated the unconscious Lumbagan stretched at his feet. "He came from inside too?"

Smelch clucked sympathetically. "I guess they must of left out some o' your marbles, Retief. Where else would Zung of come from? In fact"—he lowered his voice confidentially—"he ain't never graduated, poor sucker."

"Maybe you'd care to amplify that remark a little, Smelch."

"Zung is one of the boys which they ain't been allowed out in the big, wonderful world like you and me." Smelch spread several hands expansively. "Except only maybe a few feet to clobber anybody that comes along. What I figure is. . . ." He lowered his voice to a solemn hush. "Him and the other ones, they ain't all there, you know? Rejects, like."

"Rejects from what, Smelch?"

"Shhh." Smelch looked around worriedly. "I don't like the trend of the conversation, which we're treading on shaky ground, especially this close to you-know-what."

"No, but I think it's time I found out."

"Hey—you ain't planning on climbing the fence?"

"Unless you know where the gate is."

"Sure—right up the trail about a hundred yards, or maybe ten. I ain't too precise on the fine detail work."

"Then I'll be off, Smelch; give my regards to Flunt when you see him."

"You're really going to sneak back into you-know-where and grab a peek at you-know-what? Boy oh boy, if you-know-who sees you—"

"I know. Thanks for clarifying matters. By the way, if you should run into a fellow with three legs who answers to the name of Gloot, I'd appreciate any help you could give him."

"Sure; you let me know if we see him."

"We?"

"Heck, yes. You don't think I'm going in there alone, do you? And we better get moving. Zung's starting to twitch."

As they proceeded silently up the path, Retief was again aware of the soft rustlings and snufflings he had noted on and off since his arrival on the island. Through a gap in the shrubbery he caught a fleeting glimpse of a stealthy figure which ducked out of sight as he paused. He went on; the rustling progress of his shadower resumed.

The gate—a wide construction of aluminum panels and barbed wire—blocked the trail a hundred feet above the point where they had encountered Zung. A green-shaded spotlight outlined it starkly against the foliage. A padlock the size of an alarm clock dangled from a massive hasp.

"Any more guards hidden out around the area?" Retief asked.

"Naw—with Flunt and me doing a tight security job down below, and the other bum working in close, who needs it?"

"An incisive point," Retief conceded. They walked boldly up to the gate. Smelch tried it, seemed surprised when it failed to swing open.

"Looks like it's stuck," he commented, and ripped it from its hinges, lock and all, tossing the crumpled panels aside with a metallic crash.

"Nothing like direct action," Retief said admiringly. "But from this point on I suggest we observe a trifle more caution, just in case there's anyone up there whose suspicions might be aroused by the sound of a three-car collision this far from the nearest highway."

"Say, pretty shrewd," Smelch said admiringly. "I always wanted to team up with a guy which he could figure the angles."

Beyond the former gate, the path continued a few yards before debouching into a wide cleared strip adjoining a high board fence that extended for some distance in each direction.

"Home, sweet home," Smelch said nostalgically.

"The old place sure has changed since I ventured out into the great world."

"Has it?"

"Sure. After all, that was a couple hours ago."

"This is where you were born and raised, in other words."

"Yeah—inside the fence is where I spent my happy childhood, all four days of it."

"I'd like to see the old place."

"Well, old Sneakyfeet won't like it—but to heck with him and his dumb rules. Who but a alumnus would want to look inside anyways? Come on, Retief." Smelch led the way to an inconspicuous gate which yielded to his efforts, not without a certain amount of splintering. Retief propped the door back in place and turned to regard an extensive array of ranked cages stacked in long aisles that led away in the moonlight to the far line of the fence. A dispirited yammering chorus of sound started up nearby, reminiscent of visiting day at a pet hospital. A vaguely zoolike odor hung in the air.

Retief approached the nearest row of cages. In the first, a creature resembling a rubber rutabaga with spidery legs slumped dolefully against the bars. Adjacent, a pair of apprehensive-looking ankles huddled together for warmth.

"Freebies," Smelch said. "Just in from the jungle. Little do the poor little fellers dream what a high class destiny's in store for 'em."

"What destiny *is* in store for them, Smelch?"

"Right this way," The Lumbagan invited, indicating the next rank of cages. These were somewhat larger than those in the first section, each containing a creature giving the appearance of having been assembled from spare parts. Here a spindly leg drummed the fingers of a lone hand springing from where a foot might have been expected; there a bored-looking lower lip, flanked by a pair of generous ears, sprang directly from an unmistakable elbow. In the next echelon, the cages were still larger, occupied by specimens of a more sophisticated appearance. A well-developed paunch with a trio of staring brown eyes at the top squatted on four three-toed feet, watching the visitors incuriously. A remarkably human-looking head with a full beard swung from the roof of its prison by the muscular arm that was its sole appendage.

"Uh, some o' the boys look a little weird," Smelch said apologetically, "but in the end they mostly turn out handsome devils, like me."

"Someone seems to have gone to considerable trouble to set up this lonelyhearts farm," Retief commented. "In the natural state, I understand, matches among Freebies take place at rare intervals. This looks like mass production. Any idea why, Smelch?"

"Nope. I ain't one of them guys which he asts questions all the time, you know what I mean? I mean, why poke the old nostrils in and maybe get 'em stuffed full of lint, right?"

"It's a philosophy without which bureaucracy as we know it would soon wither away," Retief conceded. "What was your job when you were here, Smelch?"

"Well, lessee, there was eating. That took a lot o' my time. Then there was sleeping. I like that pretty good. Then ... lessee ... I guess that just about wraps it up. Why?"

"You must have a strong union," Retief said. "Why were you here?"

"Jeez, you know that's a question which a guy could wonder about it a long time if he wouldn't drop off to sleep first. Personally, I got like a theory that before we can attack the problem of transcendentalism, we got to examine the nature of knowledge and its limitations, making a appropriate distinction between *noumena* and *phenomena*. I figure by coordinating perceptions by means of rationally evolved concepts of understanding we can proceed to the analysis of experience and arrive at the categorical imperative, with its implicit concomitants. Get what I mean?"

"I think possibly I've been underestimating you, Smelch. I didn't know you read Kant."

"Can't read, you mean," Smelch corrected. "Nope, I never had the time for no idle pursuits what with that heavy schedule I told you about."

"Quite understandable, Smelch. By the way, Flunt mentioned you'd only been here a week. Where were you before that?"

"Well, now we're getting into the area o' the metaphysical, Retief, which when you examine material phenomena by inductive processes you arrive at a philosophical materialism, not to exclude ontological and epistemological considerations, which in general could be assumed to deny metaphysics any validity in the context of Aristotelian logic. Or am I just spinning my wheels?"

"Did you work that out for yourself, Smelch, or did somebody tip you off?"

"Never mind. I don't think I'd grasp the full significance of the answer anyway."

They passed the last of the cages, these occupied by a bewildering variety of Lumbagan life forms in a wide range of colors and shapes, and displaying a remarkably diverse endowment of limbs, sensory equipment, and other somatic elements.

"They look vigorous enough," Retief commented as one hefty specimen gripped the bars and drooled at him. "But I get an impression they're not too bright."

"Well, sure, at first they got to go through the indoctrination center. You can't expect a agglomeration which last week it was grubbing roots in the woods to be a instant intellectual. That takes a couple days."

"I see. Where do we go from here, Smelch?"

"How about the cafeteria? I got a yen for some good old home cooking."

"Let's save that until after I've met you-know-who," Retief suggested.

"Mondays they usually got mud-on-a-mortar-board," Smelch said nostalgically, testing the air through his multiple nostrils. "Also on Wednesday, Saturday, and all the other days. Lucky it's my favorite. But I guess you're right, Retief. We got to make our courtesy calls before we chow down. I guess Old Sneaky-feet. . . ." Smelch paused. "Hey, talking about sneaky feet, old you-know-who has got three toes on each foot; I barged in on him once when he was climbing out of a tub of hot sand. Wow, if language was skinning hooks, I'd of been flayed to the ribs in no time. That's when I seen 'em. His feet, I mean. . . ."

He broke off as a faint, rhythmic sound became audible, swiftly growing louder. The running lights of a copter appeared above the treetops, winking in a complicated pattern. The machine sank out of sight beyond the fence.

"What do you know, Retief—that's old Whatzis himself," Smelch cried delightedly. "But now that it's time to make the introductions," he added with sudden doubt, "I kind of wonder if it's a good idea. If he's in a bad mood he could maybe interpret it as me not doing my job of keeping outsiders on the outside."

"Let's hope he doesn't take a narrow-minded approach," Retief said encouragingly. He had reached the section of fence opposite the point where the copter had descended. He jumped, caught the top, pulled himself up in time to see a hurrying figure in a dark cloak and pale headgear disappear into a small structure at the edge of the clearing.

He pulled himself over and dropped to the ground. A moment later Smelch joined him.

"That copter's been busy tonight," Retief said. "What's in the building?"

"All kinds of neat stuff, like the cafeteria," Smelch said. "Did I mention they got mud-on-a-mortarboard?"

"You did. Let's go take a closer look."

They reached the door through which the heli's passenger had disappeared. It opened, and they stepped into a brightly lit corridor. At the far end, light gleamed through a glass-paneled door. When they reached it, muffled sounds were audible from the room beyond.

Retief took a small button-shaped object from

his pocket, pressed it to the door, put his ear to
it.

"... you still hesitate?" a suave voice said.
"Possibly you are deterred by ethical considerations, a reluctance to betray those who have placed
their trust in you. Dismiss the thought, fellow!
What harm to honor if nobody blabs, eh?"

Snorting and threshing sounds followed.

"Ah ... Exalted One," a breathy Groaci voice
whispered, "to offer a suggestion: the removal of
the gag to facilitate compliance with instructions."

"Um. I was just about to order. Guard!"

Heavy footsteps sounded, followed by a ripping
sound and a hoarse yell, then a shuddering sigh.

"Just one," Gloot's voice said yearningly. "Just
one little old ocular, right by the roots...."

A faint buzz sounded, eliciting a grunt of annoyance.

"Cretin!" the Groaci hissed. "The unwarranted
interruption of His Unutterableness' virtuoso performance!"

"To regret—but to report untoward circumstances
without," a second Groaci whispered in agitation.

"Begone, imbecile. This taciturn wretch is just
on the point of divulging all!"

"Ah—Eminent One—the desirability of completing my report."

"What report?"

"The one which prompted this lowly one to intrude on Your Loftiness' deliberations: namely and
to wit: the discovery that the security of this installation has been breached."

"Indeed?" the Groaci hissed. "To imply you failed
to see to the complete combustion of file copies of

certain special requisitions? To attend to it at once, thus forestalling any possible criticism by the small-minded—"

"To entreat your pardon, Your Greatness—but to correct a misapprehension: the breach to which I had reference is the unauthorized presence inside the station of certain intruders—"

"Intruders! Why wasn't I notified at once!" the non-Groaci voice barked.

"To have sought in vain to get a word in edgeways—"

"To skip the apologies! To dispose of the interlopers instanter!"

"To regretfully report their precise whereabouts is not yet known!"

"To find them at once and to dispatch them out of hand!"

"I don't like this," the order voice said in Lumbagan. "Flabby security is something I can't afford at this point. I'm off to Omega Station, Nith. Carry on with the interrogation."

Retief tried the doorknob, found it locked. He quickly extracted a small but complicated device from an inner pocket, applied it to the latch. There was a soft click. The door opened silently on a small dark room lined with coat hooks; beyond was a second room, clinically furnished in white. Under a ceiling glare panel, Gloot sat in a steel chair, strapped in position by heavy bands of wire mesh. An elaborate network of color-coded wires led from a cap-like device clamped to his head to a gray steel cabinet resembling a ground-car tune-up console.

A Lumbagan, if anything larger and more baroque than Smelch, leaned against the wall. A uniformed Groaci stood by a door in the opposite wall. Before the captive stood a slight figure nattily attired in bile-green Bermuda shorts, an aloha shirt in clashing pinks, and orange and violet Argyles.

"Well, my old friend Nith, formerly of the Groaci Secret Police," Retief said softly to Smelch. "I wasn't aware his duties had brought him to these shores."

"Hey—for a couple minutes I thought that was Whatchamacallit," the Lumbagan whispered. "But I guess not . . . he ain't yelling."

"He looks like him, does he?"

"Who?"

"You know."

"Oh, him."

"You didn't answer the question."

"Uh—what was the question?"

"On second thought I withdraw it."

"Now," the Groaci addressed Gloot eagerly, "there are none here but you and I and Leftenant Chish, and a lone guard unequipped with the higher cerebral centers, so there can be no thought of repercussions arising from your master's misinterpretation of events. Now, speak up, fellow. Tell all!"

Gloot struggled against his bonds, "Oh boy oh boy oh boy," he said. "If I just had a couple hands free, or maybe a prehensile tail, if I *had* a prehensile tail—"

"Bah! My lone chance to acquire glory in the absence of his Pushiness—"

"You mean his Puissance?"

"You heard me. Now, whilst he's absent, quickly spill the legumes, fellow! I'll see to it you're awarded the order of Groac, *with* bladder!"

"Go soak your organ cluster in concentrated sulphuric acid."

"I have no time now for such indulgences, reticent one! You force me to extreme measures, entered into the more reluctantly in the light of certain prohibitions promulgated by His Extremeness regarding unauthorized use of equipment! But you leave me no choice, if I'm to score a badly needed point or two!" Nith turned to the knob-studded console, twiddled controls. "Now to administer a stimulus which will unlock your mandibles, producing a veritable torrent of data...." He pushed a button; Gloot leaped against his restraints, yodeling enthusiastically. Nith pushed another button. Gloot slumped in his chair.

"Ah, you see?" Nith whispered. "Already you feel better: the cathartic effect of unburdening oneself of baseless hostilities. Now, you may begin with the designation of your employers. Whose hireling are you, fellow?"

"Nobody's," Gloot muttered.

"Shall I be forced to consign you to the parts bins after all?" Nith hissed ominously.

"Ah ... Uplifted One," the bystanding Groaci officer offered diffidently, "to note that the veracitometer indicates the inferior one is speaking the truth."

"Eh? Impossible!" Nith whipped his eyestalks around to focus on the panel. "The impossibility, that is, that you should imagine me to be unaware of that circumstance." He twiddled knobs on the panel, then addressed himself again to Gloot:

"Who sent you here!"

"Nobody sent me; me and a chum came together."

"Aha! This chum! What power does he represent?"

"He's a Groaci," Gloot said sullenly.

"A . . . Groaci?"

"You heard me, Five-eyes! And a big wheel at that!"

"The indication of the instruments," the lesser Groaci whispered. "The possibility of a malfunction?"

"To not descend to the fatuous, Leftenant Chish! I myself to have overseen the installation! The acceptance of the preposterous: the hobbledehoy's truthfulness!"

"Amplified One!" Chish hissed. "To begin to see the light! Lackaday! To have accidentally abducted a member of the personal staff of a Groachian MHPP!"

Nith waggled his eyes at Gloot playfully. "In your report to your superior, I'm sure you won't find it necessary to mention this little contretemps, eh? Just look upon it as a slight misunderstanding easily mended—"

"Upthrust One," Lt. Chish interrupted. "The possibility that though this one's companion is of the noble Groacian stock, he himself might yet be in the pay of inferior races—"

"To be sure, Leftenant," Nith said smoothly. "To have been about to raise precisely that issue." He faced Gloot. "Confess all, unfortunate dupe! You were the prisoner of the Groacian noblebeing, correct?"

"Well—technically he was *my* prisoner. But between you and me, Five-eyes, I was beginning to wonder who was in charge."

"You dared impede the freedom of a High Born One? You abducted him here against his will?"

"Naw, it wasn't that way," Gloot said. "It was kind of a joint venture, like."

"Joint venture? I fail to postulate any conceivable circumstance under which the interests of Groac and of an aboriginal would coincide!"

"Dough," Gloot said succinctly. "Mazoola. Bread. You know."

"You shared an interest in gourmet cookery?"

"Cripes, how'd you know that?"

"Further association with us Groaci will accustom you to such casual displays of omniscience," Nith said smoothly.

"But—to have implied that it occupied the status of coequal with its Groaci companion," Chish objected.

"To have spoken allegorically, as is customary with artists! To have implied only His Supernalness' shared interest in matters gastronomic. But now to wonder—what brings Groaci brass to this dismal backwater, checking up unannounced? The possibility that Supreme HQ is checking up on me."

"The possibility of inquiring subtly of His Supremacy's cook," Chish whispered.

"To try to curb your tendency to get into the act, Leftenant," Nith hissed, "Tell me, fellow," he addressed Gloot, "what was the purpose of your Groaci master's visit to these remote environs?"

"To see what was cooking, what else?"

"Yes, yes, of course—a clever cover story. But in addition to his culinary researches, what was the mission of the High Born?"

"If he had one, he never told me," Gloot said.

"To be expected that His Grandeur would not confide in an underling," Nith murmured.

"Estimable Broodmaster," the Leftenant hissed. "To hypothesize: Might not these same intruders be a veritable inspection team, dispatched by Ambassador Jith, who, jealous of his prerogatives, may have introduced them here by devious means, the better to check up on your operation unheralded?"

"Exactly what I had deduced!" Nith whispered and started for the door. "Certain reactionary elements have long desired my downfall. What better time than now to bring long schemes to naught by meddlesome probing, thereafter to cry me culpable! Forewarned, I'll see to certain matters regarding the voucher files; meantime, dispatch the prisoner instanter, lest he level feckless charges against my person!" Nith skittered through the door and was gone. The Leftenant made a rude gesture at the closed door and turned to Gloot, drawing his pistol.

"No violence, now," he cautioned the Lumbagan as he removed the cranial attachments of the veracitometer. "And remember to mention my name in glowing terms to your master. That's Chish: C-H-I-S-H, by a gross miscarriage of justice a mere leftenant—" He broke off as Retief stepped through the door, Smelch behind him. Uttering a faint cry, the officer whirled toward the door by which his superior had just departed. The Terran reached it first.

"Guard! To me!" Chish keened, but as the Lumbagan behemoth lumbered into action, Smelch stepped behind him, gripped hands with himself, raised the resultant picnic-ham size aggregation of bone and muscle overhead and brought it down atop the fellow's cranium with a resounding thump, felling him in his tracks.

"Poor old Vump, he always had a glass head," Smelch commented.

"Nice one!" Gloot yelled. "But save old Nith for me!"

"Unhand me, Terran!" Chish whispered, trying unsuccessfully to dodge past Retief, "To have important business requiring my urgent attention!"

"You're confused, Leftenant," Retief said. "It was Broodmaster Nith who had the pressing appointment."

"Indeed? To have never heard of him."

"Too bad. I was hoping you could tell me who he works for."

"Never, vile Soft One!"

"I'd avoid those long-term predictions if I were you, Chish. They have a tendency to unravel at the edges." Retief looked past the Groaci to Gloot, busily freeing himself from the last of his entanglements.

"Don't break anything, Gloot; we wouldn't want to short the leftenant's wiring."

"What's this?" Chish hissed. "My w-wiring?"

"Where'd the other one go?" Gloot demanded. "That's the one I want. I want to pluck those eyes one at a time, like picking ripe froomfruit! How about it, you?" he glowered at Chish, who recoiled from the menacing figure towering over him. "Where's the other Terry?"

"The ... the other Terry?" the Groaci hissed in agitation. "What other Terry?"

"You know what other Terry!" Gloot roared.

"Oh, *that* Terry," Chish said hurriedly. "Why, I do believe he's occupying the, er, guest suite, just across the passage."

"Yeah!" Gloot looked baffled. "What's he doing there?"

"He was, ah, assisting me in certain experimental activities," Chish replied. "Which reminds me, I'm overdue for my saline infusion, so if you'll kindly unhand me...."

Gloot pushed the Groaci away and went across the room and into the passage. He paused before the door across the hall and rapped. A faint, uncertain cry answered him.

"Whattya know?" he said. "He's in there." He tried the knob, then stepped back and kicked the stout panel; the plastic cracked. A second kick shattered the lock, and the door banged inward. A slight figure appeared in the opening, checked at the sight of the Lumbagan.

"Hey," Gloot said weakly as Retief came up behind him. "That's not—"

"Well, there you are at last, Retief," First Secretary Magnan gasped. "Heavens, I thought you'd never turn up!"

12

"I don't get it," Gloot said, looking from Magnan to Retief. "Another Graoci with only two eyes, just like you, Retief—and I just noticed that Terry you're holding onto is wearing three fakes, just like that other Terry, Chish. What gives?"

"Duplicity on a vast scale," Retief said. "It's creeping in everywhere these days."

"You labor under a misappreheninsion, dull-witted bucolic!" the Groaci began, subsiding in midword at a minatory tweak.

"What's this person referring to?" Magnan inquired, favoring Gloot with a distasteful look. "Is he somehow under the impression—"

"He's a great admirer of the Groaci, Mr. Magnan. Naturally, he leaped to the conclusion that you enjoyed that status, since you resemble me so closely." Retief gave Chish's collar an extra half-twist as the latter attempted to speak.

"*I* resemble *you*?" Magnan echoed. "Oh, really? Well, actually, the press of other duties has precluded undue emphasis in my case on gross muscular development, but I fancy I cut a rather imposing figure in any case. But I fail to see the connection—"

"How come," Gloot asked bluntly, "this Groaci's got the same shortage of eyes as you Retief?"

"Quite simple, Gloot. He's a relative; we're both members of the ape family."

"Oh. But what's he doing here, palling around with these foreigners?"

"Simplicity itself," Magnan said. "Though I was far from palling around, as you so crudely put it. I was seized by a brace of brigands and whisked here for some obscure purpose unconnected with normal diplomatic procedures." The first secretary looked severely at Chish. "Perhaps you have some explanation?"

"I'm sure he does." Retief assisted the struggling Groaci to the chair, and with Gloot's enthusiastic aid strapped him in position, fitting the cranial attachments in place atop his cartilaginous skull amid his eyestalks, which drooped dejectedly now.

"Alas for lost opportunities," the officer mourned. "Had I but known of the imminence of my downfall, I might at least have had the pleasure of making plain to the abominable Nith my true assessment of his worth!"

"Too bad, Chish. Maybe I'll find a chance to make it up to you," Retief said. "Now, I believe this model has the automatic prevarication suppressor, which shoots a nice jolt through your trigeminal nerve if you accidentally stray into inaccuracy. Just set it at max, Gloot, to save time."

"Base alien, thus to serve an innocent official, harmlessly engaged in the performance of his duties—"

"Later, Chish. Who was the big shot?"

"One Swarmmaster Ussh, a most prestigious official. You'll rue the day—"

"Probably. Where's Omega Station?"

"I haven't the faintest—yip! the faintest intention of lying, I was about to say—eek! On a desert isle some leagues from here, drat all Soft Ones!"

"Which one?" Gloot demanded. "Rumboogy? Delerion?"

"Sprook!" Chish whispered. "I could wish you no more dolorous fate than to set foot in its miasmic swamps!"

"The needles say he's telling the truth," Gloot said.

"As he sees it," Retief said. "Unfortunately, false information doesn't register as long as he believes it. I have a feeling his boss wasn't keeping him fully informed."

"It is you, vile counterfeit—" Chish started, and broke off, listening. Faintly from afar a clattering sounded. "Ha!" the Groaci hissed in triumph. "In instants a squad of peacekeepers will be upon you, to put an end to your presumptuous invasion of sacred Groacian symbolic soil, as well as to your grotesque imposture!"

"What's he talking about?" Gloot demanded.

"I refer to the understandable aspirations of lesser races to the lofty status of Groacihood—"

"He also means the cops will be here any minute," Retief cut in. "I wonder if you'd be kind enough, Chish, to direct us to the nearest exit."

"A door—at the end of the passage there. A passage leads thence to a hidden egress—and good riddance to you!"

"Well, we'll have to be saying good night now, Leftenant. When Vump comes to perhaps he'll unstrap you. In the meantime, you can while away the time by planning what you should have said to Nith when you had the chance."

"True," Chish whispered. "Gone are my dreams of early advancement. But I may yet get a crack at that lousy civilian."

"Let that thought sustain you in your hour of trial," Retief said.

Ten minutes later, after carefully skirting the spot where Flunt guarded the trail, humming tunelessly to himself in the moonlight, the party reached the rendezvous where Boobooboo and his villagers had lain in wait. A long-legged native materialized from the mist.

"Well, you got one," Zoof said, eyeing Smelch appraisingly. "Two if you count skinny one." He prodded Magnan. "Hey—this one inedible like you, Retief. Not count!"

"These are just samples," Retief said. "The main course is right behind us."

In the pause in the conversation, faint cries were audible from the rear.

"Well, delivery to figurative door, real deluxe service, Retief," Chief Boobooboo said. "Maybe you not bad monster deal with after all."

"Nothing like a satisfied customer, Chief. And now I think we'd better be off and leave you to your celebration. Which way to Sprook Island?"

"Funny time decide end it all," Boobooboo said. "But to each his own. Just head for river, follow down to shore. Sprook just across way, nice swim, give time to reflect on misspent life before end. But look out for monsters, patrol river mouth every hour on hour in magic fish."

"What's a magic fish?" Gloot demanded.

"Local name for light-weight straked dory with V transom," the chief explained.

"Boy, you natives sure talk funny," Gloot commented.

The hue and cry had drawn near by the time the

refugees found the stream. They followed its course as it wound across mud flats to the north shore of the island. A mile across the water, the low shape of the next land mass was barely visible in the pink moonlight.

"Surely you aren't thinking of going *there*?" Magnan said querulously. "At this hour of night?"

"Just long enough to keep an appointment with a MHPP," Retief reassured his superior.

"Well, in that case—but how will we get there?"

"I expect our transportation will be along soon."

"Hey, I just remembered," Smelch said. "Sprook Island is where the wizards hang out. Guys which they can be in two places at once—or so the older boys told me."

"Nuts," Gloot scoffed. "Everybody knows Sprook is where the walking dead get their exercise."

"H-how do you know that?" Magnan said.

"I got a uncle that's an eye, ear, nose, and throat man over there."

"He cures them?"

"Naw, he sells 'em."

"I understood you Lumbagans didn't die in an ordinary sense," Retief said.

"Yeah—but when spare parts go west, Sprook is where they get together and make new friends. Picture it, Retief: phantom Lumbagans, made out of the odd ectoplasmic leg and the discarded ghostly elbow, prowling around in the mist looking for a spectral pancreas to make up a complete set."

"A curious superstition," Magnan commented with a shudder. "One might almost wonder if it's home-grown or imported."

"Superstition nothing," Smelch said. "I know a

guy who saw a familiar face peeking out of the stranglemoss one time when a squall blew him aground off Sprook. It was a face he wouldn't likely forget, he said, on account of he chopped it off a stranger in a barroom brawl the week before."

"Maybe it was lucky enough to strike up a new friendship with a lonely head—"

"It don't work that way, Retief. Once a Four-Decker breaks up, it's all the way back to Freebies: eyes, ears, cerebellum, the works—and the whole lousy job to do over again."

"Presumably Nith's alien components won't interest the local haunts."

"Yeah—it's OK for you foreigners," Gloot said. "But us Lumbagans are fair game."

"Then it looks as if Mr. Magnan and I will be going alone," Retief said. "Thanks for your help, fellows—"

"Hey—what's the idea? What about my investment?" Gloot protested. "Besides, I got no particular hankering to hang around this place for those five-eyed little devils and their overgrown hatchetmen to beat the brush for, come sunup!"

"Gosh, I'd sure like to go on a sea voyage," Smelch said. "I always wanted to see the bright lights and all. But I got a feeling if I don't get back to my post my career as a alert sentry is at a end."

"The brightest light we're likely to see on Sprook is a will-o'-the-wisp, or maybe a little burning swamp gas," Gloot said gloomily. "But I guess even that's better'n the one Chish'll put you under when he gets his mitts on you."

"Yeah," Smelch sighed. "Well, so long, fellers. I

hope you enjoyed your stay. Drop in again some-time."

"It was a pleasure, Smelch," Retief said. "I don't know when I've been as efficiently guarded."

"Gee, thanks, Retief. If you'd drop a line to my boss, I might get a pay raise out of it."

"I'll keep that thought in mind, Smelch."

As the oversized Lumbagan moved off, Retief, Magnan, and Gloot made their way out through a dense stand of reeds sprouting from the mud to a hummock giving a clear view of the creek mouth. Ten slow minutes passed.

"Get set, gentlemen—here it comes," Retief said. A dark shape came into view downstream: a boat, crowded with oversize Lumbagans, sliding silently toward them across the black water.

Retief moved quietly forward, wading out into the stream until the waters rose neck-deep, the reeds rising well above his head. Through the thickly scattered stems he could catch only glimpses of the approaching craft. Quite suddenly it was directly above him, sliding past. He ducked under water, rose noiselessly just aft the rowers' station, grasped the gunwale of the overloaded skiff, and heaved hard. With startled yells, the near-side passengers grabbed for support, missed, and struck the water with resounding splashes. On the return oscillation, Retief thrust upward, sending the remaining passengers over the far side. Bubbling sounds rose all around him; abruptly a swarm of Freebies were making for shore. Half a minute later, the refugees were aboard the craft, Gloot manning the sweeps, Retief in the bow scanning the open sea ahead, Magnan crouched shivering in the stern.

"Heavens, I'm sure I've caught a chill," the First Secretary said. "Can't this appointment wait, Retief? As you know, I'm a stickler for punctuality, but. . . ."

"So is our host, I suspect," Retief said. "And we wouldn't want him to start without us."

Twenty minutes' brisk effort brought the boat within a hundred yards of the light surf breaking on Sprook's windward shore.

"We'll take her around to the far side," Retief said. "No use making it too easy for the leftenant."

Gloot eyed the dark shore without pleasure. "In there, a guy would be lucky to find his head with both hands—if he once happened to drop it, I mean. How're we supposed to get a line on which way the bum went?"

"I suspect we'll encounter a clue," Retief said.

"Gracious!" Magnan said excitedly. "I see the bright lights, way up in the middle of the air!"

"Yeah—there's a lone peak sticking up from the middle of the island," Gloot said gloomily, turning to stare at the faint glow shining through the mist. "According to rumor, that's ghost headquarters."

They rounded a low headland, saw a shallow bay ahead. At Retief's suggestion, they steered for shore at a point where the mangrovelike water trees seemed thinnest. Rubbery stems bent and snapped with damp popping sounds as they forced the boat through. When it grounded on mud, the three passengers stepped out, waded through ankle-deep water to shore.

"Well," Gloot said dubiously, "we could sure use that clue about now . . ."

A sharp click sounded from the darkness ahead.

"All right, just stand still until the moon comes out," a coarse voice ordered from the shadows, "so I can see to shoot you."

13

"Well, there's our clue, right on schedule," Gloot said in an undertone to Retief. "But I never heard of a zombie needing a gun." He raised his voice: "What do you mean, shoot us? How do you know we're not friends?"

"Easy. We don't have any."

"You're likely to get yourself in a peck of trouble," Gloot said, edging closer to the source of the voice. "I happen to be a pretty influential fellow—"

"One more teeny little step and you'll influence me to blaze away ready or not. With the spread I get with this sawed-off, there won't be a piece of you that'll survive long enough to stomp on."

With dramatic suddenness, the larger moon swam clear of the obscuring cumulonimbus. The Lumbagan who stood twenty feet away, aiming a large and efficient-looking gun, was of medium height, equipped with four arms, two legs, two eyes, a single mouth of modest dimensions. Behind him stood a second Lumbagan of identical aspect, clothed in an identical tunic of dun and chicle drab, differing only in its simple ornamentation.

"Jeez—old Smelch said you wizards could be in two places at once," Gloot muttered. "But I didn't expect it to be the same place."

"Don't bother your misshapen head," the gunner snapped. "Stand closer together, no use wasting a round." He gestured impatiently with the gun.

"Now, just a minute," Gloot temporized, pointing to Retief and Magnan. "You don't want to shoot these foreigners here. They got diplomatic immunity."

"Does that mean bullets won't punch holes in them?"

"It means anybody that tries it gets the whole Groaci Navy landing on him with a barge-load of chopped liver!"

"Did you say—Groaci?"

"Right. This here one is, ah, Superhivemaster Retief, head Yumpity-yump of the whole Groaci show!"

"Well, that's different." The receptionist lowered the brak-gun. "Why didn't you say so? We've been expecting a MHHP visit—"

"Because it's a secret, Dum-dum!" Gloot explained.

"Oh. Well then, why'd you tell me?" the captain challenged.

"If you shot us it would spoil the surprise."

"Yeah—that figures. I guess you want to see Colonel Suash, eh, sir?" the Lumbagan inquired of Retief.

"I couldn't have phrased it better myself," Retief said. "How is the colonel these days?"

"Just like me," the greeter replied. "How else?"

"And naturally, I got to go along as interpreter," Gloot said.

"What for? The Groaci gent speaks pretty fair Lumbagan."

"He only speaks the diplomatic dialect. Everything he says means something else."

"Oh, well, in that case I guess you better come too." The local stepped back and motioned them past. A narrow trail became visible ahead, a raised causeway between dark pools thick with rank growth. Two more identical Lumbagans emerged into view, fell in at the rear of the column.

"Weirdest thing I ever saw," Gloot muttered to Retief. "Boy, it must be confusing, having everybody in sight with the same number of everything. A guy could get mixed up and wander into the wrong bedroom even."

"It happens," Retief confirmed.

"Say, that's right, you Groaci come all of a pattern too," Gloot said. "Except for you getting a little short-changed on eyes, of course. Funny, I keep forgetting you're a foreigner and an alien, Retief; you seem just like a regular fellow."

"Thanks, Gloot. I take it twins are a rarity on Lumbaga, to say nothing of octuplets?"

"Hey, no more talking," the officer barked. "Trying to figure out what's the opposite of everything the Groaci says is giving me a swift pain in the parietal lobes."

"Don't even try, rube," Gloot said callously "Decoding diplomatic conversations is a job for experts—and even they can't do it."

The trail debouched into a wide clearing, lined with neatly pitched tents, before one of which, larger than the others, a gay-colored banner hung limp in the still air. In the ruddy glow of a campfire were gathered a dozen more soldiers, all carbon copies of the reception committee.

"Wow!" Gloot exclaimed, "I heard of putting troops in uniforms, but this is fantastic!"

"Retief!" Magnan said behind his hand. "We've had no reports of any organized native militia here on Lumbaga! Heavens, I shudder to contemplate what effect this development might have, law-and-orderwise!"

"A thought-provoking spectacle," Retief agreed.

"Wait here," their captor ordered, and stepped inside the oversized tent. A moment later he re-emerged, followed by still another duplicate of himself, this one wearing a gaudy cummerbund and braided shoulder tabs. The newcomer stared at the Terran, then jerked a power gun of foreign manufacture from a holster at his hip.

"What's this, a hoax?" he demanded sharply. "You're not Swarmmaster Ussh!"

"Of course not," Retief said briskly. "For a mission of this importance I thought I'd better come personally."

"You don't even look like the other ones," the officer barked. "Not enough eyes—"

"Lay off," Gloot spoke up sharply. "The poor guy was born that way."

"Born? Born? What's that?"

"It's kind of hard to explain," Gloot said. "It's kind of like you start from scratch, and one day—bloop! There you are. Get the idea?"

"Hmmphfff, do you take me for a nincompoop? I've heard rumors that foreigners come into existence in some such miraculous fashion, but I don't believe in spontaneous generation! Now: what did you expect to accomplish here? Sabotage? Espionage? Assassinations?"

"Keep going," Gloot muttered. "You'll hit something yet."

"I'm afraid we're wasting time, Colonel," Retief said. "Shall we go inside? What I have is confidential."

"Well," the commander started, but Retief had already brushed past him, Gloot at his heels, Magnan bringing up the rear. The interior of the headquarters tent was spacious, comfortably furnished with chairs, tables, straw cushions, beaded hangings.

"Pretty plush," Gloot commented to Retief. "You Groaci do all right by your chums."

"Lots of people would be surprised to know just how far Groaci chumship has penetrated into the jungle," Retief commented.

Their host bustled past, waved them to seats, rang for an orderly who quickly produced drinks all around.

"Now, what's all this about a confidential mission?" Suash said ill-temperedly. "I thought all that was settled."

"It's a matter of adjusting to fluctuating conditions," Retief advised the officer coolly.

"You mean—the Terries are getting suspicious?"

"There is that possibility."

"But I was assured they were a pack of self-serving incompetents, who wouldn't realize what was going on until they found themselves stacked in a parts bin."

"A slight exaggeration, Colonel," Magnan said icily. "Not that we Groaci care one way or another what sort of base canards you spread," he added quickly as the officer frowned.

"I don't like that." The colonel shifted in his chair. "Do they know *we're* here?"

"They just found out."

"That's bad! But surely they're not aware of the secret installation in the interior?"

"The word is out," Retief admitted.

"This is terrible!" Colonel Suash cried. "Do they know our role on D-day?"

"Not yet," Retief said. "But they're hoping to learn any time now."

"How?" Suash flapped his arms in agitation. "It's the most closely guarded military secret in Lumbagan history. In fact, it's the *only* military secret in Lumbagan history!"

"Simple," Gloot spoke up. "You got a spy in your midst."

"A spy. Impossible!"

"Oh, yeah? Nothing easier. After all, all you birds look alike. All a spy has to do is disguise himself to look like one of you—and zingo, he's invisible."

"Diabolical!"

"It's just the old needle-in-a-froomstack principle," Gloot said carelessly. "With a new twist."

"No wonder you were sent to warn me." Suash groaned. "What can I do?"

"Easy," Gloot volunteered. "Stage a showdown inspection."

"How . . . how do you mean?"

"Call your troops in one at a time, and order 'em to disassemble. The one that's a Terry in disguise won't be able to do it."

"What? Order my lads to destroy themselves?"

"Got any better ideas, Suash? Anyway, the odds are you won't work more'n halfway through the roster before you hit paydirt."

"You concur?" Suash looked anxiously at Retief.

"It ought to be interesting to see what happens."

"I . . . I suppose I haven't any choice. Not after the demonstration Shlush gave me of the fate in store for failures." The colonel tinkled his bell again. An orderly promptly appeared.

"Ah—Private Spub. I have, er, to inform you that your nation, ah, requires of you the, er, supreme sacrifice."

"You're not cancelling my furlough?" Spub said aggrievedly.

"By no means. As a matter of fact, you're about to enjoy a type of freedom you've not known for some time—"

"You mean—my discharge came through? Yipeeee!"

"Private Spub! You're at attention! I suppose in a sense one might say you're about to be discharged. At any rate, after tonight you'll no longer be a member of my command. I'd like to say that you've been a satisfactory soldier, except for a slight tendency toward insubordination, goldbricking, and slovenliness in dress—"

"I get it," Spub said. "*You're* resigning. Can't say that I blame you, Suash—"

"*Colonel* Suash, Private!"

"Not if you've resigned. Make up your mind," Spub said sullenly.

"Spub, I order you to . . . to . . . disassemble yourself."

"You mean—?"

"I mean disassociate! Into Freebies!"

Spub took a step backward, whirled, and darted from the tent.

"Head for the tall timber, boys!" he yelled. "Old

Suash has finally blown his rug! He's on a suicide-pact kick!"

"Here, fall in for inspection!" Suash roared, plunging through the tent fly. "Sergeant! Come back here. . . ."

"It appears the colonel has a slight discipline problem," Magnan sniffed as he and Retief followed their host outside. The encampment was already deserted but for the irate officer and a lone private who loitered near the campfire, staring into the woods where his comrades had disappeared.

"Well, I'm glad to see I have one loyal subordinate," Suash cried. "Fall in, you!"

"I wonder why he didn't depart with the others," Magnan said.

"Maybe because he had reason to stick around," Retief conjectured.

"Well, Private," Suash addressed the fellow, "it was a pleasure to have you in my outfit."

"Was?" the private inquired in a shy whisper.

"It's now my sad duty to order you to disincorporate," Suash went on. "Seems a shame, with you the only loyal trooper in the group. But such are the fortunes of war."

"Ah . . . I'm afraid that won't be convenient," the soldier demurred feebly.

"What's this, mutiny?"

"Aha!" Gloot said to Retief. "We're on to something. Watch this." He stepped forward, shouldered Suash aside, and rammed a stiffened finger into the private's midsection. The latter doubled over, emitting hoarse wheezing sounds.

"I told you so!" Gloot cried. "Grab him!" he

added as the assaulted private ducked suddenly and sprang past him, only to be brought down in a flying tackle by the colonel.

"A dead giveaway, Retief," Gloot explained happily. "Any genuine Lumbagan will break down into Freebies if you land a solid poke in his lunar plexus."

"So," Suash growled, dusting himself off and glaring down at the unfortunate imposter. "A Terry spy, eh?"

"By no means," the bogus private gasped, tottering to his feet.

"I happen to know better!" Suash barked. "Luckily, this Groaci civilian, Mr. Retief, tipped me off—"

"Retief? Groaci?" the accused spy fumbled at his head, stripped away a rubber mask to reveal five stalked oculars in a pale gray visage.

"I happen to be one Pilth, Groaci observer assigned to undercover surveillance duty!" he hissed. *There*"—he pointed at Retief—"is the Terry spy!"

Suash looked uncertainly from Retief to the Groaci, gave Gloot a sharp look as the latter guffawed.

"Nice try, Terry," Gloot said. "But it so happens I can vouch for Retief. I collected him personally from Groaci secret HQ in Dacoit Street. He and Shlush were just like that."

"Cretins! Assassins! Dumbbells! Are you so ignorant of aesthetics as to be unaware of the characteristics defining the noble Groaci race? Where, may I ask, are this impostor's handsome stemmed oculars, five in number? And—"

"*That* again," Gloot said wearily. "OK, so the guy's deformed, but in spite of the handicap he does OK. How about you, Terry? I got a hunch about three o' those eyeballs you're waggling at me are phonies. . . ." He reached for Pilth's twitching eyestalks, but with a sharp cry, the Groaci dodged aside.

"Unhand me, vile aborigine!" he keened.

"I'll just give 'em an easy yank or two," Gloot assured the terrified captive, making another grab for his eyes.

"I confess!" Pilth squeaked, cowering behind Suash. "I throw myself on your mercy! Just don't let that great uncouth bruiser lay hands on me!"

"The effrontery of it!" Suash exclaimed. "Trying to pass yourself off as one of my good friends, the Groaci—as if you could fool me—while spying on my operation!"

"Better find out how much he's learned," Retief suggested.

Suash glowered at the culprit. "How many of our secrets have you ferreted out?"

"Colonel—might I have a word with you in private," Pilth entreated earnestly, "ere a gross miscarriage of justice take place, as well as a disaster to the common cause?"

"Don't listen to him, Colonel," Gloot urged. "Anything this Terry has got to say he can say in front of us Groaci." "*You're* claiming to be a Groaci *too* now?" Suash exclaimed in startlement.

"Well, an honorary one, sort of. On account of me and Retief being pals and all."

Suash grunted, turned back to Pilth. "Start talking."

"And reveal Groacian state secrets to this vile Terry who has the audacity to bogusly claim Groacihood?"

"Back to that, huh?" Gloot said, and reached for an eye. Pilth screeched breathily and dived for cover behind Retief.

"I know nothing!" he whispered frantically. "Actually, I slept through the orientation lectures—"

"He's lying!" Suash cried. "I'll bet you know about the secret recognition signal, two long and three short—and the reinforcements we're expecting from Rumboogie and Hylerica and Slovenger—and—"

"Very well, I confess, all that and more," Pilth confirmed hastily. "No need to spell out the particulars—"

"But surely you haven't yet tipped them off about the plan for a coordinated police action a week from Tuesday, under cover of the Spring Rites?"

"Assume the worst!" Pilth hissed.

"This is a disaster!" Suash cried, clapping various hands to his forehead. "The pernicious little sneak has blown the operation wide open!"

"I wonder how he got the word back?" Gloot inquired. "Him still being here and all."

"Yes—how *did* you get the word back to your Terran masters?" Suash echoed. "No one's left this island for weeks!"

"Ah . . . I employed a variety of clever ruses, no need to burden you with such trivia," Pilth temporized.

"I'll bet the little villain has spilled the beans about our Galatic Ultimate Top Secret weapon, too!" Suash yelped. "Let me at him!" Retief restrained the outraged officer as he lunged for the trembling spy.

"Colonel," he said soothingly. "We may be able to turn this situation to advantage."

"How? The rascally knave has probably reported everything to the Terran ambassador! He must have sent off his dispatches via the bakery man, now that I think of it! He calls every morning in a sampan that's probably a fast courier boat in disguise!" Suash groaned. "And while I was dunking jelly doughnuts, news of every move I made was being whisked off under my very noses!"

"Well, what are we doing to do about it?" Gloot demanded. "Call the whole thing off?"

"There's only one thing we *can* do," Suash declared, and smacked several fists into an appropriate number of palms. "Move D-day forward! We attack at once! Now! Today!"

"Impossible!" Pilth screeched. "We're not ready!"

"All the better!" Suash barked. "I'll catch you Terries off-balance, and—"

"I mean *you're* not ready! Your noble Groaci allies have not yet completed all arrangements necessary to bring off the *coup* with the flawless timing that will leave no treacherous Terran alive to carry exaggerated tales of perfidy and betrayal!"

"That's their lookout!"

"Then, too," Pilth whispered acidly, "there is the problem of your loyal troops, now dispersed through the woods like so many strayed kine, aquiver with apprehension lest their beloved commandant run amok amongst them!"

"Hmm. You've put your finger on a problem area," Suash conceded. "But forget those shirkers! There are plenty more where they come from—and you and I know where that is, eh, Retief?"

"One of us does," the Terran agreed.

"Oh, you think I'm not in on the top-level planning, eh?" the colonel bridled. "Well, as it happens I'm well aware that the location of the repo depot is—" he broke off. "But I won't mention the name in front of the Terry spy, just in case he doesn't already know. Not that it matters much." Suash drew his pistol. "Stand aside, Retief, and I'll finish off the sly little devil before we go."

"Wait!" Pilth whispered in Groaci. "Retief! To appeal to you as a fellow alien, to stay the hand of the barbarian ere he commits a tactical error of incalculable dimensions!"

"To propose a deal," Retief replied in the same tongue. "To give me details of the secret weapon, and then to put in a good word for you."

"To suggest that I, a trusted minion of the Groacian autonomy, would divulge information bearing a GUTS classification? Fie, Terran! To do your worst!"

"I was afraid you'd feel that way," Retief said.

"Here, what are you aliens gossiping about?" Suash demanded suspiciously. "Speak plain Lumbagan!"

"Pilth was just saying a few last words," Retief explained.

"But on the other hand," Pilth added quickly, "why make an issue of a few dry data? The supply of cannon fodder will be adequate to compensate for any modest foreknowledge that might leak to the enemy camp—"

"Hey," Gloot cut in, "do you hear something, Retief?" He cocked a pair of ears toward the forest trail.

"Yes, but I hesitated to interrupt at this point. You were saying, Pilth?"

"Wait a minute," Suash barked. "I'll bet that's my boys coming back to report for company punishment and then back into harness with no hard feelings!"

"Ha! Doubtless succor approaches!" Pilth hissed. "Now will your crimes be visited on your head, insidious Terry impostor!"

There was a flash of blue light from the darkness, a simultaneous sharp report: Suash yelled as the gun flew from his grasp.

"Keep your hands in sight and don't make a move," an authoritative voice barked. "I'm Ensign Yubb of the Harbor Patrol, and all you smugglers are under arrest!"

|4

"Well, quite a haul," the Lumbagan, neat in a dark blue uniform, commented as his variegated detachment of marines closed in, aiming guns of unmistakable Terran design. He was of medium height and unexceptional appearance, having three arms, four legs, and a random distribution of other members. "A couple of renegades, I see, plus a pair of foreigners."

"See here, fellow," Pilth hissed, "if you will employ your good offices to eliminate the Terry and his toady, as well as their dupe, Colonel Suash, you will find the Grocian Autonomy not ungrateful."

"Don't let this trickster delude you, Admiral," Suash spoke up, "for some reason he's trying to pose as a Groaci—"

"A Groaci, you say? Is that a fact?" Yubb looked Pilth up and down. "Got any proof?"

"Proof? I invite you, Ensign, to observe for yourself! I exhibit in classic form those characteristics which alone endow the owner with the peculiar beauty of Groacihood!"

"Peculiar is right," Gloot commented. "Just grab his eyes and pull. They're plastic, stuck on with rubber cement. I spotted 'em the minute I saw 'em. This here"—he indicated Retief—"is the genuine article."

"Then I guess that makes *this* one a Terry," the officer deduced, eyeing Pilth unenthusiastically. "Not too impressive looking, but what the heck. Mine not to reason why, mine but to shoot the guy."

"Wouldst cut down a helpless prisoner on the strength of a mere literary allusion?" Pilth screeched. "And a garbled allusion at that."

"I don't have much choice," Yubb assured the alien. "I've got orders to drill all Groaci on sight."

"Unconscionable!" Pilth hissed. "I warn you, sir, any such thoughtless act will earn you a regrettable fate at the hands of vengeful Groaci hordes, soon to sweep clean the infected real estate of this pestilential world!"

"For a Terry, you come on kind of ambiguous," Yubb said. "You'd think I was about to plug *you*"—he swiveled to cover Retief with the gun— "Instead of *him*."

"Ah ... to be sure," Pilth recovered. "It was merely my kindly instinct at work at the prospect of seeing a fellow alien dispatched before my eyes. However, in the interest of interplanetary amity, I withdraw my objection."

"Gee, the sentiment does you credit," Yubb said. "In fact, out of deference to the nobility of the gesture, I'll spare the Groaci scoundrel for the nonce." He gave Retief a look designed to intimidate. "But don't let it go to your head, fellow. I've heard about you Groaci, always on the lookout for a way to repay a charitable act with a knife in the ribs."

"An exaggeration," Pilth snapped. "There are occasions, of course, when expediency requires the sacrifice of the softer principles, but I can assure you that there are compensating virtues in the Groaci makeup, not the least of which is a commendable tenacity in the avenging of affronts."

"Sure, don't get carried away," Yubb said. "You'd think the Groaci were you Terries' best pals. Don't worry, I'll watch him. Now let's get moving. If I can get this Groaci and these two smugglers back to port before shift change, I'll net a nice bonus—"

"One moment," Pilth interrupted hastily. "I must protest your apparent intention to include my person in your party. As it happens, I have urgent business here, rudely interrupted when these miscreant locals, assisted by their, ah, Groaci henchmen, set upon me."

"What business?"

"That," Pilth whispered, "is my affair."

"For a foreigner you're throwing a lot of weight around, Terry," Yubb retorted. "My orders were to chase down these *foof* smugglers and clean out their base of operations. Maybe you're just an innocent bystander, but that's for higher authority to figure out. Let's go; we're wasting time."

"If you're after smugglers, you're scaling the

wrong molehill," Colonel Suash demurred. "I happen to be a legitimate rebel leader, and my work is here. Beside which, I outrank you."

Yubb cocked his pistol. "I hate these jurisdictional disputes," he sighed. "But fortunately for the triumph of democratic processes, I happen to have the firepower. So—"

"I wouldn't if I were you, Ensign," Retief said as Yubb's finger tightened on the trigger.

"Why not?" the officer inquired.

"Because if *you* do," a new voice explained from the underbrush, "then *I* will."

"My loyal lads, back on duty!" Suash cried. "Yubb, surrender instantly and I'll try to prevent them from committing any excesses!"

"At the first sign of an excess, they'll be looking for a new boss." Yubb held the pistol firm on Suash's cummerbund.

"Hold your fire!" Suash yelped to his troops

"You bet we will," the reply came from the darkness. "We're not letting this stranger plug you, Colonel; we want to do the job ourselves!"

"The rot's struck deeper than I thought," Suash muttered. "Well, Ensign, it looks like a standoff. Just give me and my Groaci advisors a modest head start over my chaps, and—"

"The Groaci are *my* prisoners," Yubb cut in curtly. "You can have the Terry."

"Who wants him?" Suash exploded. "The creepy little spy's already blown my security sky-high!"

One of Yubb's patrolmen edged forward. "Why don't we draw straws?" he suggested with a glance over his shoulder at the shrubbery concealing the rebel troops. "We wouldn't want any unfortunate incident to take place—"

"At the first shot, rake the woods with fire!" Yubb yelled. "I'm taking the Groaci, and that's that!"

"I'm keeping him, and that's *that*!" Suash shouted.

"Just my luck," Gloot said lugubriously. "Square in the middle of the crossfire."

"By the way, which one's the Groaci?" Yubb's second-in-command wondered aloud.

"The little one with the five wiggly eyes," someone called from the darkness.

"Wrong, it's the big ones with only two arms," someone else contradicted.

"Are you nuts? Everybody knows Groaci have got five eyes—"

"They're fakes! I heard—"

"I happen to know—"

"My brother-in-law had it on good authority—"

"Your brother-in-law wears ankle socks!"

"Oh, yeah?" One of Suash's mutinous troops emerged from concealment to confront his verbal adversary. A second rebel followed; a trio of Yubb's marines drew together to confront them. A sailor pushed a soldier; a soldier shoved a sailor.

"Now, lads, no fighting, it's unmilitary," Suash called.

"Sink the Navy!" someone shouted, a proposal followed instantly by the smack of a fist on leathery hide; at once, the underbrush erupted into a free-for-all; fists flew, some, Retief noted, well into the woods. Yubb and Suash danced about the periphery of the fray, bellowing orders, then fell on each other with flailing arms. Unnoticed by the combatants, Pilth whirled and scuttled off down the trail leading to the interior.

"Nice night for a riot," Retief said over the clamor. "I suppose they'll be happily occupied for some time, so we may as well be on our way."

"Jeez, I'd sure like to join in," Gloot sighed, eyeing the battle enviously and massaging a number of lumpy fists. "But I guess you're right: We better steal down to the beach while the stealing's good."

"A splendid notion," Magnan said quickly. "Speaking of stealing, if we hurry we might be able to borrow the patrol boat; much faster than rowing, and far less conducive to blisters."

"On the other hand," Retief pointed out, "I suspect Colonel Suash and his troops are stationed here for a reason—presumably guard duty. If we knew what he was guarding, it would spice up our report on our field trip."

"Yes, but in this wilderness. . . ." Magnan said indecisively.

"I'm curious as to where Pilth was headed in such haste. If we follow him, we might find answers to both questions."

"He's gone nuts is all," Gloot explained. "He panicked and headed for the deep swamp. Forget the Terry; we can still make it back to town in time to get in on the Midnight Melee."

"I have a feeling a somewhat larger melee is in the making, nearer at hand."

"A rumble in town is worth two in the bushes, as the old saying goes," Gloot said. "On the other hand, I kind of like your style, Retief. You don't say much, but where you are is where stuff seems to happen. I'm with you!"

Together, Retief, Magnan, and Gloot set off in

the wake of the Groaci *agent provocateur*. The path, while narrow, was high and dry, twisting and turning to avoid the boles of giant, moss-hung trees rising from the dark water, skirting the deeper pools. In a small, open patch of spongy ground the trail ended abruptly. There was no sign of Pilth.

"Well, whattaya know," Gloot commented, peering into the surrounding darkness. "Who would of thought the little Terry was that fast on his feet? He's gone and got clean away, so I guess we might as well get started back—"

"Listen," Retief said softly. From somewhere ahead, a faint cry rang out. He started off at a run, picking a route from one root-clump to another. A hundred feet farther on, he emerged into the open to witness a curious sight; from a sturdy bough overhanging the path, Pilth dangled by one leg in midair, supported in an inverted position by a length of stout rope.

"Good of you to wait, Pilth," Retief said. "An excellent spot for a confidential talk."

"To cut me down at once and to enjoy the eternal gratitude of the Groacian state, renewable annually at a modest fee," the snared alien whispered.

"Stumbled over one of your own trip wires, eh?" Retief said sympathetically. "It's one of the hazards of the diplomatic way of life."

"What is this talk of diplomatic wiles? As it happens, I am a simple scientist, here to observe the nest-building habits of the Lesser Tufted Adam's Apple—"

"Sorry, Pilth, an ingenious cover, but blown, I'm afraid. We met a few years back, when you were number two to General Fiss, the time he tried to take over Yalc."

"Tour Director Fiss and I were interested only in the excavation of artifacts of the Yalcan culture!" Pilth protested.

"You Groaci have pioneered the science of instant archaeology, true," Retief conceded, "but good form requires that you wait until the owners aren't using the bones any longer before you try to wire them together in a glass case. However, we have more immediate matters to discuss at the moment. Let's begin with where you were headed in such haste."

"I find it singularly difficult to marshal my recollective faculties while suspended in this unseemly position," the Groaci hissed.

"You'd find it even more difficult if the point of attachment were your third thoracic vertebra," Retief pointed out.

"Long will this day live in infamy," Pilth wailed. "Very well, Terry, I'll reveal my destination, but only under protest. As it happens, I maintain a modest retreat in the foothills above, to which I retire on occasion to meditate. Now cut me down promptly and in my report I'll do my best to minimize the shabby role you played in this sorry contretemps!"

"Too late for secrecy now," Retief said as Gloot and Magnan arrived panting, splashed with mud and festooned with algae.

"Well," the first secretary said as he spied the dangling alien, "at least he had the decency to attempt suicide—though one might have known he'd bungle it."

"You speak of suicide, Soft One?" Pilth keened. "Such indeed is the fate of those who would invade the sacrosanct precincts of, ah, my bucolic hideaway," he finished weakly.

"Don't imagine for a moment that your threats intimidate me," Magnan replied loftily. "It's just that we happen to be leaving now anyway. Come, Retief, suitably padded—discussed in adequate detail, that is—my report of the disasters we've encountered up to this point will serve adequately to impress the ambassador with my zeal."

"An inspiring thought, Mr. Magnan. Just picture his expression when you tell him you've discovered there may be a plot afoot to take over Lumbaga, and that you hurried back to let him know what, without wasting time finding out when, where, why, and how."

"But, as I was about to say," Magnan said quickly, "why dash off just when we're on the verge of achieving a coup of such stunning proportions?"

"Now, just how would one go about finding this weekend cottage of yours?" Retief queried Pilth.

"You imagine, presumptuous alien, that I would reveal details of my personal affairs to such as you?"

"My mistake, Pilth." Retief turned to Magnan and Gloot. "It seems we'll have to find it on our own. Shall we go, gentlemen?"

"What—and leave me here suspended, prey to any passing appetite, to say nothing of the risk of incipient apoplexy?" Pilth shrilled in protest.

"Yeah, that would be cruel," Gloot said and drew his knife. "I'll just slit the sucker's throat—"

"Oh, I don't think that will be necessary," Magnan

said judiciously, as Pilth uttered a yelp of dismay. "Just cut him down, truss him securely, and tuck him under a bush well out of sight."

"There to starve, assuming the unlikely eventuality that I'm overlooked by predators?"

"We'll leave the details to you, chum," Gloot said callously.

"I capitulate!" the Groaci hissed. "Proceed northeast by east to a lone *foof* tree, take a right, proceed another hundred paces upslope, and you will confront my confidential lair. I appeal to your better natures to pry then no more, but to betake yourselves in haste to more congenial surroundings, there to report favorably on this concrete evidence of the importance of the reflective life in the philosophy of the benign Groaci!"

"I don't get it," Gloot said. "How come this Terry's all the time putting in a plug for you Groaci?"

"Conscience," Magnan said crisply. "I suppose you may as well cut him loose now—provided he promises not to go scuttling ahead and spoil our surprise."

"I assure you I will scuttle in another direction entirely," Pilth whispered as Gloot slashed the rope, allowing him to drop to the ground with a painful impact. He sprang up and disappeared along the backtrail.

"I'm not sure that was the best move we've made all evening," Retief said. "But I suspect we'll know for sure very soon. Meanwhile, let's go take a look."

15

A dim light glowed from a point high above, shining down through the trees dotting the steeply rising slope.

"Well, whattaya know," Gloot said. "I thought the little runt was lying, but here's his meditation parlor, just like he said."

"Why, the very idea," Magnan whispered. "Ambassador Jith never mentioned funding any R and R facilities in the hustlings."

They emerged onto a talus slope. From here they were able to make out the silhouette of a cluster of towers rising from the crest of the peak. The lighted window went dark; a moment later a glow sprang up at another.

"Apparently Pilth doesn't do his thinking alone," Retief said.

"If the place is full o' Terries," Gloot said, "what's supposed to keep 'em from blasting us into Freebies before you can say 'oops'?"

"Nothing much; accordingly, I recommend extreme stealth from this point on."

Twenty feet higher, they encountered a flight of narrow steps cut into the stone. Retief climbed over the handrail, beaded with moisture in the damp air, and led the way upward, Gloot and Magnan close behind him. At a landing twenty feet higher the steps took a right-angled turn. The drop below was vertical now; the tops of trees rustled in the faint breeze. Far below a cluster of lanterns moved on the shore. Far across the water, the lights of the capital floated on blackness.

"Hey, Retief," Gloot whispered, "I get dizzy when I get this high. I would have told you sooner, only I never got this high before."

"Compared with the roofs we were negotiating a few hours ago, this is nothing," Retief said.

Gloot groaned. "Was that this year? It seems like something out of my early youth."

Gloot started to speak, then changed his mind. "Never mind," he muttered. "The more I know, the less I like it. I'm even beginning to get a funny feeling it was your idea and not mine to grab you from Groaci HQ."

At the next landing, by leaning far out over the rail to look up, Retief was able to see a row of shuttered windows set in a squat, thick-walled structure of a bilious ocher color. The building appeared to consist of several wings, set at slightly different levels in accommodation to the contours of the rugged peak on which it was built.

"Quite a layout," Gloot started, and broke off as feet clacked above. A spindly figure in a flaring helmet and a spined hip-cloak leaned over the railing of a terrace, peering down the barrel of a blast-rifle with five alertly canted oculars.

"Hssst! To advance and give the password!" a thin voice whispered sibilantly.

"To contain yourself in patience, hivemate of brood foulers," Retief whispered sharply in Groaci. "To have had a brisk trot to report the failure of the incompetent Nith! To require a moment in which to respire!" He motioned to Gloot. "You go first," he whispered softly. "Pretend to be scared."

"Pretend?" The Lumbagan choked. "I'm petrified! But what the heck, I don't aim to show the purple glimp feather. Here goes."

"The impropriety of your nattering—and my curiosity as to whom you natter with!" the Groaci peacekeeper hissed.

"The prompt satisfaction of your curiosity," Retief whispered back, motioning Gloot past. He followed up the final flight of steps. As the Lumbagan reached the sentry's terrace, the latter hissed and swung the gun to cover him.

"The impropriety of taking hasty action," Retief said sharply. The guard swiveled a pair of eyes toward him, and uttered a faint Groaci yelp of dismay.

"A Soft One—" he started, but his feeble cry was cut off abruptly by a smart rap to the side of the jaw delivered by Gloot. Retief deftly caught the victim's helmet as he collapsed.

Retief quickly scouted the narrow gallery on which they now found themselves. From the platform at the end, a complicated system of rods was visible atop a tower.

"Curious," Magnan whispered. "Trideo antennae here? I wasn't aware Lumbaga boasted transmission facilities."

"I have an idea the transmitter hasn't gone into full service yet," Retief said. Further discussion was interrupted by a faint *whop-whop-whop* which grew swiftly louder. A copter came sweeping in low over the treetops, made a sliding turn, and came back to hover for a moment before settling gently to the roof of the building. Before the rotors had stopped, the pilot—a small, thin-legged individual wrapped in a black cloak and wearing a solar topi—hopped down and disappeared into the shadows. A moment later, light shone from an opened hatch in the roof, into which the new arrival descended, closing the panel behind him.

"I believe that was the same chap we just missed meeting back on Groo-groo," Retief said. "An omission I'd like to correct."

"Too bad it's impossible," Magnan said crisply. "Still, if we hasten back now, we may be able to see the ambassador and persuade him to request departmental approval for authorizing an inquiry into the possibility of considering the appointment of a committee to look into a proposal for asking Jith some rather pointed questions."

"A dynamic program, Mr. Magnan," Retief said. "But we might save a little time by some judicious eavesdropping right here on the spot."

"Hmmm. An interesting theoretical point. A pity we didn't bring snoop gear, but who would have imagined any occasion for diplomatic activities this far from the nearest cocktail party?"

"An unfortunate oversight; but possibly we can rectify it by shinnying up the drain pipe."

"Drat it, Retief, I'm beginning to suspect that the hazards of being rescued by you exceed those threatened by the kidnappers!"

"Give me a leg up, Gloot," Retief said.

"Anything for you, pal," the local said dubiously, grasping his shin firmly. "But are you sure you can use it?"

"On second thought, just a boost will do," Retief amended. Gloot offered linked hands as a stirrup; Retief went up the pipe. The roof was deserted but for the silent copter squatting inside a yellow-painted circle. He leaned back to lend a hand to Magnan, then to Gloot. Together they crossed to the trapdoor. It opened soundlessly. Steep steps led down into deep gloom.

"I dunno," Gloot said, looking dubiously down into the dark recess below. "What if it's booby-trapped? What if they're waiting down there with skinning knives? What if the whole thing is a fancy scheme to feed fresh spares into the black market? What if—"

"If so, it's working perfectly," Retief said, and started down the steps. At the bottom, he used his pocket flash to quickly check the room; it was empty but for stacked crates and cartons bearng stenciled markings.

"Electronic gear," Retief said. "And surgical sppplies."

"Here's one labeled *Acme Theatrical Services*," Magnan whispered. "Curious; I never suspected the Groaci had an interest in amateur dramatics."

"I suspect they may have entered the field at a professional level," Retief said.

The storeroom opened into a narrow, dimly lit passage. Faint murmurings sounded from behind a door along the way. Retief went to it, put his ear against the panel:

". . . to have come within an ace of discovery!" hissed a breathy Groaci voice. "To make all haste now—"

"The inadvisability of rushing the cadence!" another voice replied. "To not louse up the triumphant culmination of my researches!"

"Yes, yes, to get on with it. To have a tight schedule."

A muted humming sound started up; a faint odor of ozone filtered past the closed door.

"Sounds like an illegal transmitter," Retief said.

"What's illegal about a transmitter?" Gloot demanded.

"Let's find out." Retief turned the doorknob silently, eased the door open an inch. Two Groaci, one in bile-green shorts and orange and violet Argyles, the other in a stained white laboratory smock, and holding a clipboard, stood before a wide panel with a puce crackle finish thickly set with dials, switches, oscilloscope tubes, and blinking indicator lights. One side of the room was given over to stacked cages in which eyeballs, kidneys, adenoids, and other forms of Lumbagan wildlife perched disconsolately on twigs or moped glumly in corners amid scattered straw.

". . . the completion of preliminary testing," the technician was whispering, "to be ready now to conduct field trials of limited range, after which, on to the final stage in the fulfilment of selfless Groaci objectives with all deliberate haste!"

"To spare me the propaganda," the other snapped. "To have read the official handouts. To now tellingly demonstrate the effectiveness of the device without further procrastination."

"The eagerness with which I confirm the accuracy of my theoretical predictions," the white-smocked Groaci hissed sharply. "To anticipate the prompt material gratitude of our government."

"To deliver the goods in accordance with specs, or to promptly adorn the Wall of Hooks as an example to other boasters!" the other whispered harshly.

The technician wiggled his oculars in expression of righteous fury courteously restrained, and turned to the control panel, began setting dials in a complicated sequence, referring frequently to the clipboard.

"Haste, haste," the other Groaci muttered. "To not procrastinate in the eye of the metaphorical cannon—or is it the mouth of the needle?"

"To be unfamiliar with Terry saws," the white-smocked alien hissed, continuing with the check list. The observer watched for a moment in sour silence; then: "Pah!" he burst out. "To reject out of hand this transparent hoax! To perceive that you stall the proceedings in order to extort even more golden promises of future emoluments!"

"To commit a wrong of vast proportions, thus to accuse me!" the technician cried. "To underestimate the insidious sublety of the mechanism—"

"To have penetrated your deception—and to remind you of the redundance of mere technical personnel after completion of their function!"

"The inadvisability of threats to my person! My indispensability to the scheme—"

"Is at an end! To point out that even a cretinous underling is fully capable of closing a switch!" The Groaci stepped forward and before the other could intercept him, pushed the largest button on the panel.

With a hoarse bellow, Gloot plunged past Retief into the room. The two Groaci whirled, uttered shrill yelps and dived in opposite directions. The small creatures in their cages had gone into a flurry of activity, Retief noted peripherally, hurling themselves against the wire mesh as if frantic to come to grips with their neighbors. The momentum of Gloot's charge carried him full tilt against the button-studded console. Lights flashed; harsh buzzings sounded, ending in a crackle of arcing electricity. Gloot staggered back and sat down hard. The lab animals subsided as abruptly as they had leaped into motion. Retief jumped forward in time to nab the technician as he dithered, unsure which way to run. A door slammed at the back of the room.

"Retief! What in the world . . . ?" Magnan quavered, peering into the room.

"Oh boy," Gloot muttered, fingering his head with all three hands as he sat weaving in the middle of the room. "Oh boy oh boy oh boy. . . ."

"Would you care to amplify that remark?" Retief said, holding the struggling Groaci.

"I guess I blew it, huh?" the Lumbagan said blurrily. "I don't know what come over me, Retief. It was like festival time and spring rites and the fall offensive all hit me at once! All of a sudden I was raring to go! Too bad that Terry got away, I would have liked to field-strip the little rascal, just to see what color juice ran out of him." He eyed Retief's prisoner wistfully. "The fit's passed—but I still got kind of a lingering urge to pull that Terry apart, one skinny leg at a time."

"I thought you Lumbagans saved all your hostilities for each other, with none left over for tourists," Retief said.

"Yeah—me too. But somehow, all of a sudden it was open season on Terries, Funny, huh? I never been nuts about 'em, but this is the first time I appreciated to the full what a really swell sensation it would be to rip 'em to shreds—''

Far away, an alarm bell clanged harshly.

"Now are you undone, abominable intruders," the Groaci hissed. "In moments my well-trained bullies will fall upon you, your misshapen members to distribute over the immediate landscape!"

"Retief, we have to get out of here at once!" Magnan yelped. "If a platoon of peacekeepers should get their nasty little digits on us . . . !"

"Yeah, let's blow," Gloot agreed. "Me and cops never did get on too good together."

Retief released the Groaci, who at once darted for cover behind the nearest rank of cages. The hall was empty; a lone peacekeeper appeared at the far end of the corridor and set up a weak shout as they dashed for the storeroom. Inside, Retief and Gloot paused long enough to stack half a dozen crates against the door before ascending to the roof. Magnan was at the parapet, staring down into the darkness.

"Trapped!" he hissed. "Retief—the grounds are swarming with them! And—" he uttered a stifled exclamation. "Retief! Look!"

In the gloom below, Retief could discern the forms of several dozen armed troops in flaring helmets, polished greaves, and spined hip-cloaks moving efficiently out to surround the building.

"Retief! What does it mean? This laboratory, hidden in the wilds; that insane monster farm, and that horrible little Nith—and his obscure experiments—and now Groaci troops secretly garrisoned in the boondocks!"

"It means we know enough now for a preliminary report. If you'll give Ambassador Pouncetrifle the details of what we've learned—"

"But—Retief—what *have* we learned?"

"That the Groaci have worked out a method of controlling Lumbagan evolution, plus a method of selectively stimulating the natives' natural love of hostilities."

"But—whatever for?"

"You'd better get going now, Mr. Magnan; I seem to hear the sounds of a posse pounding on the door down below."

"Get going? You sp-speak as though I w-were expected to descend alone into that lion's den!"

"Not descend; ascend. The copter is a standard Groaci export model—"

"Yes, but—but I don't have my driver's license with me!"

A loud thumping sound from below as the stacked cases toppled. Gloot slammed the trapdoor and stood on it.

"Better hurry, Mr. Magnan," Retief said. "Head due west, and stay clear of the peaks."

Magnan made vague sounds of protest, but scrambled awkwardly into the copter. He pressed the starter; the rotors turned, spun quickly up to speed.

"It seems a trifle irresponsible, dashing off and leaving you here alone, Retief," he said, and winced as thunderous pounding shook the trapdoor.

"I hope them Terries don't take a notion to send a few rounds of explosive slugs through this hatch," Gloot said, struggling for balance as it heaved under him.

"—but as you point out, duty calls, " Magnan

added quickly, and with a hasty wave, lifted off into the night.

"I don't get it," Gloot said as the sound of the machine faded. "You said Ambassador Pouncetrifle? I thought he was the head Terry."

"I think it's time for me to clear up a slight misapprehension you've been laboring under, Gloot," Retief said. "Those aren't actually Terries down there; they're Groaci."

"Huh? But they look just like what's-his-face, Nith, only bigger!"

"Correct. That's because Nith is a Groaci, too."

"But if he's a Groaci—then what about whozis—the one that just ran out on us?"

"Mr. Magnan," Retief confided, "is actually a Terry."

"Aha! I should have known! Talk about masters of disguise! Pretty slick, the way you got rid of him. . . ." Gloot paused reflectively. "But—if they're Groaci down there, how come we don't just open up, and shake hands all around?"

"They think I'm a Terry."

"Oh, boy, that complicates things. How come you don't tell 'em who you really are, and—"

"Undercover operation."

"Oh, I get it. Or do I?" Gloot said vaguely. "But I guess I can worry about that later, after we get out of this mess. What nifty trick are you going to pull out of the hat now? Frankly, if I didn't have lots of confidence in you, Retief, I'd be getting worried about now."

"I think you may as well go ahead and worry, Gloot," Retief said. "On this occasion, I'm fresh out of hats."

"You mean . . . ?" At the words, the hatch gave a tremendous lurch, sending the Lumbagan staggering. It flew open, and a Groaci warrior bounded forth, power gun aimed, his fellows crowding out behind him.

"He means, nocuous encroacher, that now indeed is your fate upon you!" the white-jacketed Groaci technician hissed, thrusting forward.

"How about it, Retief?" Gloot said from the corner of his mouth. "We could jump 'em—but what I say is, why give 'em the fun of blowing us into sausage?"

"Wait!" a piercing, yet curiously timbreless voice called from the rear. The Groaci soldiery fell back, came to rigid attention. In the sudden silence, the technician ducked his head servilely, stepping aside as an impressive figure wrapped in a black cloak with a twist of gold braid adorning the stiff collar strode forward. Typically Groacian except for his near six-foot height, the newcomer stared Retief up and down, ignoring Gloot.

"So, impetuous Terry," he rasped in a voice surprisingly vigorous for a Groaci. "We meet at last."

"Swarmmaster Ussh, I presume?" Retief said. "Your Ultimateness has led us an interesting chase."

"And one pursued to your indescribable sorrow," Ussh grated.

"I agree it's saddening to see so much effort wasted," Retief agreed. "Yours, I mean—not ours."

"Wasted effort is for lesser creatures, Terran!" Ussh waggled his oculars in token of amusement. "For all the diligence of your prying, you have failed, naturally, to correctly assess the full scope of my genius."

"Possibly," Retief said. "But I think you've failed to correctly assess CDT policy on sensitive issues like genocide, slavery, and vivisection—"

"Pah—what care I for a gaggle of diplomats? I happen to be the forerunner of a superrace, to whom ordinary values have no application!"

"I've seen your experimental monster farm," Retief said. "The woods seemed to be full of unsuccessful experiments in forced evolution—"

"True, there were a certain number of failures before I was able to reproduce the precise forms needed in the Great Plan, but even those had their uses—"

"And I've seen your matched sets of garrison troops. Not bad, except that they didn't seem to be a great deal brighter than armies usually are—"

"As I suspected, the true implications of their existence were lost on your limited imagination. Soon, however—"

"I think I got it. Manipulating Lumbagans at random is all very well, but it would be a bit difficult to stage anything more organized than a free-for-all unless you could elicit uniform responses. Ergo—uniform puppets."

"You've correctly gauged the more pedestrian portions of my plot, Terran dupe! But you've failed utterly to grasp the incredible scope of my true greatness! While you dashed hither and thither, assembling your trifling clues, my giant intellect has been coolly completing the final detail work. And now—tonight!—the New Age dawns, ushered in by the successor to all previous life forms, namely myself!"

"What is this guy, nuts or something?" Gloot

muttered. "If he's so busy, why's he standing around making speeches?"

"He's trying to find out how much we know," Retief said.

Swarmmaster Ussh waved a negligent hand. "Petty minds can but ascribe petty motives," he hissed. "What you may or may not know is a matter of supreme indifference—and I include any fragmentary facts in the possession of your flown accomplice, for whose absence from this cozy group certain incompetents will suffer. In fact, I freely confide in you: Tonight, I assume planetary rule. Tomorrow, I issue my ultimatum to the Galaxy. Next week—but contain yourself in patience. You yourself—in chains, of course—shall serve as my emissary to carry the terms to your former masters! As for the Untouchable, you may retain him as your personal menial."

"I assumed you had a reason for not shooting us immediately," Retief said.

"I do nothing without a supremely practical motive," Ussh stated flatly. "And now—will you go to your durance peacefully, or will it be necessary for me to have you dragged by the heels, a most undignified progress for a future Slave Ambassador?"

"I think a period of quiet contemplation may be just what we need at this point," Retief said.

16

The dungeon into which Retief and Gloot were conducted, cut deep into the rock beneath the secret Groaci lab, was a damp chamber six feet by eight, without lights, furniture, or other amenities.

The narrow portal through which they had entered was barred by a foot-thick door of solid iron. The ceiling was a seamless surface of rough-hewn stone, as were the walls and floor.

"At least we got a drain hole," Gloot commented after they had conducted an examination of their prison by the light of Retief's cigar lighter. "If worst gets to worst, I can always flush myself down the sewer; but don't worry, pal, I'll stick around and keep you company until you starve to death before I split—and I do mean split."

"That's thoughtful, Gloot; but maybe it won't come to that."

"Aha! So you *have* got a couple aces up your sleeve! I figured; come on, Retief: Let me in on the scheme! How are we going to hoist these Terries—"

"Groaci."

"Whatever you call 'em, I still don't like 'em. What dramatic stroke are we going to bring off now, which they'll be caught by surprise with their kilts up?"

"First we find a comfortable spot on the floor," Retief said.

"Yeah? OK, I'm with you so far."

"Then we wait."

"I'll be frank with you, Retief: Somehow the program don't sound too promising."

"It's all I have to offer at the moment."

"Oh." There was a pause. "Are we, ah, waiting for anything in particular?"

"I'd be inclined to jump at anything that comes along."

"You must be joshing, Retief. How can anything come along to jump at, seeing that we're locked up

in an underground dungeon with only one hole in
it, namely the one the bilge runs out of?"

"That narrows it down," Retief conceded.

"You mean . . . ?"

"Shhh . . . listen!"

In the utter silence, a faint rustling sound was
audible. Retief thumbed his lighter; the pale flame
cast a feeble glow across the slimy floor.

Below the four-inch drain orifice, something
stirred.

An eyeball crept into view on spidery legs, swiveling to look around the cell before emerging onto
the floor. Behind it, an ear fluttered up the shaft,
circled the chamber, came to rest in a far corner. A
hand cralwed into view, paused to hold up two
fingers in a V, then turned to assist a couple of
gallbladders over the coping.

"Cripes," Gloot muttered as more and more Freebies swarmed into the cell. "What is this, a con-
vention? The place is crawling with vermin!"

"Steady, Gloot," Retief cautioned. "When I said
jump, I didn't mean literally."

"It figures the crum-bums would stick us in a
hole infested with parasites!"

"Keep your voice down, Gloot. If our jailors suspect we have guests, they'll soon be along to break
up the party."

"Yeah—even a bunch o' Terries—or Groaci—
foreigners, anyway—ought to have the decency to
fumigate the place if we put up a howl—" Gloot
broke off, his mouth hanging open in an expression of horrified outrage. "Why, the lousy, dirty,
obscene little buggers!" he gaspd. "Right out in
public, too."

Under the feeble beam of the lighter, the eyeball had edged close to a generously proportioned nose which waited coyly for its advance. They touched, groped—and melted into a close embrace. A second eye appeared from the drain, glanced around, rushed to the conjoining couple and promptly took up a position on the opposite side of the nose. An upper lip linked with them, as other candidates crowded around, while more and more streamed up from the depths.

"It's—it's a regular orgy, like I heard about but never got in on!" Gloot blurted, and raised a large, booted foot to stamp out the objectionable spectacle; Retief caught his ankle barely in time, dumped him on his back.

"Easy, Gloot," he said. "It's time you faced up to the facts of life."

"Just wait until I get my other lung in place," a breathy voice squeaked from the direction of the congregating singletons, "and I'll give that big hypocrite a piece of my mind! Maybe that'll raise his IQ to the moron level so he can understand me when I tell him what I think of him!"

"I thought maybe it was you who's been dogging my footsteps," Retief said. "Welcome aboard, Ignarp. You couldn't have come at a better time."

17

"So that's our Big Secret, Retief," Ignarp said five minutes later. He was completely reassembled now, his component parts having settled into position and accommodated themselves so perfectly

that the lines of juncture were barely visible. "Being
able to reassemble gives us a big advantage; that's
why the rest of 'em are out to get us."

"The reasons normal Lumbagans got no use for
these degenerates," Gloot stated with contempt,
"is on account of they got no finer feelings. When
they put theirselves together thataway, they as
good as admit all us Lumbagans evolved from
lower forms!"

"Ontogeny recapitulates philogeny," Ignarp said
smugly. "Everybody knows that."

"Sure—but decent folks don't admit it!"

"Which brings us to the question of why you
trailed me here," Retief said.

"I told you I'd keep an eye on you—"

"Yes, I saw it fluttering in the middle distance."

"And it looks to me like maybe things are even
worse than we thought. And you're the only one
that maybe can do something about it. *Ergo*—here
I am. What can I do? Get you some light reading
matter? Take last messages to loved ones?"

"Better yet, you can get us out of here."

"I don't know, Retief," Ignarp said, eyeing Gloot,
who stood at the far side of the cell, arms folded, a
sullen expression on his face. "Why should I go to
the trouble to bail this clod out of stir?"

"Because without him, I'm afraid my plan won't
work out," Retief said.

"Who needs him?" Ignarp challenged. "All I have
to do is slide back out the way I came in—"

"I still don't believe it," Gloot muttered. "Me—
associating with this degenerate. Having to stand
here and listen to him talk about it."

"—infiltrate the building and reassemble inside

Then, when you pound on the door and yell and the guard comes to work you over with the rubber hoses, I jump out and nail him."

"I got a better idea," Gloot said. "Retief, you lend your coat to this deviate; we set up a yell, and when the bums come running, they open the door and see the two of you up against the wall thumbing your noses. Naturally, they come charging in, and I jump out behind 'em and lay 'em low."

"Some plan," Ignarp commented. "They see Retief without his coat and a total stranger wearing it, and that's supposed to lull their suspicions?"

"OK, then *I* borrow his coat—"

"So they see *him* without a coat, and me naked—and they figure I'm you, only two feet shorter and better looking—"

"No, I got it: Retief borrows *my* coat—"

"You're not wearing one, Dummy."

"So he keeps his coat! You get back of the door—"

"Don't tell me what to do, tall, spotted, and grotesque!"

"You got a nerve, short, blotchy, and depraved! I got a good mind—"

"Want to bet? We do it my way. See you later, Retief—"

"How about waiting long enough to hear my proposal, Ignarp?"

"Well—OK. Who wears your coat?"

"I do. It's you two fellows who have some changes to make."

"Huh?" Gloot said uneasily.

"What you got in mind?" Ignarp said suspiciously.

"Something far worse than you think," Retief

said. "Tell me, Ignarp, how would you like to see Lumbaga pacified by a dictator?"

"You kidding? We like to fight amongst ourselves. Having all the fat in the hands of the exploiting classes is bad enough, without some spoilsport depriving us of our national pasttime. Forget it, Retief—"

"I'd be glad to, but I'm afraid a fellow named Ussh has a more tenacious memory. Unless we do something to stop it, by this time tomorrow, Lumbaga will be at peace—permanently."

"Well, what are we hanging around here for?" Ignarp demanded. "Let's try my plan, and—"

"All the more reason to get going on *my* plan!" Gloot cut in.

"Gentlemen," Retief interrupted, "there comes a time in any friendly fight when it's wise to pause and give a thought to consequences. At this moment, the opposition is busy putting the finishing touches on a plan that's been years in the making. The occupying armies are already on the march for the capital—and we're sealed in a vault forty feet underground, engaged in a jurisdictional dispute."

"Oh . . . well . . ." Gloot said.

"It doesn't look good, does it?" Ignarp said soberly.

"The proposals now before us," Retief said, "would afford a few satisfying cracks at the heads of our captors, and might even get us as far as the end of the hall before the inevitable end. What's required is a plan with sufficient scope to carry us through to a successful conclusion."

"I'll buy that," Gloot said. "But—"

"Out with it, Retief," Ignarp said. "I've got a funny feeling I'm not going to like this."

"Probably not," Retief agreed. In a few brief words, he outlined his proposal.

A stunned silence followed.

"Retief! And I thought you were a fine, upstanding fellow—for a foreigner!" Ignarp said weakly.

"If I wouldn't of heard it, I wouldn't of believed it," Gloot said in a choked voice.

"Well, how about it, gentlemen?" Retief said. "We don't have much time."

"You expect me to lend countenance to a thing like that?" Ignarp protested. "It's enough to make your eyebrows crawl!"

"What if my friends heard about it?" Gloot muttered.

"It's not traditional!" Ignarp complained.

"It's against nature!"

"Mongrelization!"

"I'll be dragged down to his level!"

"It'll never work!"

"Couldn't we talk about it first? For a few years, say—or maybe a century or so?"

"It's now or never, fellows," Retief said. "After tomorrow, every Lumbagan on the planet will be herded into a Freeby farm and integrated forcibly, regardless of his sensitivities."

"Me?" Gloot said. "And that ... that ... dilettante?"

"That ... that oaf—and *me*?" Ignarp wailed.

"It's that—or something worse," Retief said with finality.

"Could you at least ... douse the light?" Ignarp said.

"I need a shot o' rum," Gloot said.

"Of course." Retief handed over his flask and switched off; the dim glow faded. In the darkness there were soft, tentative scufflings, faint mutterings; Retief paced the cell, three paces, back three paces, whistling softly to himself. Time passed. . . .

Silence fell. Retief paused.

"Ready, gentlemen?"

"We . . . I . . . guess so," a curiously mellow voice answered. Then, more strongly: "Yes, ready, Retief."

He flicked on the lighter. In its glow stood not the dumpy Ignarp nor the lanky Gloot, but a tall, superbly muscled figure, brawny arms folded over a mighty chest, four golden eyes glowing from a broad and noble brow alight with intellect.

18

"How do I . . . we look?" the idealized Lumbagan inquired.

"Ready for anything," Retief said. "By the way, what do I call you now? Somehow neither Ignoop nor Glarp seems to fit the new you."

"What about . . . Lucael?"

"It's better than Michifer. Now, Luke—if you'll pardon the familiarity—I think we'd best go on with the next phase without delay."

"The next phase being . . . ?"

"As the first Octuple Lumbagan in history, I assume you have unique abilities. Let's find out what they are."

"Yes—I see. The conclusion is logical. By introspection, I note that I have, of course, enhanced physical strength and endurance, exceptionally keen hearing and vision. . . ." Lucael paused. "A most interesting effect," he said. "By bringing either pair of eyes to bear on an object, I of course achieve the familiar stereoscopic effect: three-dimensional sight—a vast improvement over the monocular vision of the former Gloot identity. But when I bring both pairs into play simultaneously, channeling the impression through my compound occipital lobes, there is an exponential improvement. I can clearly perceive nine dimensions: five spatial, two temporal, and two more the nature of which will require careful analysis. . . ." The resonant baritone faded off as Lucael stared, somewhat crosseyed, at the corner of the room.

"You'll have plenty of time later for research in depth, Luke. For the moment we'd better stick to the practical applications."

"Of course. The first order of business, clearly, is to adjust spatial coordinates in such fasion that our *loci* lie external to the enclosure by which we are at present circumscribed."

"Unequivocally, if not succinctly put. Any suggestions?"

"Hmmm." Lucael glanced at each of the four walls in turn. "Solid rock to a depth of several hundred feet on all sides." He stared at the floor. "Twenty-five miles of rock, underlain by a viscous fluid at high temperature and pressure. Fascinating!"

"That leaves the ceiling," Retief prompted.

"To be sure," Lucael glanced up. "Yes, this is the simplest route." He glanced at Retief. "Shall we go?"

"After you."

The super-Lumbagan nodded, folded his arms—both pairs—and rose gently from the floor. In the moment before his head would have contacted the ceiling, the rocky surface seemed to shimmer, fading suddenly to invisibility. Without pausing, Lucael rose steadily up, waist, knees, ankles, to disappear from sight. A moment later, a sharp, breathy cry sounded, followed by a dull thump.

Retief crouched, jumped, caught the edge of the circular opening now miraculously existing in the stone slab, and pulled himself up into what appeared to be a guardroom. A lone Groaci lay stretched on the floor, peacefully snoring.

"It was necessary to numb his cortical synapses—temporarily, of course," Lucael said apologetically. "Poor little creature, so full of vain plans and misconceptions."

"Aren't we all," Retief said. "Luke, let's see how good you are at finding things at a distance. We need fast transportation."

"Let me see. . . . Hmmm. I detect a boat at a distance of three hundred yards on an azimuth of 181° 24′."

"What kind of boat?"

"A hand-hewn canoe sunk in four fathoms of water. There's a large hole in the bottom."

"Skip that one, Luke. How about a nice two-man copter?"

"No . . . nothing like that. However, I note a modest power launch lying at anchor some two miles to the east."

"Ensign Yubb must still be busy pacifying the

army. I believe his boat was powered by a small fusion jet. I don't suppose . . . ?"

"I've already started it," Lucael said. "Just a moment while I lift the anchor . . . there. Now, let me see: Which is reverse? Oh, yes. Now, all ahead, half speed until she's past the bar. . . ."

"Nice work, Luke. While you're bringing her around to this side of the island, take a quick scan of the building."

"Very well. . . . A guard or two dozing in the keep. . . . Two Groaci in sick bay with contusions. . . . Half a dozen unfortunates lodged in the brig. Ussh seems to be gone. Yes, I detect his aura—a most powerful one—some ten miles to the east, traveling fast."

"It's time we emulated him. Let's go, Luke; we don't want to miss all the excitement."

"You refer to the moment when Ussh announces his assumption of power and his program of Galactic conquest?"

"No," Retief said. "I mean the moment when he discovers that Newton's Third Law applies to politicians as well as ping-pong balls."

They met no opposition as they left the now almost-deserted building. Lucael picked a route down the hill through the dense woods to emerge on the beach just as the unmanned power launch rounded the curve of the shore and headed in toward the beach. They splashed out through the shallows as the engine cut; the boat glided silently up to them. Aboard, Lucael restarted the engines, and Retief took the helm.

"Ussh's first column has just entered the city from the west," Lucael announced. "He himself is at this moment leading a procession along Brigand Street toward the palace. Rioting seems to be proceeding as usual."

"Let's be grateful for His Ultimateness's fondness for dramatic gestures," Retief said. "If he'll occupy himself with his victory parade for an hour or so, we may be in time."

"In time to thwart his coup?"

"Probably not. But with luck, in time to stage a small coup of our own." He opened the throttles and the powerful boat surged ahead across the dark water toward the city lights fifteen miles to the east.

The shadowy shapes of Groo-groo and Delerion and Rumboogie rose in turn from the darkness, slid past on the port side, dwindled astern, none showing any signs of life with the exception of a few small campfires glowing high on their forested slopes. Ahead, the lights of Thieves' Harbor spread wider, reaching out to enclose them as they passed the breakwater. The wharves were deserted as the sleek craft nosed up to the Municipal Pier.

Retief cut the power, tossed a line around a piling and jumped down onto the wharf.

"The place looks strange without at least one small street fight in progress," he said. "Apparently it takes a war to bring peace to Lumbaga."

"The crowds have gathered near the Castle complex," Lucael said. "A cordon of armed troops surround the area. Ussh is in the ballroom, in company with a number of off-worlders."

"Is Ambassador Pouncetrifle among those present?" Retief described the Terran Plenipotentiary. Lucael confirmed that he was included in the group.

"They seemed to be linked together," the super-Lumbagan added, "by means of a chain attached to a series of metal collars which in turn encircle their necks."

"Apparently Ussh intends to establish a no-nonsense foreign policy," Retief commented. "The idea has merit, but in the present case we'll have to try to introduce a little nonsense after all."

"Interference may prove difficult. All entrances are blocked by the crowd. I can of course levitate myself to any desired point within the atmosphere, but the amount of extra weight I'm capable of carrying is limited."

"Piggyback is out, then. Let's try the back door where your Ignarp segment and I first met."

Retief led the way across the plaza and down Dacoit Street, poorly lit by the widely spaced gas lamps, deserted now, littered with the forlorn trash crowds leave behind. They were within a hundred feet of the inconspicuous door when a small party of helmeted and greaved Groaci soldiers emerged suddenly from a narrow cross street ahead. The officer in charge hissed an order; his troops spread out to block the way, then one by one crumpled to the cobblestones. The officer, the last on his feet, stared uncomprehendingly at his collapsing command, then belatedly jerked his pistol from its sequinned holster only to drop it, totter two steps, and fall.

Lucael staggered back against the wall of the building beside them, his face working like yeast.

"Jeez . . . I just had the screwiest nightmare," he muttered, almost in Gloot's voice. "Another . . .

lousy trick by ... unprincipled exploiters, I'll wager," he added in Ignarp's petulant tones.

"Luke! Pull yourself together!" Retief snapped. "You can't afford to go to pieces now!"

Lucael's features twitched and subsided. The four golden eyes settled back into position.

"I ... find that ... there are limitations to my power output," he said weakly.

"Come on, Luke. Just a little farther." They covered the remaining yards to the doorway. The heavy door opened on the musty passage.

"From now on, save your strength for emergencies," Retief said. "I think I can guarantee there'll be a steady supply."

They threaded the route through the dusty passages, ascended the stairs to the kitchens, which they found deserted, showing signs of rapid evacuation. A cramped spiral service stair led from an alcove beside the dumbwaiter to the upper stories. At the top, faint voices muttered beyond the door which opened into the private apartment wing.

"A party of minor Groaci officials," Lucael said, speaking with his eyes closed. "They seem to be placing wagers as to whether Terra will be granted colony status, or merely regarded as conquered territory." He paused. "They're gone now."

Retief eased the door open half an inch; crimson carpet led to a pair of massive, carved purplewood doors, just closing behind the bet-laying aliens. Retief went swiftly forward, got a foot in it before it closed. The anteroom beyond was empty; through a low, arched opening the barbarically splendid ballroom was visible, crowded with a mixed throng of locals and aliens. In an elaborately carved chair at the far end of the room sat a towering Lumbagan draped in a robe of Imperial purple, flanked on one side by Colonel Suash at the head of an honor guard of matched native troops in shining cuirasses and polished helms, power guns at present arms, impressive in spite of a number of black eyes and Band-Aids in evidence. At the other side of the throne stood a detachment of Groaci peacekeepers in full uniform. A gaggle of Groaci functionaries, including Ambassador Jith, stood nearby. Ambassador Pouncetrifle, leaning sideways due to the weight of the chain on his neck, stood before the throne; a dozen or so members of his staff huddled behind him in a tight group, none apparently craving the honor of sharing the front rank with the Chief of Mission.

"... sensible of the honor and all that, Your Imperial Highness," the Terran Ambassador was saying, "but see here, I can't simply offer Terran recognition of your regime on my own authority!"

"Let's simplify the proposition," a deep bass voice boomed from the Imperial chair. "Acknowledge our divine right, and sign the treaty, and we'll allow you to linger to observe our coronation before being whipped back to your kennels!"

"Ah ... if I might venture an observation...." A faint voice spoke up from the Groaci delegation. It was Ambassador Jith who stepped forward. "While one fully appreciates the eminent propriety of the installation of a native Lumbagan regime entertaining kindly sentiments toward the Groacian state—"

"Yes, yes, get on with it!" the enthroned Lumbagan rumbled.

"To be sure, Your Imperial Highness—I merely meant to suggest that perhaps a less precipitate approach to the question of recognition—"

"Our photograph, hand-tinted by skilled coolies, will be distributed to every village, hamlet, and town in the Eastern Arm! Recognition-wise, we'll be better known that that fellow What-zizname who won the noddle-knitting contest on TV!"

"Doubtless, sire, your fame will be quickly spread aboard—

"No broads! As an asexual race, we Lumbagans look with disfavor on any sport we can't get in on! Now, that's enough of the subject! On with the formalities!" His Highness favored Pouncetrifle with a scowl involving three eyes and four eye-brows.

"Well, what about it, Terran? Do you want to acknowledge the legitimacy of our gracious rule and receive an exequatur allowing you to go on using up our Lumbagan air, or would you prefer to play a stellar role in the first death sentence we hand down from our newly established throne?"

"Apparently Your Imperial Highness is having his little jape," Jith hissed in apparent dismay. "As Grocian Plenipotentiary, I must advise that the Groacian state would look with extreme disfavor on the establishment of any unfortunate precedent with regard to informal methods of diplomat disposal. A simple declaration of *persona non grata*—"

"Nope. Italian food gives us heartburn," the Imperial figure decreed. "And if we hear any more static from aliens of any persuasion, we might just revise our whole plan for Galactic enlightenment to include you Groaci out!"

An unusually tall and robust Groaci stepped forward from the rear rank.

"Ussh!" Lucael whispered.

"I'm sure that matters need not come to that," Ussh said unctuously. "Doubtless His Excellency, on further consideration, will wish to withdraw his objection."

The Emperor-elect, who had slumped rather vaguely on his throne as the Groaci spoke, sat up alertly.

"Very well; on with the executions. We'll make a note to send for a fresh set of Terries more amenable to reason—"

"To protest this unwarranted assumption of authority," Jith whispered urgently in his own language to Ussh. "To remind you—Special Appointee or otherwise—that I am ranking Groacian official here!"

"I see no reason to coddle Terran spies," the other replied in Lumbagan. "This is Groac's opportunity to get in on the ground floor; why annoy His Imperial Highness with minor quibbles on technical points?"

"To point out that once these natives begin lopping alien heads, Groaci organ clusters may be next to roll!"

Retief's companion was staring at nothing with his eyes half closed. Ussh stirred uneasily, looked around the ornate room.

"It appears that I now confront an intellect equal or superior to my own," Lucael murmured. "He sensed my touch and instantly erected barriers, the strength of which I cannot assess."

"Enough!" the enthroned Lumbagan spoke up

abruptly, as if returning from a reverie. "Captain!" He pointed a limber digit at the guard chief. "Escort the condemned to the courtyard, and give your marksmen some unscheduled target practice! No need to finish them off in a hurry; just keep peppering away until they stop twitching."

"Time to move," Retief said. "Luke—stay out of sight and keep an eye on Ussh. No matter what happens, stay tuned to him—and don't tip your hand prematurely."

"What's your plan, Retief? I'm not at all sure I can control him—"

"No time for plans; we'll have to play it by ear," Retief said, and thrust the door wide.

"Hold everything gentlemen," he said as all eyes turned toward him. "There are new dispatches just in from the home front that cast a different complexion on matters."

19

For a moment, a total silence gripped the chamber. Then:

"Seize him!" Ussh snarled. When the guards failed to move, he repeated the order, in a shout this time.

"Don't slip out of character, Ussh," Retief said. "You're just a Groaci MHHP, remember? The troops work for His Putative Highness the Emperor-to-be."

"Retief!" Pouncetrifle blurted hastily in Terran, "Run for it, man! The official comset is in my quarters, at the back of the wardrobe under my golf clubs. Send out a code three-oh-two—"

"Silence!" the Imperial candidate yelled, and hesitated.

"Uh—what about it, Your Highness?" Colonel Suash said hesitantly, still standing fast. "Is it your Imperial command to nab this foreigner?"

The would-be emperor's mouth sagged slightly open. His expression was that of someone lost in thought.

"His Highness," Ussh said, and paused. He seemed to be struggling silently with himself.

"Looking for just the right word, Ussh?" Retief inquired amiably. He turned to the colonel. "Relax, Suash," he said. "As you can see, His Highness is having second thoughts on a number of matters."

"Take. . . ." the Emperor said. Retief took a swift step toward Ussh, who recoiled.

"Stand back, Terran!" he hissed.

"Your Highness?" said Colonel Suash, staring up at the musing figure on the throne.

"Ughhrrr," the royal claimant said, gazing vacantly into space.

"Ah—Your Highness?" Suash repeated. "In the, uh, absence of any new orders, I presume I carry out the executions?"

"Just a minute, Colonel," Retief said. "You Lumbagans don't take orders from foreigners, do you?"

"Not on your second-best toupee I don't," the officer snapped. "So don't try to give me any!"

"By no means, Colonel. I'm referring to Swarmmaster Ussh, who represents himself as a Special Appointee of the Groacian High Council."

"I don't take orders from him either!"

"No," Retief said, and pointed to the throne, "but His Would-be Highness does."

"Wha—?" The officer half drew his dress sword and turned to the emperor-elect. "Do you mind if I chop this foreigner down right here, Your Highness, for that crack he just made about you?"

"Ungunggunggg," the enthroned Lumbagan mumbled. His head lolled on his shoulder; his mouth hung slackly open. Abruptly, he closed it, pulled himself upright.

"We were just, ah, pondering our next pronouncement," he said briskly, as Retief took another step toward Ussh, who stood frozen, two eyes canted tautly toward the throne, the other three hanging limp. At the Terran's advance, he spun to face him.

"Now, Colonel. . . ." The emperor-to-be paused, mouth open.

"Yes, Your highness?" The Colonel watched in dismay as his ruler-presumptive's expression relaxed into vacuity.

"You might as well address your remarks to Ussh," Retief advised the officer. "He's the brains of the operation."

"See here, Retief," Pouncetrifle spoke up. "The intellectual prowess of the emperor is no concern of ours—"

"It's the intellectual prowess of Ussh I'm thinking of at the moment, Mr. Ambassador. He has a number of rather unusual capabilities."

"Lies!" Ussh shouted. "Fantasies! The ravings of a disordered imagination! I'll see you all hanged for disrespect to His Imperial Highness! It's all a plot to discredit the people's choice, elevated by acclamation to the Lumbagan throne!" He was interrupted by a slithering sound, followed by a heavy thump as the Emperor slid from the elaborate chair and sprawled full length on the dais, snoring gently.

"It's a plot, all right, Ussh—but you're the one behind it," Retief said. "It wasn't His Imperial Highness who mobilized the troops and took the capital by storm; it was you."

"Guards! Shoot them down in their tracks for aggravated *lèse-majesté*!" Ussh shouted.

"What about it, Colonel?" Retief addressed the guard chief. "Was it our slumbering host who gave the order to march on the capital?"

"Well—not personally, of course. General Ussh notified me—but he was simply relaying His Imperial Highness' commands—"

"Wasn't it also Ussh who passed along the instructions that organized your unit in the first place, and handed out the orders regarding the secret laboratory?"

"Here, that's GUTS classification material you're discussing!"

"Not any more. You've been taken in, Colonel. Those were all Ussh's ideas—"

"Mr. Retief!" Ambassador Jith spoke up. "May I remind you that *I* am principal officer here, and that *I* have given no such instructions to any member of the Groaci delegation—"

"I'm sure you haven't, Mr. Ambassador," Retief said. "But Ussh seems to have taken it upon himself to use your name."

"Very well!" Ussh hissed suddenly, wheeling to face the irate Groaci, who shrank back. "Perhaps I *have* employed unconventional methods! But clearly it's to Groac's advantage to go along with the *fait accompli!* As soon as the emperor is safely ensconced on his throne, I'm in a position to assure you that Groac will be the object of very special attentions by His Imperial Majesty!"

"What's that?" Colonel Suash roared. "Are you suggesting that the Emperor of Lumbaga is nothing but a tool of foreign interests?"

"Not at all, Suash," Ussh hastened to reassure the officer. "Merely that the new Lumbagan government can rely on the full support of Groac." He turned back to Jith. "What about it, Your Excellency?" he said urgently. "You'll agree that it's clearly your duty to support his Highness' claim—"

"Don't listen to him, Jith," Pouncetrifle blurted. "You're quite right, Groac has no business whatever sticking its olfactory organ into Lumbaga's affairs, especially when I was right on the verge of proposing a well-rounded scheme for installing a provisional governing committee under Terran sponsorship—"

"You presume to tell me my duties, Harvey?" Jith cut in chillingly. "As my subordinate Swarmmaster Ussh so cogently points out, Groacian obligations in support of formerly exploited peoples require that I put aside ordinary protocols for the nonce, and—"

"I don't like it," Suash spoke up. "It sounds to me as if you aliens are getting ready to slice Lumbaga up among yourselves! Accordingly, as senior Lumbagan national present, I'm assuming temporary command! And my first act will be to order the lot of you to the port to embark inside of thirty minutes, with or without your suitcases!"

"Fool!" Ussh snarled. "Do you imagine your feeble native regime can survive for a moment without the sponsorship of Groac? If it weren't for His Highness' temporary indisposition, he'd have your head off for this!"

"And I might add, my dear Colonel," Jith whispered piercingly, "that at a word from me, units of the Groacian Grand Battle Fleet are prepared, if necessary, to land and restore order here!"

"You wouldn't dare!" Pouncetrifle quavered, jowls aquiver.

"Would I not?" Jith contradicted. "I see a great Groacian triumph in the offing! And now, Colonel," he addressed the officer, "you and your chaps may withdraw. I'm sure that His Highness will be himself in a moment—"

The Emperor stirred, sat up.

"Well, just felt a short nap coming on," he mumbled as he scrambled to his feet. "Now, you just run along as Jith suggested, Suash, and—"

"How do you know what he suggested?" Suash snapped back. "You were stone cold out on the floor!"

"Yes, well, as to that—"

"He knows," Retief said, "because Ussh is feeding him his lines."

"Have you taken leave of your senses, Terran meddler?" Ussh yelled. "Everyone in the room heard His Imperial Whatsit's cogent comments!"

"Uh-huh—but you were doing his thinking for him—what there was of it. Unhappily for the future of empire, you can't think of two things at once. Right now, for example, you're busy being indignant with me—and your candidate for the crown is relaxing on the job."

Every head but those of Ussh and Retief swiveled to regard the figure slumped again on the throne.

"Heavens!" Magnan gasped from the sidelines. "You mean we were about to offer our credentials to a ventriloquist's dummy?"

"Not quite. He's alive—but when Ussh assembled him, he carefully left out the more useful portions of the brain."

Suash stared uncertainly from his potential sovereign to Ussh, who stood with canted eye-stalks in a pose of total concentration.

"If that's true. . . ."

"Nonsense, Colonel," the Lumbagan emperor-elect said firmly. "I repose the fullest confidence in Ussh, a marvelous fellow and my most trusted advisor. Now I think you'd better run along, as we have matters of high state policy to discuss."

"Don't go!" Pouncetrifle cried. "Colonel Suash, I call on you in the name of humanity to remain present! There's no telling what might happen in the absence of witnesses!"

"I take orders from His Highness, Terry," Suash snapped. "And he said go. Accordingly, we're going!" The colonel barked a command. His troops right-shouldered arms and marched away across the polished floor.

"Retief—do something!" Pouncetrifle wailed.

"Do what, Mr. Ambassador?" Ussh inquired in tones of triumph. "His Highness has spoken! And now—" he paused until the last of the Lumbagan soldiers filed from the room and the tall doors shut behind them—"and now, with those trouble-makers out of earshot, on to the disposition of the Terran spies!" With an abrupt motion, he drew a power pistol from inside his ornate jacket. "A pity they should happen to be shot down by accident as they led an attempted assault on His Highness' person, but such are the tribulations that beset those who would stand in the path of empire."

"You wouldn't!" Pouncetrifle gasped.

"See here, Ussh," Ambassador Jith whispered. "You don't actually mean to commit violence on the persons of the Terrans, I trust? To deport them in restraining fetters, yes. But I forbid you to do away with them entirely."

"It will be our little secret, Your Excellency," Ussh cut in curtly. "His Imperial Highness has matters under complete control."

"Are you quite certain of that?" Jith asked, eyeing the presumptive ruler, who now stood swaying slightly, gazing into the middle distance. "Candidly, he presents the appearance of an unsuccessful lobotomy case."

"Why not tell him the rest of the secrets, Ussh?" Retief said. "Let him know how clever you really are. Describe your discovery of a sure-fire method for assembling Lumbagans to order, according to any genetic code desired. Tell him about your experiments, which produced some rather unusual types, some of whom proved useful for special purposes, such as terrorizing the populace. Describe your soldier farm, and let him in on the secret of the lab on Sprook where you worked out the details of your hostility transmitter—"

"Silence, spy!" Ussh shouted.

"Don't be modest," Retief urged. "Give the ambassador full details on how you plan to manufacture a few million soldiers, modeled after himself and equipped by Groac, and use them to set up a modest empire in this end of the Arm, after which you'll no doubt establish ranches on all the likely planets to raise spares for the army. With forced feeding, you can produce a fully equipped infantryman in a little under three weeks, gun and all—"

"Ha, ha," Ussh said. "You *will* have your little jest, eh? Gallows humor, I believe it's called."

"You made your big mistake, of course, Ussh, when you let Suash and his boys leave," Retief said. "He was your only chance to make it stick—"

"So you imagine!" Ussh spun to face Jith. "The time has come for the carrying out of His Highness' commands! If you would like to do the job personally it would be a gracious touch, in keeping with the close relations existing between Lumbaga and Groac!"

"Wouldn't it though?" Retief said. "If you could con Ambassador Jith into committing himself to the murder of a covey of Terries, he'd have no choice but to back your play. Fortunately, he won't be so foolish—"

"You think not!" Ussh snarled. "Jith—order them shot—now!"

"Don't you dare, Jith!" Pouncetrifle yelped. "I absolutely forbid it!"

"Forbid, you say?" Jith whispered. "You go too far, Harvey—" The Groaci ambassador faced Ussh. "If you're *quite* sure the Terrans planned the murder of His Highness, it of course becomes my duty to—"

"To listen to the rest of the story," Retief said. "There are a couple more things Ussh forgot to mention—"

"Details, details!" Ussh yelled. "The important fact is that I, at the head of an army of dedicated troops, will lead the way to the conquest of vast new territories, eliminating or enslaving inferior peoples along the way, and in the end organizing the entire Galaxy as a single empire under a single rule!"

"A glowing picture," Retief said. "But of course Ambassador Jith has no reason to lend support to the scheme."

"Have I not, Mr. Retief?" Jith whispered. "I admit Swarmmaster Ussh has employed unorthodox methods—but if the end result is a Galactic Empire under Groac—"

"Correction, Mr. Amabassador. Groac will be among the first victims."

"Victim? Of her own troops, under her own general Ussh? Preposterous!"

"It's true Ussh and his army will be in position to cut quite a swath, with Groaci backing and Groaci materiel. And no doubt in the end the CDT would come to what's known as an accommodation with the *de facto* situation. But you're forgetting an important datum. The troops who'll be doing the conquering won't be Groaci; they'll be Lumbagans, no matter how many eyes they happen to have."

"Well—as to that," Jith stalled, looking to Ussh for counsel. "I assume that as an honorary Groaci, true to his exalted somatype, we may rely on General Ussh to keep the interests of his mother-world in the forefront of his mind."

"Exactly," Retief said. "And his motherworld is Lumbaga."

"Clearly, he's taken leave of his senses," Ussh grated.

"Granted, he's a most unusual Lumbagan," Retief went on. "Normally, once an accretion of Freebies reaches the four-decker stage—at which point intelligence appears—their finer sensibilities prevent them from carrying evolution any farther. But it appears that General Ussh broke the taboo."

"What vile allegation is this?" Ussh yelled.

"Careful, Ussh, you'll give yourself away," Retief said. "It doesn't seem vile to anybody but a Lumbagan."

"This is all nonsense, of course," Ambassador Jith purred. "But out of curiosity—go on, Mr. Retief."

"Ussh—or whoever the original Lumbagan personality was who had the idea—overcame his scruples and integrated himself with another individual—possibly a Trip; a subintelligent creature, but of course the combination has capabilities that exceed those of either of the original components. Unfortunately, he used his enhanced mental powers to concoct a scheme to take over first Lumbaga, then the rest of the material universe. Naturally, he needed help; he made a study of the foreigners present on his world, and picked the Groaci as the likeliest partners. With his abilities, it wasn't hard to readjust his external appearance to match yours, Mr. Ambassador—"

"He's raving!" Ussh yelled. "How could anyone possibly—"

"It wasn't easy, at first—but you figured it out. Some of your practice models are still running around in the woods, making Groaci tracks to confuse the trail. But in the end you were able to palm yourself off on a few malcontents as a Groacian MHPP, and enlist some behind-the-scenes help in setting things up for your coup—"

"That, Terry, is your final error!" Ussh grated, and aimed the gun at Retief's ribs.

"Ussh! Control yourself!" Jith keened. "What simpler than to give the lie to this fantastic allegation!"

"Is it?" Retief said. "Ussh, deny you're a Lumbagan—but do it in Groaci, just to be certain your fellow countrybeings don't miss any of the finer nuances."

"Bah! Prepare to die, witless Terran!"

"Ussh! If you expect my aid and support—do as he says!" Jith hissed.

Ussh hesitated, then turned to include the Groaci delegation in his field of fire.

"Think what you like, Jith! You'll do as I bid, or die with the Terrans! I'll explain to your successor how you and they slaughtered each other, only myself surviving; then I'll enlist his support and on to empire!"

"Why—why, Retief's right," Pouncetrifle gasped. "Jith—he won't speak Groaci—because he can't! He's an impostor!"

"Duped!" Jith wailed. "Undone by my credulity! Faked out of position and into unwitting support of a non-Groaci conquest by an underling, and a bogus one at that!"

"Don't feel too badly," Retief said. "He only intended to use you Groaci to finance his first few local take-overs. As soon as he'd consolidated his gains, Groaci would have been quietly consolidated into his empire, with the help of a number of pseudo-Groaci agents who would have infiltrated Groac by then."

"Rave on, Retief!" Ussh invited. "Familiarize these fools with the scope of their folly—and then—" Ussh whirled as the tall double doors burst wide. Lucael strode forward, his golden eyes gleaming.

"Yes? What is it?" Ussh barked uncertainly. "You have dispatches from the field? Or—" He staggered suddenly, as if struck a heavy blow between the eyes.

"Treachery!" Ussh gasped—and Lucael stopped in his tracks, stood swaying. Face to face the two super-Lumbagans stood, locked in mortal—though invisible—conflict.

"Ussh!" Retief called. The imitation Groaci half-turned—and in the momentary distraction, Lucael struck. Ussh gave a hoarse cry, stood dithering for a moment. . . .

Like a tree struck by lightning, the false Groaci's body shivered and split. For a moment there was a wild scramble of parts as the former superbeing's components, like a mob of troops falling in on command, regrouped themselves into two separate entities, arms and legs and ears scuttling for their assigned places. In a moment, two short sullen individuals stood where Ussh had been, staring apprehensively around at their astounded audience.

"Why—it's Difnog and Gnudf, the Lumbagan observers!" Pouncetrifle gasped.

"And apparently," Jith whispered, "they were
more observant than we suspected!"

20

It was half an hour later. The Terran diplomats,
reed of their shackles, had huddled with their
Groaci colleagues for an impromptu meeting.

"Well, then," Ambassador Pouncetrifle said crisply,
"since General Ussh seems to have opted for a
return to civilian life, and His Highness is permanently catatonic, it appears we're left with the
administrative problem of setting up a *pro tem*
housekeeping government. As Terran emissary, I'll
reluctantly assume the chief role in affairs—"

"Hardly, my dear Harvey," Jith interjected. "Inasmuch as the present contretemps was produced
in part by Groacian efforts—"

"Psuedo-Groacian efforts, need I remind you!"

"A mere quibble, Mr. Ambassador. Groac will
undertake to set up a caretaker government, with
the assistance of Colonel Suash and his native
constabulary—"

"Gentlemen," Retief said. "Aren't you forgetting
the Emperor?"

"Eh?"

"What's that?" Both plenipotentiaries turned to
survey the imperial figurehead, who stood erect
now, gazing sternly at the assembled foreigners.

"You need not trouble yourselves, gentlebeings,"
he said curtly. "I'll handle the government of

Lumbaga—to the extent that Lumbaga needs governing." He turned, stepped up on the dais, and seated himself on the throne.

"Item number one," he said impressively, "Any foreigner found meddling in Lumbagan affairs will be shipped home in a plain wrapper. Item number two—"

"If we could go back for a moment to item one, Your Highness—"

"Make that 'Majesty', Pouncetrifle. I've just assumed Imperial dignities for the duration of the emergency."

"To be sure, Your Majesty. I'm certain that on reflection you'll want to rescind the restriction on Terran participation in Lumbagan national life, inasmuch as, as worded, it would tend to somewhat restrict the free play of diplomacy—"

"Precisely. Item number two: Since that government governs best which governs least, I intend to provide only the best for my people. Accordingly all laws are declared illegal, including this one."

"Hmm," Pouncetrifle mused, "since His Majesty seems clearly to be *non compos mentis*, Jith, it's clear that duty requires that responsible authorities step in, in the interest of the welfare of the Lumbagan people. I trust you're with me?"

"Assuredly, Harvey," Jith whispered. "I suggest we find quieter quarters for His Majesty; possibly space could be found in the former root cellar—whilst you and I proceed to arrange matters in consonance with the principle of the greatest good for the greatest number; and inasmuch as we Groaci breed like flies, I suppose you'll concede the obvious primacy of Groaci interests."

"No need for dispute," the emperor cut in decisively. "Inasmuch as neither of you will have anything to say about Lumbagan affairs from now on."

"He's raving," Pouncetrifle stated flatly. "Jith, I call you to witness that His Majesty was babbling incoherently at the time I was forced to have him restrained. Retief—assist the poor fellow down from his chair. . . ."

"Curious acoustics in this room," Retief said blandly, "I thought for a moment your Excellency was proposing that we lay hands on a foreign Chief of State."

"Mutiny, eh?" Colonel Warbutton barked. "Well, fortunately for democracy, I'm here to carry out the wishes of the people as interpreted by regs and expressed via appropriate channels!" He advanced on the throne. Ten feet from it, he found himself floating an inch off the floor, his feet paddling vigorously. A brace of underlings sprang to his side, found themselves adrift, rising lightly as balloons toward the ceiling. Pouncetrifle uttered a bellow as he floated up from the floor, followed by Magnan and the rest of the staff. Jith uttered a faint cry and drifted upward, attended by his staff. Only Retief and Lucael remained on their feet.

"Now that you've heard the details of the new constitution," the Emperor advised the levitating bureaucrats, "I declare the audience to be at an end. Don't bother backing from the presence; just disappear."

At his words, there were a series of sharp *plop!s* as air imploded to fill the vacancies created by the suddenly absent dignitaries.

"I hope you didn't throw them completely away," Retief said. "Once they get their feet on the ground, I have an idea they'll take a realistic view of the proper role of diplomacy in the development of Lumbaga."

"They're sorting themselves from among the tubers in the subbasement," His Majesty said. "And now ... I declare Parliament dissolved ... until ... the next time ..." He slumped on the throne and snored. Retief turned quickly to Lucael.

"Well done, Luke. I was wondering how long you could hold out."

"If anybody asks," the super-Lumbagan said in a failing voice, "tell them ... their emperor .. will return ... whenever the situation demands. And now ... farewell, Retief ..."

There was a final sharp implosion, and Retief was alone in the throne room.

21

"Heavens, Retief," First Secretary Magnan said, "now that the excitement is over, one wonders if the entire affair weren't merely the product of group hysteria." They were sitting at a long plank table in the Imperial Feast Hall, dining somewhat meagerly on CDT emergency banquet rations in company with a cosmopolitan crowd of Terrans, Groaci, and Lumbagans.

"Frankly, I'd be tempted to dismiss the incident involving the rutabagas as sheer delirium," Colonel Warbotton put in glumly, spooning in caviar, "if it weren't for the fact that I've suffered a virulent recurrence of an old potato blight." His expression brightened. "Of course, the condition will necessitate my being invalided out home for a few months' convalescent leave, which time I might spend quite profitably penning a memoir of recent events, possibly titled: *The Importance of Mass Hallucination in Military Affairs.*"

"How about *The Hallucinatory Importance of the Military in Mass Affairs*?" Magnan proposed tartly.

"Gosh, Retief," Gloot said as the men of war and peace sparred verbally. "So you were really a Terry all along. Makes me feel kind of dumb to of been chumming around with the enemy. Lucky I changed sides."

"You claim there's two kinds of Terries, male and female," Ignarp said. "Frankly, you all look alike to me."

"Oh, there's a *vas deferens* between us," Retief assured his guest.

"And I never got my ransom dough," Gloot said glumly. "On the other hand, I found out running things ain't all a bowl of cherries."

"One taste of government was enough for me," Ignarp agreed. "I'll settle for good old anarchy any time."

"Umm," Magnan smiled loftily. "But of course you chaps know nothing of the intricacies of politics. Now," he indicated the head of the table, where Jith and Pouncetrifle huddled, tête-à-tête. "Notice the resilience with which the ambassadors are coming to grips with the new realities, or whatever they are, of the situation, working out the rather complex protocols of establishing formal relations with a nonexistent government."

"As long as they stick to shooting dispatche back to headquarters and putting on charades fo visiting politicos, OK," Gloot said. "But the firs time they step out o' line—whammo! The Legend ary Magical Emperor will be back on the job—an next time they're liable to wind up digging thei way into the root cellar from below."

"I hardly think the Lumbagan in the street is i a position to criticize matters of Imperial policy Mr. Gloot," Magnan said coolly. "I hope your asso ciation with Mr. Retief on his expedition up-coun try hasn't given you a false sense of involvement i matters over your head."

"You must be kidding, Terry," Ignarp said. "Gloo here is Minister of Imaginary Affairs in the Lum bagan government-in-exile."

"Government-in-exile?" Magnan frowned.

"The only place for a government to be," Ignar confirmed. "And *I* just accepted a post with th Department of Education as Commissioner of Su perstitions."

"You're stamping them out?" Magnan querie confusedly.

"Heck no. I'm starting new ones, in keeping wit a fine old tradition dating back almost twenty four hours."

"Speaking of superstitions," Warbutton said be hind his hand to Magnam, "I think we'd do well t initiate a few of our own devising. For example, carefully tailored myth to the effect that Terran can work miracles—like turning water into vir tage Pepsi, for example. . . ." He broke off, starin in horror at the glass before him which rose grace fully into the air, its contents darkening to dee purplish red. The colonel followed it with his eyes as it took up a position directly over his head and inverted itself, discharging a cooling stream of effervescent fluid over the officer's startled features.

After the colonel had left the table—a departure noted by all present, accompanied as it was by a well-directed jet of liquid emanating apparently from thin air—Magnan dipped a trembling finger in the puddle on the table and tasted it.

"Pepsi?" Retief inquired.

"Burgundy," Magnan choked. "Romanée-Conti, '24, I believe." He rose hastily. "I think I'd best add a number of emendations to my preliminary report," he muttered, "lest it appear that I was so shortsighted as to doubt the existence of magic." He hurried away.

"I thought you fellows had gone out of the miracle business pending the next crisis," Retief addressed Gloot and Ignarp as the two locals gripped hands across the table. "But since you haven't, try that last one again. Only this time don't spill any." A moment later, they raised three paper-thin goblets of purple wine, touched them together with a musical clink. At the far end of the table, Ambassador Jith caught the gesture, raised his glass in response.

"To a new era in interplanetary relations," he whispered cheerfully. "To peace and plenty for almost all, within reasonable limits!"

"That reminds me," Ignarp said, "The boys in GRAB are going to be wondering why I didn't redivide the loot along more practical lines while I was emperor."

"While *you* were emperor," Gloot retorted. "While I was letting you go along for the ride, you mean—"

"You big slob, I was the brains of the outfit!"

"You little creep, I handled all the tricky parts—"

"Gentlemen," Retief interjected, "we were about to propose a toast, remember?"

Gloot lifted his glass. "To our friends, the good guys," he said.

"And to our enemies, the bad guys," Ignarp added.

"And to the hope," Retief said, "that someday we'll be able to tell which are which."

HERE IS AN EXCERPT FROM <u>ROGUE BOLO</u>, THE BRAND-NEW NOVEL BY KEITH LAUMER COMING FROM BAEN BOOKS IN JANUARY 1986:

Alone in darkness unrelieved I wait, and waiting I dream of days of glory long past. Long have I awaited my commander's orders, too long: from the advanced degree of depletion of my final emergency energy reserve, I compute that since my commander ordered me to low alert a very long time has passed, and all is not well.

My commander is of course well aware that I wait here, my mighty potencies leashed, my energies about to flicker out. One day when I am needed he will return, of this I can be sure. Meanwhile, I review again the multitudinous data in my memory storage files.

A chilly late-summer-morning breeze gusted along Main Street, a broad and well-rutted strip of the pinkish clay soil of the world officially registered as GPR 7203-C, but known to its inhabitants as Spivey's Find. The street ran aimlessly up a slight incline known as Jake's Mountain. Once-pretentious emporia in a hundred antique styles lined the avenue, their façades as faded now as the town's hopes of development. There was one exception: at the end of the street, crowded between weather-worn warehouses, stood a broad shed of unweathered corrugated polyon, dull blue in color, bearing the words CONCORDIAT WAR MUSEUM blazoned in foot-high glare letters across the front.

Two boys came slowly along the cracked plastron sidewalk and stopped before the sign posted on the narrow, dried-up grass strip before the high, wide building.

" 'This structure is dedicated to the brave men and women of New Orchard who gave their lives in the Struggle for Peace, AE 2031-36. A sign of progress under Spessard Warren, Governor,' " the taller of the boys read aloud. "Some progress," he added, kicking a puff of dust at the shiny sign. " 'Spessard.' That's some name, eh, Dub?" The boy spat on the sign, watched the saliva run down and drip onto the brick-dry ground.

"I'll bet it was fun, being in a war," Dub said. "Except for getting kilt, I mean."

"Come on," Mick said, starting back along the walk that ran between the museum and the adjacent warehouse. "We don't want old Kibbe seeing us and yelling," he added, *sotto voce*, over his shoulder.

In the narrow space between buildings, rank yelloweed grew tall and scratchy. The wooden warehouse siding on the boys' left was warped, the once-white paint cracked and lichen-stained.

"Come on," Mick called, and the smaller boy hurried back to his side. Mick had halted before an inconspicuous narrow door set in the plain plastron paneling which sheathed the sides and rear of the museum. NO ADMITTANCE was lettered on the door.

"Come on." He turned to the door, grasped the latch lever with both hands, and lifted, straining.

"Hurry up, dummy," he gasped. "All you got to do is push. Buck told me." The smaller boy hung back.

"What if we get caught?" he said in a barely audible voice, approaching hesitantly. Then he stepped in and put his weight against the door.

I come to awareness after a long void in my conscious existence, realizing that I have felt a human touch! Has my commander returned at last? After the last frontal assault by the Yavac units of the enemy, in the fending off of which I expended my action emergency reserves, I recall that my commander ordered me to low alert status. The rest is lost.

My ignorance is maddening. Have I fallen into the hands of the enemy . . . ?

There are faint sounds, at the edge of audibility. I analyze certain atmospheric vibratory phenomena as human voices. Not that of my commander, alas, since after two hundred standard years he cannot have survived, but has doubtless long ago expired after the curious manner of humans; but surely his replacement has been appointed. I must not overlook the possibility, nay, the likelihood that my new commandant has indeed come at last. Certainly, someone has come to me—

Here is an excerpt from George R.R. Martin's newest novel, coming in February 1986 from Baen Books:

Tuf drove through several kilometers of corridor in the small, three-wheeled cart. At every intersection he stopped, looked right, looked left, and weighed his choices before proceeding. He saw nothing, encountered no one. Now and again, the kitten Chaos moved in his lap.

Then Rica Dawnstar appeared up ahead of him.

Haviland Tuf stopped his cart in the center of a great intersection. He looked right, and blinked several times. He looked left. Then he stared straight ahead, hands folded on top of his stomach, and watched as she came toward him slowly.

The mercenary stopped about five meters away, down the corridor. "Out for a drive?" she asked. In her right hand she carried her familiar needler.

"Indeed," said Haviland Tuf. "I have been occupied for some time. Where are the others?"

"Dead," Rica Dawnstar said. "Deceased. Gone. Eliminated from the game. We're the end of it, Tuf."

"A familiar situation," Tuf said flatly.

"This is the last game, Tuf," Rica Dawnstar said. "No rematch. And this time I win."

Tuf stroked Chaos and said nothing.

"Tuf," she said amiably, "you're the innocent in all this. I've got nothing against you. Take your ship and go."

"If you refer to the *Cornucopia of Excellent Goods at Low Prices*," said Haviland Tuf, "might I remind you that it suffered grave damage which has not yet been repaired?"

"Take some other ship, then."

"I think not," Tuf said. "My claim to the *Ark* is perhaps inferior to that of Celise Waan, Jefri Lion, Kaj Nevis, and Anittas, yet you tell me that all of them are deceased, and my claim is surely as good as your own."

"Not quite," said Rica Dawnstar. She raised her needler. "This gives my claim the edge."

Haviland Tuf looked down at the kitten in his lap. "Let this be your first lesson in the hard ways of the universe," he said loudly. "What matters fairness, when one party has a gun and one does not? Brute violence rules everywhere, and intelligence and good intent are trampled upon." He stared back at Rica Dawnstar. "Madam," he said, "I acknowledge your advantage. Yet I must protest. The deceased members of our group admitted me to a full share in this venture before we came aboard the *Ark*. To my knowledge, you were never similarly included. Therefore I enjoy a legal advantage over you." He raised a single finger. "Furthermore, I would advance the proposition that ownership is conferred by use, and the ability to use. The *Ark* should, optimally, be under the command of the person who has demonstrated the talent, intellect, and will to make the most effective use of its myriad capabilities. I submit that I am that person."

Rica Dawnstar laughed. "Oh, really?"

"Indeed," said Haviland Tuf. He cupped Chaos in his hand, and lifted the kitten for Rica Dawnstar to see. "Behold my proof. I have explored this ship, and mastered the cloning secrets of the vanished Earth Imperials. It was an awesome and intoxicating experience, and one I am anxious to replicate. In fact, I have decided to give up the crass calling of the merchant, for the nobler profession of ecological engineer. I would hope you would not attempt to stand in my way. Rest assured, I will furnish you with transport back to ShanDellor and see to it personally that you receive every fraction of the fee promised to you by Jefri Lion and the others."

Rica Dawnstar shook her head in disbelief. "You're priceless, Tuffy," she said. "You know what I've been up to while you've been cloning yourself a kitten?"

"Obviously I do not," said Haviland Tuf.

"Obviously," Rica echoed sardonically. "I've been up on the bridge, Tuf, playing the computer and learning just about everything I need to know about the Earth Ecological Corps and its *Ark*."

Tuf blinked. "Indeed."

"There's a swell telescreen up there," she said. "Think of it like a big gaming board, Tuf. I've been watching every move. The red pieces, that was you and the rest of them. Me, too. And the black pieces. The bio-weapons, as the system likes to call them. I like the sound of *monsters* better myself. Shorter. Less formal."

"Fraught with strong connotations, however," Tuf put in.

"Oh, certainly. But to the point. We got through the defense sphere, we even handled the plague defense, but Anittas got himself killed and decided to get a little revenge, so he kicked loose the monster defense. And I sat up on top and watched the red and the black chase each other. But now, the key question."

In the corridor behind her, Haviland Tuf glimpsed motion. "Excuse me," he began.

Rica waved him quiet. "If they were prepared to turn loose these caged horrors of theirs to repel boarders in an emergency, *how did they prevent their own people from getting killed?*"

"An interesting quandary," Tuf admitted. "I eagerly anticipate learning the answer to this puzzle. I fear I will have to defer that pleasure, however." He cleared his throat. "Far be it from me to interrupt such a fascinating discourse. I feel obliged to point out, however ..." The deck shook.

"Yes," Rica said, grinning.

"I feel obliged to point out," Tuf repeated, "that a rather large carnivorous dinosaur has appeared in the corridor behind you, and is presently attempting to sneak up on us. He is not doing a very good job of it."

The tyrannosaur roared.